ANGELS FALL

by

Baron R. Birtcher

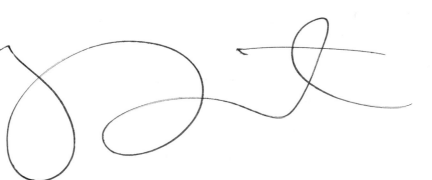

IOTA
PUBLISHING

IOTA Publishing
92 Corporate Park
Suite 110
Irvine, CA 92606

For information address IOTA Publishing,
92 Corporate Park, Suite 110, Irvine, CA 92606

Library of Congress Control Number: 2007929390

ISBN 978-0-9793720-1-8

First IOTA Publishing hardcover edition 2008

IOTA Publishing is a trademark of CIMI Associates Inc.

10 9 8 7 6 5 4 3 2

Cover design by OrangeRoc
Production by Sanford Associates, Inc.

Manufactured in the United States of America

For information regarding special discounts for bulk purchases, please contact IOTA Publishing at Business@IOTAPublishing.com.

For Christina

Prologue

The explosion blew the windows out of six houses, hurled the engine block of Dave and Rosalie's 1973 Olds Cutlass through the hood and embedded it on their front lawn. A long column of greasy smoke trailed into the cloudless sky.

I didn't know about any of that at the time. I was on the witness stand in one of the cramped hearing rooms in the Hawaii County Courts building. Neither did Rosalie. She was in the gallery watching my testimony.

"Please state your name and occupation for the record."

The room was packed with an angry, strident group of anti-development militants that the judge had already threatened with ejection as I was being sworn in. These were Rosalie's people.

"Mike Travis," I answered. "I operate a private yacht charter business."

"Your address?"

Since I live aboard my sailing yacht, I gave them the address of Snyder's bar, where I get my mail.

"And you're also the owner of a coffee farm here in Kona?"

"Part owner. Kamahale Plantation." Which was the reason I was here. Technically, my business partner is a seventeen-year-old girl. Edita Orlandella. I wasn't about to let her testify with all the outrage and media bullshit surrounding this case.

Reiko Masuda, the plaintiff's attorney, stepped in front of the heavy wooden table and crossed her arms.

"Will you please tell the court what happened on your coffee plantation on May 2 of this year?"

My eyes skimmed across the faces at the back of the room. A hundred years earlier, these people's ancestors had held a vigil on the soft grass that lined the steps of Iolani Palace, for Liliuokalani, Hawaii's last reigning queen. The naked faith I saw in those faces made me want to look away.

"Human remains were discovered inside a lava tube that runs beneath part of my property," I answered.

"Discovered by whom?"

"By me."

Ms. Masuda nodded and took a step closer to the stand. A hint of the perfume she wore drifted on the air stirred by the ceiling fans that rotated slowly overhead.

"And how old were these remains?"

"I'm told they were roughly a thousand years old."

"A thousand years old," she repeated, hooking a long black lock of hair behind her ear.

"That's my understanding."

"What did you do after you found them?"

"I looked for more remains, found none, then contacted a kahuna."

She cocked her head, and I caught a flash from one of the gold earrings she wore. "Why did you do that?"

"To have him bless the site, bless the body, and re-bury the bones in a more suitable place."

She used the stillness of the gallery, the silence, like a tool. "More suitable place? How so?"

"The ancient Hawaiians believed that once the human body had expired, its mana—its spirit—was meant to return to the dust of the earth. It was important to the continuity of their family."

"Are you a native Hawaiian, Mr. Travis?"

"I am. My mother was half-Hawaiian."

"And she raised you with these beliefs?"

I shook my head. "I was raised Presbyterian."

"I see. Nevertheless, you contacted a kahuna to tend to the remains. Did you continue conducting business on your property while this was going on?"

"No."

I could see Rosalie smile as I answered; there were approving nods among the spectators.

"Why not?" Ms. Masuda asked.

"I didn't feel it was appropriate. I thought it would be disrespectful."

She allowed a puzzled expression to crowd her features, again letting the silence speak.

"But you yourself don't subscribe to these, ah, pagan beliefs. Why wouldn't you simply call the coroner and have him dispose of the remains? Or ignore them completely and go about your business?" She shot a hard look toward the developer's counsel table as she waited for my response.

"Because this person, whoever it was, had been placed there with the expectation of returning to the earth. You don't have to subscribe to any particular set of beliefs to know what the right thing to do is. It's our heritage."

"Objection." It was the first word I'd heard spoken by any of the three dark suits seated at the defense table.

"Relax, counselor," the judge said. "I recognize opinion when I hear it."

Reiko Masuda went on as though there had been no interruption.

"Were the remains of the body that you discovered on your property related to you in any way?"

"Not that I know of," I said.

"There was no DNA testing done, then?"

"Not when they were in my possession."

She moved slowly across the polished floor, her face locked in concentration. She took a position directly in front of the judge, then turned to face me again. "Yet you still saw fit to render proper respect to the descendents of this person, in the ancient tradition."

"In the tradition with which he or she was laid to rest. Yes," I said. "I felt that it was the only appropriate thing to do."

"No further questions."

A murmur of satisfaction roiled up from the gallery as Ms. Masuda returned to her chair. Opposing counsel came forward, eyed me for a long moment before he started in on me. His face was pale, skin stretched tight against the bone.

"You haven't always been a charter captain, have you?" he began.

"No."

"What was your former occupation?"

"A detective with the L.A.P.D."

He arranged his face in a smirk that came nowhere near his eyes. "Not an outfit that's shown a tremendous amount of social sensitivity in recent years, is it?"

"That's enough," the judge interrupted. "Move on."

"Do you know either Mr. Ogden Krupp or AOK Development, Mr. Travis?"

"No."

"You've never met?" Both his tone and expression called me a liar.

"I just said I didn't know him."

"Are you aware of Mrs. Makahanui's case against Mr. Krupp and his company?"

I looked at Mrs. Makahanui where she sat beside Ms. Masuda at the plaintiff's table. Her long gray hair was pulled up into a tight bun on the top of her head, a red hibiscus tucked neatly into it. She smiled at me with her caramel-colored eyes, her square face molded into an expression of quiet dignity.

"I'm aware that his bulldozers uncovered a number of human bones and burial sites on his development—"

"Move to strike—"

"—And that Mrs. Makahanui and her group had some of the remains DNA tested and proved her standing as a blood relative from one of the areas Mr. Krupp disturbed."

"Move to strike," the attorney repeated.

"You asked the question, counselor," the judge said.

"Are you aware of the condition of the 'remains' to which the DNA testing was done?"

"I don't follow your question," I said.

"Let me restate it then: are you aware that the DNA test was conducted on a fishhook?"

Anxious shuffling emanated from the back of the room, and the judge shot them a warning glare.

"Yes," I said. "Ancient Hawaiians often made fishhooks from human bone."

"Then let me ask you, Mr. Travis, at what point does a human being cease being human and become nothing more than an ordinary tool?"

I felt the prickle of angry heat rise on my neck. "That's out of line."

"I beg to differ, Mr. Travis. It is the crux of the case," the attorney responded. His lips stretched into a tight, stitched line. "You people, and this court need to understand that Mrs. Makahanui's DNA match to a fishhook is neither sufficient or substantial enough a claim to shut down a billion-dollar golf resort project—"

There was a collective intake of breath, and a palpable, seething rage blew through the room like a hot wind. But the attorney continued on unabated.

"—A project, I hasten to add, that will have an enormous positive effect on the local economy."

I thought Rosalie was going to come over the railing as the judge hammered his gavel and tried to restore order.

"That's enough, counselor. Move on. Now."

The developer's attorney waited until the room was quiet before he spoke again. "Are you aware that there have been very serious threats of bodily harm made against Mr. Krupp, the developer?"

"No."

He waited a beat, and arched his brows in disbelief. "No?"

"No," I repeated.

He turned away from me, took a deep breath, and threw me a change-up.

"During your tenure as an L.A. cop, did you ever have occasion to fire your weapon?"

"Excuse me?"

"You heard the question."

"Yes," I answered.

"More than once?"

"Yes."

He blinked rapidly, as if he were shocked. "Have you ever killed anyone, Mr. Travis?"

"You know I have," I said, fighting to keep the anger from my voice.

"Do you have a permit to carry a weapon in Hawaii?"

"Yes."

"Have you ever discharged your weapon since retiring as an L.A. cop?"

"Yes."

He feigned a look of both surprise and disgust. "Really? Have you killed anyone since your retirement?"

The dry rattle of palms outside echoed in the silence that enveloped the room. My eyes drifted to the revolving shadow of the ceiling fan on the worn linoleum floor.

"Yes," I said. It sounded like a whisper.

He let my answer hang for a long moment.

"Have you ever made a threat against Mr. Krupp or his company?

"Absolutely not."

He shot me a mocking glance. "Are you sure, Mr. Travis?"

"I don't make threats, counselor," I said, looking him dead in the eye. "They're a waste of time."

*   *   *

Rosalie was three steps behind me, trying to keep up as I strode to my Jeep.

"Mike, wait up," she said.

I stopped in my tracks, the late afternoon sun throwing long shadows across the hot pavement. "I told you I didn't want to do this, Rosie."

"You did fine."

"That asshole made me look like the fucking muscle for the tree-hugging Mafia."

She recoiled as if I had struck her.

"I'm sorry," I said. "You know this isn't my thing, Rosie. I don't like what they're doing down there any more than you do, but I didn't help your cause. Not even a little."

"Somebody's got to stand up," she said. "And it's not just my cause."

I stopped dead. "Don't ever talk to me about standing up," I said, growing angry again. "Not ever."

She sighed an exhausted apology as she climbed into the passenger seat so I could drive her home. We sat in silence as we waited for a break in traffic. I watched a carload of teenagers blow through a stop sign and toss and empty quart bottle of beer out the window and into the weeds along the shoulder. Rosalie shook her head, squinting into the sunlight as I turned onto the highway.

We had no way of knowing that the thick column of black smoke rising from the tangle of monkeypod and jacaranda trees in the distance was the burning hulk of Rosalie's car, even as we drove toward it. Or that thirty hours later a bunch of teenage kids would go a step too far, and four people would die. I wish there was. I wish there was a way I could have known as I stepped up into the Jeep that afternoon that I'd end up being dead center of the whole goddamned thing.

-1-

I eased back the throttle on the *Chingadera's* twin outboards and let the skiff glide to a stop in the seaward flats behind the line of waves that formed up on La'aloa Bay. I kept my eye on the back of a nice six-footer as it peeled off the point in a sweet left break while Snyder leaned over the bow, watching the bottom through crystalline turquoise water. He shielded his eyes against the glare of the sun that was creeping up behind the volcano as he searched for a sandy place to drop the hook.

"Right here, Mike," he called over his shoulder. He tossed the anchor as I kicked the engines into a slow reverse, felt it bite, and finally take hold. He pulled the slack out of the line, guided it through a chrome eyelet in the skiff's gunwale, and tied off on the cleat between his bare feet.

The motors gargled into silence as I switched off the ignition. A cool white mist blew back from a newly cresting wave and fell on my bare shoulders like rain. I took the last swig of Mango Ceylon and nodded toward shore. Snyder followed my gaze as I set down my empty mug.

"You're gonna wish you brought a helmet," I said, and we watched five other dawn-patrollers drop in on the same spot.

"Full-body armor, more like."

It was the first weekend since school had begun again, and the place was jammed with teenage surfers wringing the last sweet drops out of summer and what remained of the recent south swell. For a moment time collapsed, and I was back here again with Ruby and Tino in those final few days before leaving our family's summer home and heading back to my high school on the mainland. I had that feeling I used to get in the pit of my stomach, wondering if things would be the same when I came back the next year, if they'd ever be the same again. The unexpected memory of Ruby, my first love, snapped me back to the present.

"Age and guile," I said, "beats youth and speed every time."

Snyder laughed. "Yeah. Let's just keep telling ourselves that."

I pulled the rash guard over my head like a tight T-shirt, secured the leash, and slipped over the side with my board. I pulled myself up astride it, fixed my eyes on the slopes of Hualalai, on the stands of coconut palms and plumeria along the shoreline, and watched the morning sun beat back the last remains of the night.

*   *   *

It was after ten by the time Snyder and I had the skiff back inside Kailua Bay, where my 72-foot blue-water sailing yacht, the *Kehau*, lay at anchor. I never failed to feel a flush of paternal pride every time I saw her.

I'd designed every inch of the yacht myself, had her constructed by one of the best builders in Southern California, and launched her in time for my retirement from twenty years as a detective with the L.A.P.D. The Plan was that I would live aboard, hooked to a private mooring in Avalon harbor off the L.A. coast, and offer the occasional upscale private charter to SoCal fat cats, or whoever might be appropriately long on cash and acceptably short on attitude. I shouldn't have been surprised to discover that, in California at least, that was a very thin market.

But that wasn't the thing that had truly fucked The Plan. I did that myself.

I hadn't even been retired a year when my former partner, Hans Yamaguchi, called me back to consult on a serial-murder case. What drove the last nail into The Plan was that I agreed to help him. The resulting Lizard King murder case ended up making us both more famous than we'd ever wanted to be, and for entirely different reasons, left a dark and empty place inside me that still aches when it rains.

After that, I said to Hell with California and sailed *Kehau* all the way to Kona, Hawaii, my mother's birthplace, the place where I'd spent every summer of my life until I turned eighteen. I'd come here this time for anonymity and a new beginning. Anonymity got blown to shit in no time at all. The new beginning I got to keep, though I came that close to losing that, too. I am reminded of it every morning when I wake up and see Lani's long, black hair spilled across the pillow beside me, hear her soft breath as I close our stateroom door, climb the stairway to the upper deck and watch the sun come up. It is there, as I sit alone with a steaming mug of Mango Ceylon, that I try to let go of the vapor-trail remnants of a job that had once consumed nearly every waking moment of my life and filled the ones I had left with memories of perps and perverts and violent death.

But that's only part of the truth. The nine-millimeter in the nightstand and the Beretta Bobcat stashed in the galley drawer told the rest. There's a limit to how far you can run.

"What's the deal with the bags?" Snyder asked. We were standing on the *Kehau's* stern deck, amidst several pieces of luggage.

"No idea," I said.

I stepped down into the main salon and got a clue in a hell of a hurry. Lani was sprawled on the banquette, hair matted and flat against her sweating brow. Her eyes were moist and yellow, her brown skin had turned ashen gray and looked paper-thin.

"My God, Lani, what's going on?"

"Sick," she whispered. "Flu, I think."

I made a move to pick her up and carry her below.

"Let me get you back into bed."

She put out a hand to ward me off.

"No. The rocking. It makes me…"

She didn't have to finish. I could see she was fighting a rising gorge.

"Then come above with me, Lani. You need some fresh air. It'll make you feel better."

She let me take her hand and lead her up the stairway, out into the open. Snyder cleared a space on the seat that ran along the stern rail, and she lay down again, throwing an arm across her eyes. I untied the overhead canvas, rolled it out, and gave her some shade, but it didn't look like it helped much. I placed my hand against her brow and felt her damp, simmering fever.

The first time I'd seen her, two years ago, she was tending bar at the Harbor House, a backwater semi-dive at the foot of the boat basin that smelled of beer and cooking grease and salt air. I had been at sea for over two weeks, making the crossing from the mainland, and she looked like every sailor's Polynesian fantasy. I couldn't take my eyes off her face, her hair, her skin. I thought of her too often in the days that followed, hoping, in a way, that the image would fade. But two weeks later, I met her again. Down at the beach by the old airport. It was a birthday party for somebody we both knew. Wooden torches spilled pools of yellow light along the strand as dozens of people milled contentedly amid tables full of food and coolers brimming with ice and beer.

But it is that night I will always remember, the night among the crowd at Shaloma Marks' birthday, when Lani came in off the beach and almost made me forget who I was. She was tall and dark-skinned, with long, thick black hair that fell to her waist, and the trim body of a dancer. A light dusting of sand speckled her ankles and the tops of her feet, and she smelled of the sea and the sun. That night, it was like no one else was there. We talked and drank until the party had long since been packed away, and the moon rose over the ragged summit of the volcano.

"You gotta take her ashore, man," Snyder said now. "This south swell's making it worse."

"Already called," Lani began. She swallowed dryly, struggling to finish the thought. "Already called Rosie. Going to stay with her."

Dave and Rosalie had rented a house not too far from town, just off the upper road, overlooking Honokohau Harbor. The same house where shattered windows were now covered with sheets of unpainted plywood, and the plaster was singed black with smoke.

"Forget it, Lani," I said. "I'll check you into the King Kam, right here by the bay. I can look in on you." It was bad enough that Dave and Rosalie had chosen to stick around after what had happened; I sure as hell didn't want Lani any closer to the threat of violence than she already was.

Unlike me, Lani had been married once before, but it hadn't lasted long. Three years. He'd been a part-time fisherman who turned a one-time fascination with crystal meth into a full-time lifestyle. The marriage lasted just long enough to scrape away the last patina of whatever innocence she had brought into it, but she came out of it with a quiet strength, devoid of any hint of self-pity. She called herself a romantic realist, although, even then, I know I hadn't completely believed her.

But recently, there had been a kind of coming-undone that shadowed her face when she looked at me, like she'd discovered one more crack in the little bit of hope she still allowed herself. And deep in that shadow was a piece of something I might have put there, something I couldn't even call by name, couldn't erase, couldn't take back, and couldn't lock away.

"I'll be okay, Mike. Rosie's all right now, you said so yourself."

"That's not exactly what I said."

"Whatever." She waved my objection away with a weak toss of her hand. "Please don't argue. It's where I want to be. Please, Mike."

I watched her for a long moment as she lay there in the late morning sun, knowing I would do damn near anything she asked.

"Give me a hand with her bags," I said, and headed down the ladder into the skiff. Snyder handed them over to me, then helped steady Lani as she made her way into the *Chingadera* on legs that looked about as sturdy as string cheese.

*   *   *

Two hours later, I was sitting at Snyder's bar, drinking an Asahi on ice, waiting for Lolly, his waitress, to bring my mail out from the back office. The place was pure Hawaii-kitch, right down to the blue Malibu lights that cast heavy shadows across the faces of carved tiki-gods, and the woven palm thatch awning that jutted out over the long hardwood bar. A pair of bronze hula-girl lamps stood at either end, hips swaying smoothly to the music that came from the jukebox tucked back in the far corner.

Snyder was busy behind the rail, a row of empty shot glasses lined up between him and the tourist couple he was talking to, all sunburn and matching aloha-wear. I would have had them figured for the blender-drink crowd, but Snyder was waxing eloquent about tequila instead, pouring a sample of various brands in each glass. Snyder knew more about tequila than any bartender I'd ever met, but I had never asked him why.

He finally made eye contact with me as the couple lifted the first of their shots to their lips.

"Hey, man," he said. "Lani doing any better?"

"She'll be alright. Got her settled in Dave and Rosie's guest room. Fell asleep as soon as her head hit the pillow."

"Seasick, maybe? It's been a hell of a swell."

"She's been living aboard for three months, and I've never seen her like that."

"Bummer," he said. Then, an afterthought: "Well, whatever it is, you don't wanna catch it yourself. Always some kinda crap going around."

"That's what she said."

He caught the concern in my eyes. "Don't worry about her, man. She'll be okay."

Rumor was that Snyder was a retired pot grower from Humboldt County. It was said that the liquor license for this place was in his mother's name, to create some distance from some kind of trouble, either legal or illegal, past or present. I'd also heard he spent some time down in

Mexico, but that, too, was a little vague. I didn't care. Rule number one in the tropics: never ask. If they want you to know, they'll tell you. Hell, practically everyone here comes from somewhere else. And if things were cool back home, they'd probably have stayed there.

I squinted against the shaft of sunlight that pushed Addison Gimball— Addison Dunbar Gimball, to be more precise—in from the sidewalk and through the batwing saloon doors at Snyder's front entrance. He belonged to a crowd that liked to use all three of their names, the kind of people who named their kids Skip or Chad or Tiffany. But he'd recently taken to slumming down here with the regular folk. Snyder tossed a glance toward the door, looked at me, and rolled his eyes.

Gimball was one of a newly-minted breed of snowbirds who were building homes with price tags that had so many commas you'd think they were quoting the cost in Japanese yen. To make things worse, his house was being built inside the guard-gated resort development that had been at the heart of the spate of recent protests and legal actions that had prompted my testimony against the developer, Ogden Krupp.

"Mike Travis! What're you doing here in the middle of the work day?" His voice was heavily laced with that trying-too-hard-to-be-pals tone newcomers always seemed to spill all over the rest of us. "You boat guys do work Saturdays, right?"

Gimball was hard to miss, and like a train wreck, equally hard to ignore. He was a few inches shorter than me, six feet tall, maybe two-fifty's worth of single-malt Scotch gut, and had a ruddy-faced golfer's tan. Every time he took off his white straw hat, there was a new feat of engineering on his head. Today, it looked as though he'd dyed his hair some new and heinous shade of red, then weaved it into some kind of sculpture. This one could be in the Comb-Over Hall of Fame.

Out of respect for Snyder's business, I stifled the first response that popped into my mind. "Everybody's got to be somewhere," I answered instead.

Snyder intervened before things had a chance to go south. He stepped over to the stick with a beer glass in his hand. "What'll it be, Mr. Gimball?"

"Whatever Travis is having," Gimball said. He drew a Gitanes menthol from the box in his shirt pocket.

He was an easy man to dislike, maybe too easy; the school dork all grown up, with more money, now, than brains. Maybe he'd earned it, more probably not. He seemed to come from the kind of background that valued inherited wealth more than the other kind. In truth, somewhere down deep, I felt sorry for him. He was all affectation and bluff, a loud and blundering intruder that had come to represent, to me at least, a new kind of carrier of an old strain of illness come to infect Hawaii all over again.

Snyder slid Gimball's beer across the bar. "How's that new house coming along?"

Gimball pulled a face, puffing his sun-reddened cheeks. "They're still protesting," he said. The words rolled out on a blanket of gray smoke. "Nothing but loudmouth hippies and whale-savers. I swear to God, I don't know why in the hell they have to get so worked up over a few damn bones."

I couldn't tell if he knew I'd testified, and I wondered which of those categories I was supposed to fit into. I debated not saying anything at all but couldn't let it go.

"Human remains," I said.

"Excuse me?"

"They're not just bones, Gimball. They're human remains. That's an ancient burial ground you're building on down there. You're dragging tractors all over people's ancestors."

As always, he'd let the ash of his cigarette grow so long I couldn't take my eyes off it. Irritated me to distraction, like almost everything else he did. I glanced around for an ashtray.

He started in about the lawsuit, how the judge had ruled that the development could continue despite the archeological finds, and how good it was for the economy.

I tuned him out. It was an old speech, more of the same arrogant bullshit from people who barged into anyplace that looked like paradise, expecting the locals to swap their heritage for a few minimum-wage jobs and a golf course whose greens fees cost more than most of their cars. I'd already heard enough.

I took a last look at his lengthening ash, tossed off the rest of my Asahi, and stood up to leave.

"Tell Lolly I'll come back later for my mail." I slipped a bill across the bar for Snyder.

"Can't stick around?"

I shook my head. "Gotta go meet Tino."

Snyder understood.

Addison Dunbar Gimball was still yammering as the doors swung shut behind me.

-2-

I climbed up into my jeep, an '87 wrangler that lani calls *Pilikua*, which, loosely translated, means "giant." It's rigged with 33-12 off-road tires with a six-inch lift. The body is painted the same bright orange as a traffic control cone. Functional, but not too subtle.

Wind whipped the loose canvas top as I made a left off Queen Ka'ahumanu Highway, onto the winding two-lane road that cut upward through hundreds of acres of lava-strewn pastureland, a light rain sprinkling my windshield. Massive stands of mango trees sprung up among the tall grass and papaya, and filled the air with the scent of new flowers and wet soil.

Two hundred years ago, this land still belonged to a sovereign monarch. It had been sectioned-off into narrow strips that ran from the summit of the volcano all the way to the shoreline, and was tended by loose associations of villagers. It was a brilliant system that allowed each village access to all the fresh water, crops, animals, and fish that occupied every elevation within its boundaries. But four generations later, it was gone, lost in a bloodless coup that ultimately placed the islands into the hands of foreign merchants and missionaries. The natives had been an isolated people for so long, they were vulnerable to the diseases the new bosses brought with them, and less than a hundred years later, nearly 90 percent of the native population had been killed off by smallpox, measles and gonorrhea.

I thought about Addison Gimball and his "bones," and it made me want to drive all the way back to Snyder's just to kick his fat ass.

*   *   *

Tino was standing outside the wooden shed we used as an office, hands on his hips, watching my Jeep slam along the loose dirt road, a dusty contrail hanging in the air behind me. My friend is constructed of geometric patterns, his head a wide oval balanced on a solid square torso between broad shoulders. He has legs like tree stumps, and his whole body rocks from side to side when he walks. A thick tangle of black hair stuck up in unruly tufts, and he was wearing only a pair of tattered blue shorts, a white T-shirt, and rubber sandals.

I pulled up next to his rusted Ford pickup and parked in the gravel lot.

"Howzit, bruddah?" he asked in the easy pidgin he used. He jabbed a stubby finger at his watch. "You early."

"Little bit."

"Eh, you come eat yet? Edita, she down eating lunch wit' da guys."

"I'm okay for now. Don't let me interrupt."

"Come full arready," he said, rubbing a rough brown hand across his gut.

I followed Tino down a short path that opened onto a clearing we'd carved from the dense rows of coffee plants. Edita was eating with four other people in the shade of a huge monkeypod tree, at a table that had once been a spool of telephone cable. I recognized Raul and Salina Soto, though they had their backs to me, and figured the other two for their teenage sons, Ben and Ken.

"Uncle Mike," Edita said and dropped her sandwich on the table. She ran over and threw her arms around me in a bear hug. Golden light dappled her smooth, dark complexion.

"Take it easy there, sweetheart, all this coffee-picking is making you stronger than you think."

She punched my arm playfully, and showed me a brilliant smile, one that looked more like her mother's every time I saw her.

Raul Soto made a move to stand. "Mr. Travis," he said around a mouthful of sausage and rice.

"Sit, sit," I said. "Enjoy your break."

The Sotos were among the last reminders of old Kona, when whole families would spend long, hot months working the coffee fields together. It was hard work, picking and hauling the heavy bags of cherry, then hand-trimming each plant until the sunlight hit each branch just right, maximizing the next year's crop. It wasn't until the late '60s that local schools stopped scheduling their "summer vacation" for the August to November harvest season to accommodate those families and their work on the various plantations.

"Lookin' good, Mr. Travis," Raul Soto said. "Maybe seventy pounds a tree this year."

A small tractor—a "Mule" in the vernacular—was parked in the shade beside the table, its bed half filled with burlap bags emblazoned with the Kamahale Plantation logo. Each sack brimmed with fresh-picked coffee cherry, a deep cranberry color, each one the size of a small grape. In the weeks to come, the rich smell of coffee would fill the air as the cherry was pulped, dried and roasted. When the trade winds blew just right, they'd carry that fragrance all the way down into town.

I looked at Tino beside me. "Not bad for two-year-old trees."

"Right on," he smiled. "They comin' along real good."

When I glanced back into the Mule's flat bed and caught the logo on those bags, I wished my mother could have lived to see them for herself. She had loved Tino like a son. To her, he was always the little boy who lived next door to our summer home on the bay at Honaunau, the very home she herself had been raised in as a child.

But I believe she would have appreciated the symmetry of how we ended up here. I'd gotten Tino out of a jam once, and in return, he had bought this small coffee farm on the slope of Hualalai, overlooking Kona village. Two-thirds ownership he gave to his daughter, Edita. The other third he gave to me. He named it Kamahale Plantation, out of respect to my mother's family name. It was a gift of gratitude I couldn't refuse.

I turned to the bay below, where a fleet of brightly-colored outrigger canoes sliced through the smooth turquoise sea. In earlier centuries, these same boats would have been steered by thick-muscled men and bare-breasted women paddling out to greet a merchant vessel, their narrow hulls overflowing with pineapples and breadfruit and flowers.

"Dad's been working hard," Edita said now, bringing me back.

Her face and forehead were smeared with dirt where she'd tried to wipe the sweat away.

"Looks like you have, too."

"Only on weekends," she said shyly. She took my hand in both of hers, and pulled me toward the shade of the big tree. "C'mere, lemme show you something."

I followed her over to where two other cars were parked beside the Mule.

Edita pointed to an old Toyota sedan that I'd last seen driven by her mother, just hours before she'd been murdered. "What do you think?" she asked. Edita had repainted it and replaced the missing hubcaps.

"Nice color."

"They call it 'Cayman Green.'"

"Looks great."

"And check this out—" she tugged at me again, but Tino interrupted.

"Uncle Mike got no time for that now—"

"No, no," I said. "It's okay." Edita was like a daughter to me, and about the only kid I'd ever met that I actually liked.

She'd come a long way since the first time I'd seen her, hunched and crying, hiding in the back of a closet. She had just discovered her mother's shattered body, shotgunned to death, along with several others, on the floor of the house next door to her own.

For a while after that, Edita and her father had kept to themselves, or rather, people kept apart from them, as if violent death was something that might be contagious. Then, one by one, they shouldered through crowded memories, created new routines, and survived the passage of painful anniversaries. They became father and daughter again, repairing the fabric of their lives.

"Close your eyes," she said, took my hand, and led me slowly toward the big monkeypod whose branches threw shade over the makeshift lunch table. When she told me to stop, I was standing in a warm patch of light, feeling the sunshine and shadow play across my eyelids.

"You remember when you found that burial site up here?" she asked.

I told her I did.

"Remember what you told me about tradition and stuff?"

"Yeah." I was beginning to feel unprepared. I didn't always like the sound of my own words coming back to me.

"I made you something," she said. I could hear the smile in her voice. "Okay, open your eyes."

When I did, I saw the words she'd painstakingly carved into the gnarled trunk:

RUBY ORLANDELLA

—

LA'AKEA KAMAHALE
Aloha Pau Ole

The first name belonged to Edita's mother, the second one belonged to mine. Aloha pau ole. With love forever.

I stepped forward, slowly ran my fingers over the letters she had etched there. They were the color and texture of dried tobacco leaves against the furrowed gray bark.

"It's my favorite tree," she offered. "We're all a part of it, now, see? For always."

A gust of warm air scrolled through the branches overhead, the long moment of silence broken by the bleat of francolins in the distant undergrowth.

Edita looked at me. Her expression held a whisper of concern. "Are you okay? You like it?"

I hauled in my memories, swallowed dryly. I drew Edita to me and kissed the top of her head.

"It's perfect," I said.

*   *   *

A fine mist drifted out of the clouds, blurring the gray distance to the village below as Tino and I stepped out of the office a few hours later. We'd gone over the books, checked the orders for bags and labels, and reviewed the week's payroll. Outside, we stood in the gravel lot, taking the day's last look into the fields where the Sotos and Edita were still at work.

"Ruby would be proud," I said.

"What, you mean all this?" His eyes swept the view of the Plantation.

"No. I mean Edita. She's a good girl."

Tino toed the loose soil and nodded.

"She's seventeen, arready. She don' make no trouble like me when I come 'dat age."

I remembered Tino at seventeen and had to smile. "She's a hard worker. A real good kid."

"She's a Junior in high school. Maybe soon come college." There was sadness in his awkward shrug. "Then who knows when I see her, eh?"

"You've got a couple more years before you need to worry, Tino. Try not to get too far ahead of yourself."

He nodded agreement, and the cloud lifted from his eyes.

"You right, brah."

But I knew his heart, the root of his concern, and in truth, I shared it. Because you really never knew. Things changed in the blink of an eye, things that held the power to alter everything, things you never saw coming. The whole of my life as a cop had been based on that fact—you just never fucking knew. I tried to shake it off as I looked down the slope across the canopy of jungle, where the lights of town began to glow through the haze.

"Take it easy, Tino," I said.

He shook my hand in both of his.

Maybe it's a good thing that we can't see into our own futures; there's no time for fear, or even hope. I've looked back on that moment a hundred times since then, at the simplicity of it, having no idea how quickly it was all going to change.

"You, too, Mikey," he said.

No idea at all.

-3-

A brief and bitter sunset gave way to a gray, colorless night as I pushed the jeep through town.

The nagging cloud of foreboding that had come over me at the Plantation enveloped me like a stench, and I pressed the pedal to the floor in hopes that the wind would blow it away before I got to Dave and Rosalie's. Maybe it was Ruby's unexpected incursion on my memory that brought it on, maybe something else, an alarm going off in my subconscious. Half way up Alii Drive, I pulled off at a lei stand, picked up some flowers to take to Lani.

I glanced off toward the bay, where the *Kehau* rocked gently on her moorings, then beyond her, in the direction of Tahiti, the Marquesas, and the thousand islands that dotted the South Pacific. But tonight, my mind wouldn't conjure tranquil lagoons and coral atolls. Tonight there was only a starless sky and a dim horizon, obscured by colorless clouds.

*   *   *

I parked in front of the house, behind the burned depression in the asphalt left by the blast that had destroyed Rosalie's car. Sheets of unpainted plywood and clear plastic still covered the windows that faced the street, but the shadow of scorched paint along the front wall had been freshly concealed.

Rosalie met me at the door, a finger pressed to her lips.

"She's sleeping," she whispered as she let me in.

"Any better?"

"I think so. We'll see how she does tonight."

"Thanks for—"

"Stop it," she interrupted. "Let's get those flowers in some water."

I watched as Rosalie trimmed the stems and arranged the flowers in a vase she'd taken from a kitchen cabinet. When she was satisfied, she filled it with water and walked me toward the rear of the house to the guest room. Lani was sleeping soundly, wrapped tight in tangled sheets, so I placed them on the bedside table as quietly as I could then backed out, closing the door behind me. Even in the dim reflected light, I could see she looked a little better, though I knew the renewed color in her face was most likely fever.

I followed Rosalie down the narrow hall that led back to the kitchen, stopping to look at the photos that lined the walls: Dave standing beside an 800-pound blue marlin; Rosie speeding toward a whaleboat in a Greenpeace Zodiac; Dave in his scuba gear, surrounded by mantas in a dreamlike underwater dance. There was a recent shot of Rosalie collecting an award from the World Wildlife Fund. She'd succeeded in forcing the Navy to shut down a series of low-frequency sound wave tests that had caused the deaths of at least a dozen dolphins.

"Nice work," I said. "Congratulations."

She shrugged. "It's never over."

"No, it isn't." She didn't know we weren't talking about the same thing.

"Drink?"

"Why not?"

She filled two tumblers with ice and Absolut and handed me one as she stepped out onto a lanai that overlooked the boat harbor. In the distance, I could hear the low rumble of jets resonate from the airport.

"Where's Yosemite?" I asked. Yosemite Sam was Dave's nickname. His unruly gray-blond hair, gravel voice, and long, drooping mustache obviated the reason.

"Night dive tonight."

"Crappy weather for it."

"'Ya goes where the man tells 'ya,'" she growled. It was a credible imitation.

I leaned against the rail and pulled at my drink in silence. The air was still, balmy, and ripe with the tropics. In my peripheral vision, I saw Rosalie watching me. Her face was tight across her high cheekbones, serious.

"You're a big guy, Mike, but you can't carry it all."

My expression spoke the question I didn't ask.

"The world," she said. "You look like you're carrying it all by yourself tonight."

"It's a feeling I get sometimes. I don't know why. It's been on me since this afternoon."

Her eyes were unreadable, still locked on mine. I wanted to change the subject.

"Your neighbors talking to you yet?"

"Not so much."

I nodded slowly, looking out into the deepening darkness. "Your windows… you gotta get those fixed, Rosie, it's not safe. You need me to stay over again, I will."

"I know, Mike," she said. The smile that crossed her lips was sad, but the gratitude in her eyes was real. "The first three nights was enough. There's nothing to protect me from, now that the verdict came down. Those assholes get to build their golf course and scrape away burial sites. The rest of us…" she shrugged, brought her drink to her lips. "Besides, we've got an alarm system now."

"Any leads on who did it?" I asked.

Ice rattled in her glass as she stirred it with her finger, ignoring my question. Autumn had brought the night down early over the village, and I followed the lights of a departing airliner until it was swallowed by the growing overcast.

"You ever gonna let it go?" she asked finally.

She had her back to the railing, and I turned to face her.

"Let what go?"

She pursed her lips for a moment, weighing whether to say what was on her mind, then looked down to the boat harbor below.

"Being a cop," she said.

I took another drink. It burned all the way to my gut.

"I don't think you ever stop being a cop, Rosie."

"Even if you want to?"

Especially when you want to. A mendacious thought, I knew, and it tasted bitter on my tongue. "I'm working on it," I said instead.

Rosalie slowly nodded. "Were you a good one, at least?"

I wanted to tell her that it depended on who you asked, but that would have been glib, and unworthy of our friendship. I hadn't been a *dirty* cop, hadn't ever taken cash from a narc bust, had never taken a kickback or a bribe. But I'd seen naked guilt in the eyes of a suspect in the interview room, been mad-dogged by low-rent dealers in shitty little bars, and smacked the smugness off both kinds of faces with everything from a phone book to the butt of a Beretta nine. I'd saved the life of a two-year-old boy whose own father had shot him with a crossbow, and nearly beaten a child-molesting pimp to death with my bare hands.

"I was the only kind I could have been."

Her eyes filled with private thoughts, then turned to watch as flying insects spiraled in, hungry for the light.

"You *became* the only kind you could have been," she said. "It left a mark."

I have long held the belief that Homicide cops are a different breed, and as far as I was concerned, there were only two kinds: the ones who looked at what they did as a skill, and those who saw their jobs as nothing short of a mission. The first kind wants to be smarter, more skillful than the ones they hunt down. To them it's a game, competition. The rest are avenging angels, warriors living dangerously close to the edge, who knew with certainty that there was always something new to lose. Time has shown me both the truth and the vanity of that belief.

"I know," was all I could say.

*   *   *

Dave came in a half hour later.

He was wearing one of his trademark T-shirts. This one said *NEVER MISS A GOOD CHANCE TO SHUT UP.* Amen, I thought.

Rosalie caught up to him in the kitchen, threw her arms around his waist, and kissed him. "How was it out there?"

"Dark as a gopher's asshole."

"Classy," I said.

"Hey, Travis," he grinned. "Rosie takin' good care of your main squeeze?"

I rattled the ice in my glass. "Been taking care of me, too."

He gave her a playful smack on the ass. "That's my girl."

She flipped him the bird. Another *Ozzie and Harriet* moment at Yosemite's place.

I placed my empty glass in the sink and headed for the door.

"Stick around, bro. You don't have to leave."

"I still have to stop by Snyder's for my mail." I took a pen and paper from the desk by the door, wrote a short note to Lani, folded it in half and handed it to Rosalie. "You mind giving this to her for me? Tell her I was here?"

"Of course not." She stood up on her toes, and kissed me on the cheek. "And think about what we talked about."

I squeezed off a smile and walked out to the Jeep. I didn't want to tell her that it's the one thing I think about most.

*　*　*

A close and sultry breeze drifted in through the portholes as I sat aboard the *Kehau* sorting my mail. Snyder's had been elbow-to-elbow by the time I stopped in, and I hadn't felt like sticking around.

I tossed the junk mail in the can beneath the sink and poured another three fingers from the bottle of Absolut I kept in the freezer. I took one last look at my cell phone bill and stashed it in the drawer underneath the nav table, then shut the lid on my laptop, opting to ignore my email.

An old album by Blind Faith, one of Lani's favorites, was playing on the local rock station, so I switched on the outside speakers and took my drink out to the transom to listen. I kicked back on the captain's chair, propped my bare feet on the wheel, and lost myself in Winwood's reedy voice singing *Can't Find My Way Home*. I tried to remember the first time I'd heard it; seventh grade, back in 1971, in a girlfriend's room, when rock lyrics were just one more mystery to decipher. I wondered how Lani had come to know it, being a good ten years younger than me, then swallowed the thought with a quick vodka chaser. I focused instead on the memory of her voice when she sang along with the part she said she liked the most.

By the time the song wound down, I was empty again, feeling the stab of her absence in the quiet that followed. I stared back at the lights on the shoreline, heard the dull rumble of the waves against the seawall, and the snippets of music floating out from Lola's, where Lani tended bar most days.

The frayed ends of whatever it was that had grated on me all afternoon had finally arrested what was left of common sense, so I poured myself another stiff drink and brought it back on deck with my old Martin acoustic. I switched off the stereo, and after a quick and dirty tuning job, I slammed through every song I could remember, until my fingertips were as numb as my brain.

-4-

I was up before the sun, feeling better than I had a right to, all things considered. I threw on a pair of swimming trunks, and walked bare-chested into the galley, where I washed a pair of aspirin down with a cold diet Coke. A preemptive strike.

I could feel the humid press of the low overcast in the stillness of the morning, and the south swell from the last few days had become a flat, gray mirror. Before I had the chance to think of all the reasons not to, I dropped to the deck and did my daily hundred push-ups. The sit-ups would have to wait for another day. As I caught my breath, I went to the galley, filled the teapot, and put it on the stove. I set the heat on low so it wouldn't boil over while I took my morning swim.

The water was cool against the heat of my skin, shocking my still-sleeping brain into a first rush of wakefulness. I treaded water for a minute, did a quick scan for incoming craft, and made a beeline for the blinking light out on Keahuolu Point. When I got as far as Captain Bean's mooring buoy, I turned and headed back to the *Kehau*, about a half-mile round trip that cleared what remained of the cobwebs in my head.

I dried off in the galley, poured a mug of Mango Ceylon, and got back on deck in time to watch the sunrise, my touchstone, my talisman.

*   *   *

It was noon when my cell phone rang.

My fingers were slick with gun oil, the pieces of the field-stripped Beretta laid out on the table before me, ready for cleaning, so I let it kick over to voicemail. Salt air was hell on guns, but I took comfort in the routine, even looked forward to it: the feel of the finely-tooled components in my hands, the smell of the oil. I took my time as I handled the parts, lubricated the slide and takedown levers, reassembled the sideplates and guidance rods, replaced the springs, then put the whole thing back together again. When it was done, I checked the clip for a full load, slid it back in place, and set the safety. I was about to start in on the .25 Bobcat when the phone rang again. This time I picked up.

"Travis, it's Snyder. Where the hell you been, man? Been trying to reach you for half an hour." At least I wouldn't have to check my voicemail.

"Cleaning my pistol."

He laughed. "Is that what y'all are calling it now?"

"Good one," I deadpanned.

"What's the word on your lady?"

"I looked in on her last night. She was dead to the world."

I had woken up in the middle of the night, my stomach a pit of hot ashes. Unable to sleep, I picked up a photo album, leafed through the pages. In shot after shot, I noticed, I had caught her in motion, hauling *Kehau's* sails, or running toward me on the beach, her hair blown back in the wind. There was one I couldn't stop coming back to. I had caught her unaware, lips parted, her words forever lost beyond the range of shadows and light.

"Try not to sweat it, she's gonna be okay," he said. "Hey, listen, man. You got somebody here looking for you."

"Who?"

"A kid."

I thought I'd heard him wrong. "What kid?"

I heard him pull the phone away from his ear and call across the bar to his waitress. "Hey, Lolly, ask the kid his name again." To me, he said, "Hold on a second."

I did. Lolly said something to Snyder that I couldn't quite make out.

"Kid's name is Miles. Says he's your nephew."

"Fuck."

As I mentioned before, kids are not my thing. I'd never seen the upside of parenthood, if there was one. It was challenging enough keeping my own shit in order.

But Miles was the eldest of my brother's two kids. The other was a daughter, Lindee, a couple years younger. My brother, Valden, and I have what would euphemistically be called "issues," so contact with my niece and nephew had been sporadic, at best. I didn't even know how old they were now. Teenagers, though, I was sure. Still, it was odd, even for Valden, not to have called to tell me the kid was coming.

Snyder cleared his throat. "You still there, Travis?"

"Yeah, sorry. Is he alright? Miles, I mean."

"Seems okay to me. I got him set up with a burger, and Lolly's keeping him company."

"Thanks, bud. I'll be right there."

*   *   *

When I got to Snyder's, Addison Dunbar Gimball was there, imported cigarettes and all. I tried to ignore him as my eyes adjusted to the dark. Easier said than done.

Snyder was busy at the stick, as usual, but it didn't stop Gimball from running his mouth off about the challenges of installing expensive masonry. God only knew how long he had been at it before I arrived.

"And to make matters worse," Gimball was saying, "I'm having nine kinds of hemorrhoids getting my Travertine marble down to the house in one piece."

"Uh huh," Snyder said.

"Had to become an expert on the stuff myself. Don't think there's a damn soul in this town I can trust with a job as big as mine. Hell if I know how you all put up with all the ineptitude around here."

Snyder turned and began dusting the liquor shelves behind him. I caught his expression in the mirror.

"Damned stuff comes all the way from Portugal," Gimball went on. "Comes all that way without any damage, but once it gets here? I'm telling you, if I wasn't on top of every single thing…"

Snyder's eyes slid from the mirror and landed on Gimball. "Portsmouth?" Snyder asked.

"What?"

"You said something comes from Portsmouth?"

"I said *Portugal*," Gimball said. "The marble! My Travertine. Christ, Snyder, I thought you were listening."

"Turkey," I said as I passed the bar and made my way to the back of the room, where Lolly was waving at me.

Gimball shot me a look. "Excuse me?"

"Turkey, Gimball," I said. "Not Portugal. Travertine marble comes from Turkey. Sometimes Iran." Expert. My ass.

"Oh," he said testily. "Whatever. Regardless, it's been a grade-A bitch getting it off the barge, onto the trucks, and installed in one piece. I mean, I can't believe how damn little work gets done around here—"

"Snyder," I interrupted. "Don't you ever worry about brain damage? Listening to this kind of bullshit? For Chrissakes, at least have some consideration for the rest of your customers."

Snyder tried to camouflage his grin in a fake fit of coughing, while Addison Dunbar Gimball's face went redder than usual. I turned away before I was forced to hear him start up again and headed for Lolly at the table in back.

Lolly Spencer looks like a page from a Swedish fashion magazine. Tall, blue-eyed, all legs and blonde hair. My nephew's attention was locked onto her chest region when she stood up from the table to greet me. She gave me a kiss that was just over the border from chaste, and definitely wouldn't have happened if Lani had been there.

"Aloha, Miles," I said. "I'm surprised to see you, to say the least."

His eyes darted from Lolly's chest, slipped off my face and landed somewhere near his now-empty plate as he gave me a limp teenage handshake.

Long, baggy pants hung halfway down his ass and pooled around a pair of tennis shoes that were so huge and ugly, they had to be expensive. At least he'd taken off his moth-eaten knit ski cap and stuffed it in the pocket of the black windbreaker that lay across the back of the chair beside him. Aside from the zits, the wispy peach-fuzz facial hair, and the spiky black dye-job, he would have been a good looking kid. A real fixer-upper.

His hands were still greasy from French fries—I hoped—and he folded back into the slouch he'd been in when I arrived. "Hey, Uncle Mike."

"It's been nice talking to you, Miles," Lolly said. She gestured to a spiral notebook beside his plate. "And thanks for showing me your drawings. They're good."

His pale complexion reddened from the neck up.

"I'll leave you with your uncle now," she smiled. "I'm sure you've got a lot of catching up to do."

He grunted something that probably translated as "goodbye" or "thanks" or "see you later" in his world, but I couldn't be sure. It sounded more like, "Ungh hunhr."

"So, Miles—" I began.

"Milo," he interrupted, abruptly picked up the sketchpad, and shoved it into the backpack on the floor beside his feet.

"What?"

"Milo. I like to be called Milo."

"Uh huh," I said. "So, what's the deal here, Miles? What's going on?"

"Whaddaya mean?" A hint of defensiveness.

I spread my hands, gestured around the room. "I mean, I didn't know you were coming."

"It was sort of, uh, last-minute."

"How'd you find me?"

"Off my dad's Rolodex. In his study."

It clicked then. "Your dad doesn't know you're here, does he?"

He shook his head slowly, staring a hole in his plate.

"You ran away?"

"Not really," he said, then briefly caught my eye. "Sort of, I guess. Yeah."

"You in trouble?"

He shook his head.

"Miles."

Watery blue eyes looked out from a complexion that appeared even more pasty against his dyed-black brows.

"This is going to take a long, long time, we keep at it this way," I said. "Start putting your words a little closer together, bud."

"Can we get outta here?"

"Sure," I said, and wove my way between the tables and back to the bar.

Miles gathered his belongings and followed me as I caught Snyder's attention. I handed him a ten for my nephew's burger and fries.

Snyder waved it away. "Forget it." He leaned against the back rail, sighed audibly as he took up a more comfortable stance. My friend was settling in for more of Gimball's ongoing bitch about how challenging his life had become.

"Thanks," I said, and led my nephew out into the afternoon glare.

*   *   *

"Cool boat, dude," Miles said once we were back aboard the *Kehau*. "Totally chill."

"Thanks."

"You live here? All the time?"

"All the time."

"That is so cool."

He stood beside me on the aft deck, sweating, his luggage—a soiled orange backpack and skateboard—at his feet.

"I'll show you the stateroom where you'll sleep tonight. Bring your gear."

I led him down the stairs, through the salon, the galley, then down the companionway that opened onto four separate staterooms. I gave him the one farthest from mine.

"The head is right here, through this door."

He stifled a fleeting smile. "Head?"

"Bathroom."

"Oh."

"There's a shower in there, too. Why don't you clean up, and I'll see you topside when you're finished."

I used the time to move the Bobcat, the compact .25 caliber pistol I sometimes carry in the custom-fitted pocket of my surf shorts, from its hiding place in the galley to the nightstand beside my bed. A little less handy for unexpected emergencies, but a hell of a lot more safe from curious fingers.

I made a call to Rosalie's, in hopes I'd catch Lani awake. She was.

"You sound good," I said. "Feeling better?"

"I think so. It's hard to tell, 'cause I haven't been up very long. But, I slept like a stone."

"Get the flowers I left you?"

"And the note," she said. Her laugh was husky. "You're a naughty boy."

"A little incentive to get well."

"I'll hold you to it."

"No pun intended," I said. She laughed again. It sounded good. "So, when can I bring you home?"

There was a pause, followed by a sigh.

"Oh, Mike. You know I love you, but the thought of being on a rocking boat right now? I don't think I could take it."

"I understand. It'll pass."

"I'm seeing Dr. Russell tomorrow morning, though. I'll let you know what he says."

I heard the shower pump kick off, so I knew I didn't have much time before Miles was finished. I told Lani, as quickly as I could, about my surprise visitor.

"That's sweet," she said, when I was finished.

"What is?"

"That your nephew came to you."

I had thought of a number of ways to describe the situation, but "sweet" hadn't come up for me. I didn't know how the hell I was going to run my business, look after Lani, and keep an eye on my nephew, too.

"I don't know, Lani. I'm not a kid guy. They're born crying and crapping themselves, and from what I've seen, it doesn't look like it ever gets much better."

She was quiet for a beat too long, and I knew I had crossed a line.

"It'll work out fine," I said into the void of our conversation. It was lame, but it was something.

Even over the phone, her silence was nearly tangible.

"I miss you, Mike," she said, finally. "I'll call you after I see the doctor."

I snapped the phone shut, and Miles was back in the galley, showered, but somehow looking every bit as oily as he had when he arrived. The dye in his hair appeared to have leaked, staining the line of his brow like mascara that had run. He was wearing the same baggy pants, striped boxers riding high above the waistline, and a white wife-beater underneath a polyester bowling shirt that made me sweat just looking at him.

"You gotta be hotter than hell," I said.

"I'm alright."

"Lose the shoes, at least. You can go barefoot."

He started to peel them off, but I didn't want to smell the inevitable. "Do that down below. In your stateroom."

He was back in no time.

"How old are you, Miles?"

"Seventeen next month."

I went to the refrigerator and brought out two bottles of Asahi.

"You New York City kids ever drink beer?"

He struggled with another small smile, his eyes locked on the bottles in my hand. His expression told me he thought this might be some kind of trick, some kind of test.

I popped the tops off both, and handed him one. "Let's go topside. You owe me a story."

-5-

"I hate him," Miles said.

His face was flushed with heat and twisted into an expression of helpless rage.

I knew who *him* was.

The thought crossed my mind that Miles had found out about one of his father's ugly little secrets. It hadn't been too long ago that I'd had to take some extreme steps to keep one of Valden's indiscretions from going public.

"Explain," I said. But for the fact that we were sitting on the bow of my yacht, our legs dangling over the crystal water of Kona Bay, I felt like a cop again. It's like I had told Rosalie at her house: it wasn't, for me at least, something I could just scrub off.

"He's just such an *asshole*," Miles said. "The whole 'family' thing. It's all crap. It's a pain in the ass, and a big fucking lie."

His anger hung in the still air between us, impotent.

"Go on," I prompted.

"You know what I'm saying."

"Pretend I don't."

Miles took a swig of beer, and looked me full in the face for the first time since he had arrived. "You *oughtta* know. You changed your name. You don't even go by 'Van de Groot' anymore."

He was right about my name, if not my motives. I was born Michael Travis Kamahale Van de Groot, but by the time I turned nineteen, I was just Mike Travis.

"There's an old saying, Miles: 'Not to know what happened before you were born is to remain forever a child.'"

His eyes swept the horizon before they landed on me. He didn't say anything.

"You hearing what I said?" I asked.

"Yeah." The defensiveness was back.

"How much do you know about Van de Groot Capital?" I asked.

A sheen of defiance crossed his face. "It makes mad cash, I know that much. I've seen the magazine covers."

"One of the biggest venture capital firms in the world."

"Don't start—"

"What? You don't like being rich?"

Miles turned away, looked off toward town, and watched the line of cars crawl along Alii drive.

I waited him out in silence. In the distance, the slick black flukes of a humpback whale broke the surface and glinted in the hazy sun, leaving a scar on the slow rolling swell.

My nephew turned toward me again, sighed. "He keeps a big calendar-book-thing in his study. He writes *everything* in it. My sister and I sneak in there sometimes just to see what he's going to make us do next, what party he's going to drag us to, just so he can look like Mr. Family Man. It's all so weak. He can't even have a regular conversation with us without planning it in advance."

I squinted against the glare and watched the whale nudge her newborn calf to the surface, teaching it to breathe on its own.

"Like what?"

"Like, right before I left, I saw on his calendar for tomorrow: 'Talk to Miles and Lindee about Hopes vs. Dreams.' I mean, like he's getting all *Focus on the Family* and shit."

"What is it really about?"

"My drawings."

"What about them?"

He shook his head, and his face colored with renewed irritation. "He says art is for homos and heroin addicts. That they never make any money."

That was Valden. Trying to describe all the things that were fucked-up about my brother is like trying to describe what's yellow about a lemon.

"I mean, my dad's been gone on a business trip for almost three weeks this time—hasn't seen me run cross-country, not even *once* in the last two years—but he's gonna schedule this Big Talk. It's a load of crap, and it blows."

The humpbacks broke the surface together this time, just off the point. A small huff of condensation floated into the air, another larger one slightly behind it. I watched them silently as my nephew's emotions gathered steam.

"Then there's these parties we're always supposed to go to, so he can show everybody what a great *family man* he is. Like this Wednesday? It says, 'Fund Raiser for Senator Summers. Bring kids.' My sister and me have been working up an excuse to miss that one for a month."

I knew my brother well enough to know that Miles was telling it straight. But it was the kid's sense of worth hanging there between us, and I wanted to offer something.

"A man's character is his fate, Miles."

"What's that supposed to mean?"

"I think your dad's trying to make things easier for you, Miles. Get you in front of the right people."

"Yeah," he snorted. "That's what Mom says, but it's bullshit. He does it for himself."

"Maybe. But you don't have to choose to be like him. That's what I was saying. Your character determines your fate, bud."

He took a pull from his beer that ran down the corner of his mouth. He wiped at it with the back of his hand.

"What about you?" he spat.

"What? You think that's the reason I changed my name."

"Yeah. And I don't blame you. Look how well it worked out for you. Look how you live."

His voice was carried off in a gust of warm wind as he took in the wide plain of the horizon, then turned his eyes to the mirror of water between his dangling bare feet.

"You think I like everything I've had to do in my life?"

"You?" he chuffed. "What do you ever do that you don't *want* to?"

I took a deep breath before I responded. "You better dial back the 'tude a couple notches, pal. You're gonna run out of friends."

"Well…"

"I don't think you know that tune, Miles. I don't think you're hearing all the notes."

"Oh, yeah? How's that?"

I reached down the collar of my shirt and took hold of the medal that hung from the gold chain around my neck. The family crest. "I noticed you have one of these, too."

He nodded.

"You know what it says?" I asked.

"No."

It figured. Fucking Valden. "Finis Origine Pendet."

"So?"

"That's Latin. It means: 'The end depends upon the beginning.'"

I watched his lips move, silently repeating the Van de Groote family motto.

"You follow what I'm telling you?" I asked. "The end *depends* upon the beginning."

There is a vortex that sucks up behind the children of great wealth; a near-invisible contempt behind the smiles of the people you meet, the same people who act like they can't do enough for you, as long as there was something in it for them, some future kickback from the old man for favors granted you. But that was supposed to be a secret, something you were never supposed to discover, or even notice—never feel crawling, like centipedes, squirming underneath your skin every goddamned day of your life. The *quid pro quo* was your self-respect.

"I didn't change my name so I could run away from anybody, Miles," I said. "I did it because I was tired of getting my ass kissed, tired of being known as The Rich Man's Son."

My nephew faced me, scanned my face for a trace of deceit.

"I changed my name after I started college," I went on. "So I could know for myself that the things I did afterward—like becoming a cop—were done on my own merit, not as some favor to my father."

"That's exactly what I'm saying," he said, a note of victory in his voice. "I just wanna bail. I want to quit school."

"And do what, Miles?" I knew that this kid had never done a real day's work in his life.

"I don't know. Maybe just draw; you know, be an artist."

"Want to hear something my grandfather used to tell me?"

He eyed me warily. "Okay."

"He told me, 'You gotta work like hell to keep from working.' Turns out he's right."

Miles' blank expression told me I hadn't gotten through. I tried again.

"You can either work with your hands—digging ditches, pulling weeds, slinging bricks—or with your brains. In the long run, working with your brains is one hell of a lot easier. That means getting a diploma first, or you never get to make the choice yourself. The world will make it for you."

But I knew he had no idea what real work was, no basis of comparison. He'd never broken a sweat that didn't come from running track at a private high school. A couple days in the coffee fields would make a few more years of school look like a pretty good trade-off.

The whales broke the surface one last time. A fine spray of white water drifted against the horizon as they prepared to sound. A lone frigate bird, floating on the slipstream, circled the sea above them.

"The end depends upon the beginning," he said.

I nodded. Maybe you do get through once in a while. "When's your dad getting back from his business trip?"

"Tonight."

"What about your mom? She's probably worried as hell."

He shook his head. "She's up at Oyster Bay for the weekend. She doesn't even know I left yet."

"You've got to call and tell them you're okay, Miles."

"No way. Not yet." There was something broken, disconsolate in his tone. "Please."

I wondered if Valden had any idea what his chase for success, the kind that was measured by capital accounts and cover stories, was costing him. I drained the last of my beer in one long pull, looked again at my nephew, and made up my mind.

"Whatever you do," I said. "You're not going to sit here on your ass feeling sorry for yourself."

I saw the pulse leap in his neck. "I know," he said, but his voice made it clear he had no idea what I had in mind.

"Here's the deal, Miles, two things: First, before tomorrow night is over, one of us is calling your father to tell him where you are. It can be you, or it can be me."

"And what else?"

"And in the morning, you go to work."

His face brightened. "Here? On the boat?"

I shook my head, pointed toward shore, upslope.

"Picking coffee."

"What?"

"You heard me."

He shook his head in disbelief. "That sucks."

"That's the deal," I said. "Take it or leave it."

He grabbed the chrome railing and pulled himself to his feet, staring out over the slick surface of the sea where the whales had been just a few moments before. He drained the foam out of his long-necked bottle, then reared back and threw the empty as far out into the bay as he could. It bobbed for a few seconds, briefly reflecting the dim yellow light of the sun, then sank out of sight, like a stone.

Miles stalked to the stern, hands thrust deep into the back pockets of his baggy pants. I turned my eyes out to sea, searching a while longer for the whale and its calf. But they were gone.

-6-

I woke my nephew at six the next morning.

The five-hour time difference between Hawaii and New York worked in his favor, but despite it being almost midday in Manhattan, he looked like he could roll right over and sleep for another twelve hours.

"Get dressed for work, Miles. We're leaving in an hour."

He pulled the pillow over his head and turned his face toward the bulkhead.

"Get up," I said. "I'm making breakfast."

"Not hungry," he mumbled.

I yanked the pillow off his head and smacked him with it. "Get your ass outta bed, goddammit. We made a deal."

His face was scrunched up like a dried-apple carving, and he squinted at me through sleep-reddened eyes.

"Okay," he whined. "Jesus."

A few minutes later, the smell of sizzling bacon brought Miles up from below. He pulled up a stool at the bar counter and watched in silence as I cracked a half-dozen eggs into a bowl. I whipped them together with some milk, then pressed the plunger on the toaster.

"Why does my father hate you so much?"

A hell of a conversation starter. I turned, glanced at him over my shoulder, then poured the beaten eggs into the pan that had been heating on the burner.

"Is that why you came to me?" I asked. "To piss off your dad?"

He shrugged. "Maybe."

It hadn't always been that way between Valden and me. There was a time when I thought my older brother could do no wrong. But it all started to change the year after our mother died. I hadn't thought about it in a long, long time.

"Why do you think he does?"

"'Cause you're nothing like him."

Throw the kid a fish. At least he got points for being perceptive. For a guy who didn't like himself very much, my brother Valden had almost no tolerance for people who weren't like him.

"I'll tell you something about being different, Miles. People aren't much different than most animals. You take one out of the pack, tie a ribbon on his tail, then let him go? The rest of the pack'll try to gnaw that fucking tail right off."

* * *

The office door was open when we got to the Plantation. Tino's truck was parked in the gravel lot, but he was nowhere to be found.

"It's cold up here," Miles said. A slow breeze rattled in the banana fronds and wild bougainvillea.

"Tell me about it at lunch time."

He followed me down the path toward Edita's tree, caught sight of the Mule parked in the turnaround, and ran to it. He threw a leg over the saddle and made sputtering motorcycle noises with his mouth. "Sweet. Do I get to drive this thing?"

The pickers' bags lay on the spool table under the tree, like heavy-duty knapsacks with one long shoulder strap. I picked one up, tossed it to him.

"You get to drive one of these."

He climbed off the Mule and eyed the sack with an undisguised absence of enthusiasm.

"Put the strap over your shoulder and rest the bag on your opposite hip."

"Like this?"

"No," I said, adjusting the belt across his chest. "Like that."

"Oh, man," he whined. "I look like freakin' Juan Valdez."

I hooked a thumb back toward the shed where I'd parked the Jeep. "Go get a pair of gloves out of the office."

"What for?"

"Miles, why is it you think every pitch is a curve ball?"

"What's that supposed to mean?"

"Either do what you're told when I tell you, or forget it."

"I just asked 'what for?' Chill out."

I picked up one of the three-foot sticks from among the others on the table. "Come with me," I said, as I strode out into the orchard. "This is called a 'holding hook.' Watch closely."

The stick I'd brought with me was made of guava, maybe an inch thick. At one end was a loop of wire, at the other was a metal hook. I slipped my foot into the loop, reaching up with the other end. I placed the hook near the middle of a branch full of ripe coffee cherry, gently brought my foot to the ground, and bent the bough down toward me.

"This leaves both hands free for picking. Get it?"

Miles nodded.

"You've got to be careful not to pull down too hard, or you'll break the branch off."

He looked at me blankly.

"That's a bad thing," I said. "You don't want to break off the branches."

"I'm not an idiot."

"We'll see," I said. "Now, give it a try."

I didn't know whether to laugh or feel sorry for him as he fumbled with the gear. When he finally got the hook in place, he pulled down too fast, and the branch came loose, smacking him roughly across the face.

"Try it again," I said.

He did, and that time it held.

"You only want to pick the ripe cherry," I said. I held a sample between my thumb and forefinger. "The ones that are that deep red like this one."

Miles reached into the bush and picked off a cherry. He held it up for me to see.

"Put it in the bag."

"Piece of cake," he said. A red welt was beginning to show where the branch had scratched him.

"Glad to hear it. That basket you're carrying holds about twenty pounds. A decent picker should pick about two hundred pounds a day. So, fill that thing ten times before the day's over, and you'll be doing all right."

"No sweat."

"Then get to it," I said.

He reached in, picked another dozen or so before he recoiled and quickly jumped away. The holding hook came loose and whipped the limb back at my nephew hard enough to drop him on his ass.

"What the fuck was *that*?" He pointed into the tree.

"Long skinny thing?" I grinned, holding my hands about five inches apart. "About like that?"

He nodded, eyes wide.

"Centipede," I said.

"Do they bite?"

"Oh, yeah," I said. "Like a sonofabitch. Hurts like hell."

He sat there in the red dirt, puffed his cheeks, and exhaled a loud sigh.

"You wanna do what I asked you and go get the damn gloves now, Miles?"

*   *   *

"What's this, got a new picker?"

"My nephew," I said. Tino and I were sitting on the spool table watching Miles, about twenty yards away. He was still wrestling with the same tree I'd started him on half an hour before. "His name is Miles."

Tino scratched his head. "He done any work like this before?"

I shook my head. "I don't think he's done any kind of work before."

Deep lines formed between his eyes. "He gonna come bust up da trees, brah."

"Any damage, take it out of my end. Take his wages out of my cut, too."

Tino didn't look too pleased. "The Sotos," he said, shaking his head.

"Don't worry, Tino. If the Soto boys make it hard on him, that's Miles' problem. Little reality in his life won't kill him. Time the kid pulled his shit together."

"If you say so."

"And don't you take it easy on him, either."

"You one mean-kine uncle," Tino said, laughing.

Cool morning air stirred in the trees, and the fragrance of white ginger mingled with the sounds of wild canaries hidden deep inside their branches.

"I brought his lunch. It's in the cooler in the office. I'll come back this afternoon to pick him up."

"Let's hope he don't come up dead."

"Just try to keep him away from anything sharp."

Tino was still laughing as I climbed into the Jeep and headed back to town, pushing the long shadows of the rising sun down the rutted road before me.

-7-

The dive gear I planned to use on my wednesday charter was spread out on the deck of the *Kehau*, wet and glistening in the sunlight. I dropped the hose I'd been using to wash the equipment, pushed my dark glasses to the top of my head, and reached into the shadow of the bulkhead to turn off the spigot. The boat rolled easily beneath my bare feet as I stowed the long tube of hose and looked up at the smooth, glaring sheet of sky.

I was about to go below to fix a late lunch when it hit me, a half-formed recollection that dropped on me like a weight.

It must have always been there, lurking, hanging off the limbs of my brain like moss, like a dream. But when I tried to reach out, it pulled away, broke from the branches, and left only remnants of a boy's gapped and stuttering memory.

*   *   *

1973. Early September.

Her name is Stacy Thorne.

It is my first year of high school, a year I've looked forward to since Valden started here two years before me. Every morning during junior high, I would sit in the car and watch the older kids, like an exotic and unfamiliar species, when my mother dropped my brother off for school. I would stare out the car window in a kind of fear-tinged wonder at the girls whose sweaters stretched and pulled in shapes that girls my age weren't yet even hinting at, and at the boys who were able to grow sideburns and beards. My brother was one of them, and the chasm between our worlds, at those moments, never seemed wider.

But our whole lives changed in the few weeks that led up to my first year of high school. My mother died from drowning in the bay that fronts our summer home in Honaunau, and my father has become lost in his work with the family firm, Van de Groot Capital. As his absences from home grow longer, our houses get larger, just like the household staff he employs.

At some level, I know he, too, is drowning himself: in possessions, in prominence, and, finally, in liquor. The change is so gradual it goes mostly unnoticed, but Valden is basking in it. He is a junior this year, and between the new convertible Beemer my father has given him, and his starting position in varsity football, he is wading in a sort of celebrity of his own making. The rich kid whose mother died. The girls are real suckers for it, he says.

Stacy Thorne is her name, blonde and pretty in a simple way I will always associate with innocence. She is a cheerleader, a junior like my brother. I see her at school every day. And though it may only be the trick of perception, for me, as a freshman, she seems completely unapproachable, untouchable.

"You're Mike, right?"

She is standing in our driveway, waiting for Valden to come out from the garage where he's parked his new car alongside my father's Bentley and Jag.

"Yeah," I answer, my voice sounding oddly uncertain. "You're Stacy Thorne."

"Yes, I am." She smiles, and holds out her hand. It is soft and warm, and I feel the heat rise to my face. "Nice to meet you, Mike."

My brother comes around the side of the house, feet crunching loudly on the dry leaves that whirl in eddies of cool autumn wind.

"Hey, get your own girlfriend, Tadpole," Valden says. My face takes on a deeper shade.

He weaves an arm around her waist and pulls her to him, kisses her with one eye open, watching me watch him. "Mmm," he says, licks his lips. "Cherry."

"Strawberry," she giggles. She brushes at her mouth with the tips of her fingers.

"We're gonna be studying in my room," he says. "So leave us alone, and try not to be a pain in the ass."

Stacy gives Valden a little shove. "Don't," she says. "He's sweet."

"Yeeaaah," he drawls. "Right."

My brother takes her hand and pulls her toward the front door. As he opens it, she turns back, gives me a little wave and one last smile. "Bye, Mike. See you around."

I wish it were true.

She follows me into my sleep that night.

*   *   *

I hung the dive gear out to dry in a limp afternoon glare.

Another low-pressure system was moving down the chain from Oahu. I could feel it. A thin shelf of gray cloud hugged the shoreline and stilled the air beneath it. In the distance, toward the horizon, the sea was deep blue and dotted with bright sun. But there in the bay, beneath the cloud cover, my shirt stuck wetly to my skin. It might have been the weather, or the unexpected assault of memory. Maybe I was still worried about

Lani staying up at Rosalie's. I don't know, but I felt like I was dragging an empty bucket through the water.

I still needed to fill the scuba tanks from the compressor I had aboard, but when I looked at my watch, I saw it was almost four o'clock. It would have to wait until tomorrow. I peeled off my shirt and went below to shower before going back ashore. There was a stop I needed to make before I picked up my nephew.

*   *   *

Half an hour later, I passed through the glass doors of the Kealakehe substation, into the air-conditioned chill. A uniformed officer sat at the reception desk behind wire glass. He was a bullet-headed young guy with a thick neck and close-cropped hair. The name on the brass tag above his pocket read *H. Pahoa*.

"Detective Moon around?" I asked.

He looked at me curiously before he answered. "I know you?"

"I don't think so."

Pahoa shook his head. "I seen you around."

"Is Moon here or not?"

He punched in a three-digit number without taking his eyes off me, and spoke into the receiver. A moment later, Moon appeared at the door.

He led me back to his desk in the bullpen, offered me the perp seat as he rocked back in his swivel chair, laced his fingers behind his head. "You look like you got something on your mind, Big City."

"Who's on Rosalie's car-bombing?"

Moon shot a look over his shoulder at Captain Cerillo's office and sat a little straighter in his seat. "I don't know."

"Bullshit."

He shook his head. "'C'mon, Travis, you know how it works. You can't come in here kicking sand in everybody's faces."

"Who's on it?"

Moon glanced at the white board on the far wall. A list of names ran down one side; case names, dates, and status were printed in neat block lettering beside each one. The word *Pending* appeared in the column beside Rosalie's name. "Scott Riley," Moon said. "And he's not here."

I was about to ask what the hell "pending" meant as the Captain's door swung open. When I looked over, he motioned me over with a come-ahead wave. Despite the captains' bars on his collar points, the dark uniform and the triangle of starched white T-shirt underneath made him look like a traffic cop.

He closed the door behind me as I stepped inside his office.

"You gotta stop driving nails into my guys' heads, Travis."

"Then make a priority of finding who the hell tried to flash-fry my friends."

He bit back something he was about to say, then went around the back of his desk and looked out the window at the traffic heading up toward the resorts on Queen K Highway.

"You have any idea how many people want a piece of that woman? Any idea how much hate mail she gets every month?"

"How many of those people have access to explosives, Captain? You got a developer blowing rock three days a week at that golf course down south. Anybody checking him out?"

Cerillo turned away from the view and looked hard into my face. "You want a job? You want to be a cop again? Fill out an application. Otherwise, stay the fuck out of it."

"Then arrest somebody. In the meantime, I got a couple of friends who say a novena every time they put the key in their ignition."

He showed me a condescending smile as he slid into his swivel chair. "Maybe you don't know this, but we don't get a lot of car bombs on this rock. We got forensic limitations. We got procedures to deal with."

"Fuck procedures. You need help, you should ask for it."

"I ever need help, I *will* ask for it," he said. "Meantime, go back to your boat, Travis. Before you track shit all over my case."

"You don't have a case." I stood to leave. "You know, I'd hate to think somebody on your squad's in Krupp's pocket."

Cerillo stood up so fast his chair slammed against the wall. He leaned across his desk, his weight resting on balled fists. His eyes were black stone. "That is not something you want to say again."

I held his gaze, feeling the vein throb in my temple. "It's not something I want to believe, Captain. But every time I ask somebody what's happening on Rosalie's case, all I hear is crickets."

-8-

Tino was sitting on top of the spool table, a half-empty bottle of water between his feet, flipping pages, and making notes on the clipboard he held in his hands. He was locked in concentration and didn't look up until I took a seat beside him.

"How'd it go with my nephew?" I asked.

Tino tilted his pencil in the direction of the field. "Still at it."

The sun crept below the low clouds off to the west, a dim orange ball that revealed itself briefly before dipping beyond the horizon. The last of the fading light slipped between the leaves of Edita's monkeypod tree and stenciled the dirt with pale shadows.

I looked at my watch. "It's past five."

"The Sotos, they come finish by t'ree o'clock," he shrugged. "But this guy."

Miles came out from among the coffee trees, shuffled heavily under the weight of the picker's bag that hung off his shoulder, and made his way toward the Mule that was parked in the turnaround. We watched him pour the contents into a half-filled burlap bag and turn wordlessly back toward the field.

"Where're you going?" I called to him.

His face was blank with fatigue and smudged with muddy sweat. "Got two more bags to go. You said ten a day, right?"

I caught Tino's glance out of the corner of my eye and ignored it.

"I said experienced pickers could do about ten bags a day."

"Well, I only got eight so far, counting that last one."

Tino started to say something, but I cut him off with a shake of my head.

"It's getting dark," I called out to Miles.

"I can still see."

I nodded and watched him trudge off between the rows of trees and disappear into the shadows.

Tino reached for the cap of his water bottle and screwed it back on as he got to his feet. "That boy not the best picker I ever seen, but he one stubborn bugga for sure."

"The Soto boys give him a hard time?"

Tino nodded. "Plenty stink-eye, talkin' some trash."

"How'd Miles handle it?"

Tino answered by pointing into the field where my nephew had gone to continue picking. "Just like his Uncle Mike. One stubborn bugga."

I smiled as Tino walked away, shaking his head.

*   *   *

It was dead dark by the time Miles threw in the towel.

A fine evening breeze blew down off the slopes of Mauna Kea. It cooled the night and filled it with the scent of tuberose and white ginger, and the whistle of coqui frogs that hid themselves deep inside the wild ferns and croton.

I heard his feet scuff the loose red soil as he approached, and I caught the first whiff of something pungent and overpowering.

"Jesus, Miles. What the hell is that smell?"

Even in the dimness I saw the indignity he tried to hide by turning away.

"Turkey shit," he said. "The Soto brothers stuffed my shoes with turkey shit."

"How the hell—" I began. "Never mind. Just wash 'em out before you get in the Jeep."

"I already did."

"Do it again."

*　　*　　*

It wasn't until we were back aboard the *Kehau* that I got my first look at Miles in good light. He was covered with dried streaks of mud, sweat, and a web-work of tiny scratches on his arms and face. His eyes were red and shone with fatigue.

"You look like you went three rounds with a weed whacker."

Miles shrugged and showed me a tight, humorless smile.

"How was it?" I asked.

"Hot."

"The Soto boys give you much trouble?"

"You mean besides the shit in my shoes?" My nephew's eyes slipped to the carpet. "A little. Said I was a limp-dick *mahu*, and that I picked like a *haole* faggot."

"Gonna go back tomorrow?" An unintended edge of challenge crept into my voice.

He looked directly into my face. "Yeah," he said.

I nodded. "Good."

He started down the stairs toward his stateroom, then turned abruptly, like he'd just remembered something. "About that call."

The call to his father in New York. I was sure he'd been fixated on it all day. "What about it?"

"You said either I could make it, or you'd do it for me."

"That was our deal."

He waited a beat, weighing his options one last time. I knew he dreaded making contact with Valden after running off the way he had, and I couldn't say I blamed him. The only choice left was whether to face the music himself or have me stand proxy. The proverbial high- or low-roads.

"I'll do it," he said. "Just lemme take a shower first."

He pulled his lunch cooler from his backpack, handed it to me, and headed below trailing a sigh that was so deep I thought he might pass out.

*   *   *

I had a pair of steaks on the barbecue when he came back topside. His face had a shiny, just-shaved look, the skin around his eyes drawn tight.

"Can I borrow your phone? The batteries for mine are dead."

"Sure. It's on the navigation table at the foot of the stairs."

He nodded mechanically. "What time is it in New York, anyway?"

I looked at my watch, did the math. "About eleven."

He gazed past me toward the lights along the shore, the flickering of bamboo torches at the waterline. He inhaled deeply and went back into the galley for my phone.

The night was still, quiet, and the smoke from my cooking fire streamed lazily into the darkness as I stabbed the bloody meat with a fork. I glanced below, through the open hatchway. Miles stood at the bottom of the stairs as he dialed the number, his back to me. He stared through portholes that were dusted with fine sea spray, toward the village. I could hear every word he said.

"Is Valden Van de Groot there?"

There was a long silence as he waited, then: "Will you tell him his son call—? Yeah, I'll hold."

He turned then, looked up the stairs toward the transom, toward me. I nodded to him. His attention returned to the phone call. "Miles," he said to whoever had come back on the line, then paused another second. "M-I-L-E-S. Right. He can reach—" His expression melted into something that was more frustration than relief as he was interrupted yet again, waited another long few seconds. "Just tell him I'm with Uncle Mike. He has the number."

Miles snapped the phone shut and walked slowly back to the nav table. He gently slid my cell back into the charger. His movements were exaggerated, overly careful, confined and contained, as he came back out into the night.

"Listen—" I began, but he cut me off.

"It was the service. Dad's 'unavailable' right now."

"You did what you agreed to do. You told him where you are. You held up your end."

"Yeah," he said softly.

"Steaks'll be ready in a few minutes."

"I don't think I'm hungry."

"C'mon, Miles. Have a seat up here, take a few breaths."

He shook his head. "I don't think so. I think I'm gonna go to bed."

I looked into his face for a moment, read what was in his eyes, then nodded. "Okay, kid. See you in the morning."

"Yeah," he said and started down the stairs.

"Hey, Miles?"

I heard his footsteps stop mid-stride. "Yeah?"

"It isn't about you."

The sea lapped gently at the hull of the *Kehau.*

"Sure feels like it is."

"I know it does. But it isn't. It's just your dad's way."

"G'night, Uncle Mike."

"G'night, kid."

*   *   *

My phone rang an hour later.

I had finished my dinner, cleaned up, made a steak sandwich for Miles' lunch, and just settled in for an Asahi nightcap. If I hadn't thought it was my brother returning his son's call, I would have let it go. But that night was full of surprises.

"Travis," I answered.

"Hey, pardner," the voice said. "Interrupting anything?"

"An after-dinner beer. Nothing I can't pick up where I left off. What's up, Hans?"

"I'm calling for your brother."

"You got the wrong number. He's not here."

Hans sighed. "I mean, I'm calling on behalf of your brother."

"You're a fucking hoot, Hans," I said, instantly regretting the tension in my voice.

"Valden's son, Miles, left him a message a while ago."

"What's that got to do with you?"

Silence spun down the line at me.

"Jesus. You're working for him," I accused.

"I've been working on a couple of projects for him."

"For Chrissake, Hans."

"It's not that simple, Mike."

"I know. I was there."

"Then you know how it is."

"He's pimping you, Hans. He's turning you out, and you talk like you owe it to him."

"I owe it to my wife."

"If Mie knew you were getting in bed with Valden, she'd kick your ass out of the house."

"She does know. He offered me a position as head of security for VGC."

The silence was mine this time.

"Did you take it?" I asked finally.

"I'm thinking about it. Where's Miles?"

"Tell Valden to call him himself. Miles is his fucking son."

"That's what he's paying me to do."

A dry, empty noise escaped my throat, and I felt the deck roll beneath my feet.

"Then you better watch yourself, Hans. You're about two steps up the food chain from a crack-whore. Next thing you know, you'll be giving blow-jobs at the bus station."

-9-

1973. Late September.

The pool house is crowded, close and stale, thick with cigarette smoke. The air indoors is rife with the odor of beer and sweat and cheap perfume. Wall-mounted speakers are blaring the loose and jamming "Can't You Hear Me Knocking" by the Stones.

My father isn't due back home for another two days, and Valden has commandeered the pool house for a Saturday night high school blowout. There must be a hundred and fifty people here, spilling out the sliding glass doors and onto the lawn that encircles the swimming pool. Valden is inside, tapping a fresh keg, and manhandling his new girlfriend, Stacy Thorne.

The song breaks out from a long sax solo and into the guitar licks that take the side all the way out to the label grooves. I hear the crack of the needle lifting from the vinyl then touching down again on the new live album by Deep Purple. It opens with an earsplitting "Highway Star" and I wonder that the Waldrons, our elderly live-in houseman and cook, don't come down and make Valden shut down all the racket. But I know why. It's been less than a year since we lost our mother, and they're not about to disrupt The Boys if they're having a good time. As long as nothing gets broken and nobody gets hurt. It's the unspoken rule, and in the absence of my father, it means that anything goes. Valden wears it like an emperor's robe, this newfound freedom, this bizarre celebrity, all the perks that go with being young, rich and bulletproof. As for me, I'm only a freshman. I'm just glad my brother hasn't made me look like an asshole in front of all these people.

"Hey, Mikey," she says, and taps me on the shoulder. I startle. I didn't see her coming.

"Stacy," I say.

"You wanna dance with me?"

I glance over at my brother. He's holding court at the beer keg and doesn't see her talking to me. "Sure."

We push through the crowd of squirming bodies and begin to dance just as the song segues into a slow blues "Child In Time." Stacy reaches out, wraps both hands around my waist and pulls me close. I feel the heat of her, smell the fresh scent of her hair and the sway of her body. I also feel people watching, but I try to ignore it. She looks up into my face and smiles, resting her head on my chest as she moves with the music. I am suddenly aware of how few other people are dancing beside us now.

Valden grabs my shoulder.

"Don't get your undies in a bunch, Tadpole," he says. "Dancey time is over."

"Don't be mean, Valden," Stacy says. There's a beery shine in her eyes that I hadn't seen at first.

He takes her hand and leads her away, back into the crowd inside the pool house. He steps behind the built-in bar, pours something pink and unctuous from the blender and hands it to Stacy. As she tips the plastic cup to her lips, Valden peers through the haze of cigarette smoke, and sees me watching him. He makes a gun out of his thumb and forefinger, points it at me and winks. His friends laugh.

Stacy Thorne doesn't see a thing.

*   *   *

It's past midnight, and the music continues to blare into the darkness.

There's been a change in the crowd. The inexperienced drinkers have puked and left. Now, it's only Valden's close friends, some older guys from junior college, and a handful of potheads who remain. I can smell a sweet smoky odor coming from behind the pool house, trailed by giggles and muffled conversation.

Somebody puts the new Traffic album "Shootout at the Fantasy Factory" on the stereo, and the whole night takes on a bizarre, surreal ambiance. I know I've had too much beer, but I don't feel sick. I feel like I'm watching the whole thing on a movie screen. It's like I'm there, but not there, too. The music sounds good, and the girls look even better. Everywhere I look, there're couples making out.

It is late September, and an Indian summer warms the night, touches the air with the smell of freshly cut grass and magnolia. Music rolls out across the breeze.

I wander inside to refill my beer from the keg that sits in an ice-filled garbage can in the middle of the floor in the tiny kitchen. The Waldrons are going to have a hell of a time cleaning up this mess. But they won't say a word to my father.

I pump the keg, end up getting as much foam as beer when I go to fill my cup. I don't really care. I glance around for Valden and spot him in the corner with a couple of assholes from the football team. Stacy Thorne is nowhere in sight.

I think about her, about how she smelled, how it felt when she danced with me earlier, her head resting on my chest as we moved to the music. I look over again at my brother, catch his eye, try to ask where Stacy went, but he's ignoring my sign language, and the music is too loud for me to yell over.

I wave it away. Forget it. Valden shrugs and goes back to making jokes with his buddies.

I push my way through a knot of people in the hallway and head for the bathroom. The door is shut. I try the handle. It's locked. I hear something inside. Sounds like someone crying. I knock. Nothing. I knock again, then pound harder on the door.

It flies open. The light is off, but Stacy is inside. She's got her back against the sink, wiping her mouth with the back of her hand. Shiny pink lipstick smears the back of her hand and spreads across her mouth like a wound.

Someone else is in there, too. He pushes past me, shoves me out of the doorway. He looks pissed off. It's one of the guys that Valden was talking with earlier. Tall skinny guy. Bad skin. I've seen him around, but I don't know his name.

I step inside, speak to Stacy. "You okay?"

She nods.

I hand her a tissue.

"You might want to, uh…" I say, pointing to my own mouth. She looks in the mirror and begins to fix herself up.

I take her hand and head back out into the party. I push past the hallway crowd again, back toward where I last saw Valden. Stacy follows me, my hand enfolded in both of hers. She's holding on tight.

The skinny guy is up in my brother's face, but Valden backs him off, jabbing a stiff finger in his chest. My brother's at least a head shorter than the other guy, but Valden's flexing his beer muscles in front of his friends.

"That wasn't the deal, man," I hear the skinny guy say. "I want my twenty bucks back."

"Fuck you," Valden laughs.

"That wasn't the deal. She wouldn't even kiss me for Chrissakes. She's too fucking drunk, man."

Stacy heard it too. She lets go of my hand and moves around me so quickly I didn't even register what was happening. Stacy Thorne reels back and plants a vicious slap on my brother's face. Valden rears reflexively, like he's going to slap her right back. I grab his wrist and hold it in midair. His friends start to laugh. So does my brother.

"Take her home, Tadpole," he says to me. "She's drunk."

She's crying as we walk across the lawn, her arms wrapped tightly around herself. She won't look at me.

I sit with Stacy in my father's Jaguar. It is still parked in the garage, in the dark. Long minutes pass without a word.

*   *   *

An early morning rain has washed the empty streets. Uneven brushstrokes of neon and swamps of soiled luminescence reflect beneath the streetlights as I finally drive her home. The dim flicker of lightning shows inside the clouds that hang low over the hills and punctuates our heavy silence. I want to reach across and touch her. I want to make it right.

I turn to look at her, but her face is vacant, eyes still shining with humiliation in the dim glow of the windshield, and I know there is nothing I can do. There is nothing, not even the promise of sunrise that is only two hours away.

-10-

It was the third straight day of dead calm and gray skies—the kind of weather that makes you want to slide back into bed after lunch and take long naps, but you know you'll only wake up feeling worse, disoriented and lethargic.

I was already exhausted from a night assaulted by dreams and that lingering black feeling in my gut, but the harder I tried to recall the details, the deeper the images receded. My conversation with Hans the night before was like shards of glass in my brain, and Valden still hadn't called by the time I drove Miles to the Plantation for his second day of work.

On the way back down into town, I stopped by Rosalie and Dave's to check on Lani, but she had already left for her doctor's appointment. As I climbed into the Jeep to leave, my phone rang. It was my Wednesday charter. They were canceling on me. The man balked when I reminded him of my 48-hour cancellation policy and seemed to take offense when I suggested that life could sometimes be a bitch, and I'd be keeping his deposit.

By the time one o'clock rolled around, the only bright spot in the day was an invitation to join Tino and Edita for a barbecue at their house that night. The only thing that could have made it better was if Lani had returned my calls.

*   *   *

The lunch crowd at Snyder's had thinned by the time I dropped in, so I took my usual seat at the rail, facing the door. Old habits die hard, if ever at all.

Snyder was leaning over the bar, talking to a guy about our same age wearing Army fatigue shorts, a tank shirt, and a long dark ponytail. He excused himself from their conversation and moved down the bar as soon as I sat down.

"Hey, Mike," Snyder called out. "Lunch?"

"Yeah. Fish sandwich and a beer."

He passed the order back to the kitchen, then reached into the cooler for an Asahi, popped the cap, poured the contents over ice, and pushed the glass over to me.

"You guys know each other?" Snyder asked me. He nodded toward the guy in the fatigues.

The guy swiveled in his chair and offered me his hand. "Who hasn't heard of Mike Travis?" he said as we shook. I recognized his voice immediately.

"Radical Rod," I said. "From the radio, right?"

He smiled. "Seven to midnight, on the station that rocks the rock, man."

His face was tan and deeply lined, hair showing gray at the temples. A pair of Oakley sunglasses hung from a cord around his neck.

"I caught the Blind Faith set you played the other night," I said. "Nice."

"Memory Lane. Always reminds me of college."

I nodded, tipped back the Asahi and wiped the foam from my lip with the back of my hand.

"Rod went to UVA back in the day," Snyder put in. "Law."

The DJ shot him a look like he'd just been outed. I figured they might have known one another from Snyder's previous life.

"You're a lawyer?" I asked.

"Nah," he smiled and picked his glass up off the bar. "Never sat for the Bar exam."

"You believe that shit?" Snyder said to me. "Guy goes summa cum laude from Stanford, gets his JD from Virginia, and never sits for the goddamn Bar."

I lifted my glass in his direction. "My hat's off, Rod," I said. "I'd rather have a daughter that's a hooker than a son who's a lawyer."

He laughed, leaned across the aisle and touched his glass against mine. "Tell it to my family. They're still pissed off about it."

I stood and headed for the back of the room, digging into my pocket for change. "Welcome to the club," I said as I fed a handful of quarters into the juke. Joe Walsh kicked on as I strode back to my seat.

"You used to be on in the mornings, didn't you?" I asked. Idle conversation was helping push back the shadows that had been crawling around my head all morning, dim shapes hiding in corners I couldn't reach.

"Yeah," Rod smiled. He glanced sideways at Snyder, then back at me. "They moved me to the night shift after I started doing my 'Air Traffic Reports.'"

I remembered it then. The State was receiving some big money from the Feds in exchange for having the cops run a series of marijuana interdiction operations on local growers—Operation Green Harvest, they called it—often conducted by helicopter.

"What was it you'd say?" Snyder said, imitating a news-jock voice. "Something like, 'It's a clear and sunny one, and the birds are flying south this morning.'"

Rod nodded, smiled. "'So keep your eyes to the sky, and some shoes on your feet.' I used to play stuff like 'Let Me Roll It' afterward. Hell, I figured it was a public service."

"Guess the station didn't see it your way," I said, sliding into my seat again.

"Guess not."

Joe Walsh faded out as Keith Richards' choppy guitar licks opened "Gimme Shelter" on the box as Lolly brought my sandwich out from the kitchen. Then, without warning, the hairs stood out on my neck when Jagger began to sing.

> *Rape, Murder*
> *It's just a shot away, it's just a shot away*
> *The flood is threatening my very life today*
> *Gimme, gimme shelter or I'm gonna fade away*

Something jogged loose inside me, seared my subconscious and spiked through my brain. A jolt as real as a physical blow that flashed for an instant then receded into darkness. It felt like lightning in my veins.

I looked down at my lunch plate with no appetite at all.

*   *   *

I took the skiff back out to the *Kehau* and packed a few things in a duffel before going up to the Plantation. I didn't want to waste time coming back to the boat before heading out to Tino's for dinner, so I grabbed some soap, deodorant and cologne, and looked for some fresh clothes for Miles.

Everything he had was balled-up and stuffed into the bottom of his backpack, and it looked like an explosion at a Salvation Army store. I had an hour or so before I needed to collect him, so I stopped by Coconut Willie's and bought a handful of Aloha shirts and a couple pairs of shorts for the kid. I snagged a shirt or two for myself while I was at it. I figured if my nephew was going to be in town for a while, he might as well be comfortable.

I slid my sunglasses off my head and back into place as I came out to the sidewalk into the late afternoon glare. I glanced at my watch and decided I had just enough time to stop by the market to buy a few things to take to Tino's.

The temperature cooled as I drove the winding road up the side of Hualalai. I felt the wind on my face and in my hair, my mind drifting. I looked out across a field of rocks and tall grass, and watched a flock of mynah birds light out from the shade of a poinciana, make a broad circle, then land again in the outstretched arms of a mango tree. I could hear their squawks over the Jeep's growling engine noise as they fought for space in the branches.

I turned my attention back to the rutted road just as the Mule, Tino astride it, darted out from between the rows of coffee. I slammed on my brakes in a cloud of red dust and gravel. Tino did the same, and the Mule slid to a stop at the edge of the field, dumping a bag of fresh-picked cherry into the dirt.

He looked up as the air cleared, squinting through the haze at whoever the hell had almost killed him. "The fuck, brah!"

I climbed down from the Jeep. "Jesus, I'm sorry, Tino."

He was still breathing hard, eyes wide. He switched off the engine and swung down off the muddy tractor. The silence of late afternoon hung heavily in the air for a few long seconds as our ears adjusted to the sudden quiet.

I picked the half-empty burlap bag up out of the dirt and set it back on the Mule with the ones that had somehow managed to remain in place. "I'm sorry, Tino," I said again.

"You awright?" he asked.

"Yeah," I said, pissed at the mental distraction that had been dogging me. "I've had my head up my ass all goddamned day."

"No worries," he said as he clapped me on the shoulder. "Help me get this stuff back in the bag, yeah?"

We both knelt in the dirt, using our hands to shovel the spilled cherry into the sack. When we finished, Tino looked at me, an expression of concern in his eyes.

"Cool head, main thing, you know?" he said, and drove the Mule up to the shed.

I followed in the Jeep, parked, and walked down to the spool table in silence. The Sotos' cars were still in the turnaround, but I didn't see any sign of either them or Miles. I heard Tino shut down the tractor, so I hiked back to the shed to help him offload the day's harvest.

"It's after four," I said. "What're the Sotos still doing here?"

Tino looked off into a far section of the field. "These guys, I dunno. Got a real humbug for Miles."

"Call 'em in," I said. "I'm getting hungry."

Tino went to the side of the shed, took hold of a thin rope, and rang the hell out of the rusty bell that was bolted to the outside wall. My ears hummed when he finally stopped, but I saw the three young men emerge from among the trees and trudge up the path toward us. I couldn't make out the words, though I could hear the voices of the Soto brothers as they harassed Miles from six paces behind him. All their talking stopped when they reached the shed, and each in turn dumped the contents of their pickers' bags into an empty burlap sack.

Ben Soto was the first to come out, his long, narrow face crusted with a thin layer of dust. White teeth flashed as he tossed me a grin and a head-nod greeting, then headed for the water-jug to pour himself a cup. His brother, Ken, came out a moment later, a mirror image of his twin, but for slightly longer black hair. Ben handed Ken a fresh cup, then walked over to their car. Ken greedily gulped his, then sauntered down to take a seat beneath Edita's tree, where his brother met him with a fresh pack of cigarettes.

I took the bag with the toiletries I'd brought from the *Kehau* into the shed and handed it to Miles. His face was lined with dirt and sweat, his shirt torn and heavy with grime.

He turned when he heard me enter.

"Hey," he said.

"I brought you some stuff from the boat. And a towel. There's a shower around back."

He eyed me for a second before hanging his picker's bag on a nail hammered into the wall. "What for? What're we doing?"

"Going to Tino's for dinner."

He was about to complain, then thought better of it. "I don't have any clean clothes."

"I brought you some of those, too."

Ten minutes later, he came back around from behind the shed, hair soaked and plastered to his forehead, a towel held firmly around his waist. His forearms and face were burned a ruddy brown, but his chest and legs still glowed pasty white, a ghostly T-shirt imprinted on his skin. I tossed him one of the bags of clothes I'd bought at Coconut Willie's. He turned without a word and carried it back toward the shower enclosure.

The Soto brothers were talking animatedly, hands flying as they spoke. Ben leaned back, dragged the last of his cigarette and fired up a fresh one from the butt. They were still there, sitting at the spool table when Miles came out from the shower. He was wearing a new pair of Island Pro sandals, surfer shorts, and an aloha shirt printed with palms and pineapples. It was the moment Ben and Ken had been waiting for. They both lit up with catcalls and hoots.

Ben made a loud kissing sound and said, "You so *pretty!*"

Ken howled with laughter and started in on Miles, too. "That is one *mahu* shirt you wearin' brah! Da boys gonna love you plenny!" The twin brothers balled up their fists, gave each other a pound as they reared back laughing.

"Shuddup, *lepo*," Tino said, and lobbed a dirt clod toward the table. "How 'bout you two stop making ass."

The clod burst harmlessly at the brothers' feet as Ken dropped his cigarette. He ground it into the dirt with the toe of his work boot.

My nephew's cheeks turned an angry red, and he shot me a look from the corner of his eye. I took the bag of dirty clothes he held, walked back around the side of the shed, and dropped them into the Jeep. I reached into one of the other bags I'd brought from the shop and withdrew one of the new shirts I'd bought for myself. It was identical to the one Miles was wearing. I slipped out of the one I was wearing, put on the new one, and walked back around the shed.

When I came back into sight, Ben and Ken nearly swallowed their tongues. The abrupt silence was filled with the creaking of tree branches and the far-off garble of wild turkeys.

Tino took one look at me, then at the Sotos' slack faces, and nearly busted a gut.

"So whaddaya think?" I held my arms out at my side, palms up. "I look one *mahu*, too?"

Ben and Ken Soto cleared their throats and glanced awkwardly at one another.

"Wassamatta, cockaroach?" Tino laughed. "No wanna talk stink no more? No like make beef with the boss?"

Ben looked at Tino, then at me and Miles.

"Minors, brah," Ben said, his cigarette held loosely between his lips. He smiled and raised his hands in surrender. "No big t'ing. We jes' kidding aroun', yeah?"

I shrugged, tapped Miles on the arm and started walking to the Jeep. Tino was still laughing as I cranked the ignition and pulled out of the lot.

The sun was a bright orange ball on the horizon, and the first flickering lights of the village shone through breaks in the stands of poinciana trees. I turned my head and caught Miles looking at me.

"What?" I asked.

He took a moment to answer.

"That was cool," he said. "What you did back there."

I tossed off a shrug and shifted into third.

"I don't know what you're talking about," I lied, then turned my attention back to the road. But not before I saw the smile that stole across my nephew's face.

-11-

We turned off the main highway onto a single-lane surface road that veered down toward the jagged coastline. My headlights sliced through the growing darkness, catching the reflected glow from the eyes of mongoose as they darted for cover in the weeds. Dense groves of coffee and macadamia nuts blanketed the mountain behind us, while the spindled trunks of papaya and palms sprung from patches of purple and white orchids that grew wild along the edge of the road.

About four miles farther on, a yellow sign marked the entrance to a private road where the pavement crumbled away and turned to dirt. A canopy of ancient ficus overgrew the road, and the air smelled of sea salt and wet soil. I pushed the Jeep across rutted tire imprints that cut deep into the red-brown earth until the road came to an end in a wide cul-de-sac that was carved from the heart of a coconut grove.

I pulled to a stop beside Edita's Toyota and killed the engine. The fragrance of plumeria laced the humid sea air and triggered an inescapable rush of memories, memories I had called upon for years when I was back in L.A.

But there would always be something else here, too. I could still see the red strobes of the ambulance glancing off the clean white siding of my family's old house. The cops. My mother's body on a gurney, covered by a thin sheet. An indelible piece of my past, laid down like tripwire.

I looked off into the dark space between our old house and that of our neighbor, Tino, and recalled happier times. All the games we played as young children. As we grew older, it was Spin the Bottle with Laura deStefano and Ruby Duke, who would later end up married to Tino Orlandella. The excitement of first touch, innocent.

"Uncle Mike?" Miles said. His voice cut through my thoughts, through the rushing sound of water on the shoreline and the brittle wind in the coconut palms overhead.

There were other ghosts, too.

Like the last time I had seen Ruby Orlandella alive.

She wore short cutoff jeans and a sleeveless white cotton blouse. The legs of the dancer she had been were still well-toned, a familiar hibiscus tattoo encircled her ankle. Her long copper hair was tied back in a pony-tail, loose strands across her cheeks.

Twelve hours later, she was dead. Two blasts from a shotgun had left her lying in a pool of her own blood on the floor of my family's old home.

"Let's go on in," I said to Miles, inclining my head toward Tino's place.

We climbed down from the Jeep, collected the grocery bags from the back, and headed across the sandy soil of the parking lot the two houses shared.

Tino's house had been built in the mid-1930's, a classic Hawaiian coffee shack, constructed of wood with a corrugated metal roof that had long since rusted to a ruddy brown. A pair of well-worn wicker chairs sat on the lanai beneath the casement windows, glowing warm and yellow from the light inside. The front door was propped open with a chunk of sun-bleached coral, and I heard the muffled sound of voices in the kitchen as we stepped up onto the lanai and kicked off our slippers.

The smell of a cooking fire rolled in from the backyard, through the kitchen window, and out to where we stood knocking on the weathered doorframe.

Edita came out from the kitchen, a damp dishtowel in her hand, barefooted and smiling. She pushed absently at the tiare blossom that threatened to come loose from behind her ear as she glanced from me to Miles.

"This is my nephew, Miles," I said. "Miles, Edita."

His cheeks reddened a little as she showed him a smile that could stop your heart, and he juggled the grocery bags cradled in his arms.

"Nice to meet you," they said simultaneously, causing Edita to giggle and Miles to blush an even darker shade of red.

At the sound of strange voices, Poi Dog began barking. He burst in from the backyard and into the living room, taking the corner at a full run. As always, he misjudged his own speed, his rear end slipped out from under him, and he slid across the hardwood floor and into the wall. The dog recovered his footing and came to me, all tongue and wagging tail.

"That's Poi Dog," Edita said to Miles.

Poi Dog broke away from me and began to sniff my nephew.

"Nice dog," Miles said. "What is he?"

"A poi dog. A mutt. A little bit of everything."

I took the grocery bags from Miles just in time for him to take Poi Dog's face in his hands and remove its long nose from his crotch.

His face reddened again.

"Where'd you get him?" Miles' voice was brittle, tense with self-consciousness and awkward conversation.

"I brought him back from town when he was just a puppy," Edita told him. Somebody was giving them away outside the store. My dad was kinda mad at first, but he finally let me keep him."

From the back of the house, I heard the muffled sound of a closing door. A minute later, another girl emerged from the short hall that led to the back bedrooms.

Edita introduced us. "This is my friend Cady Logan."

Cady was a *haole* girl, sandy-blonde, short and slender, and looked younger than Edita. Her smile revealed one slightly crooked front tooth, and she brought a hand to her lips to hide it. I liked the directness of her eyes as she shook my hand.

"This is my Uncle Mike, and his nephew, Miles," Edita finished.

"Katie, was it?" Miles asked, another hopeful conversation-starter.

"No. Cady. C-A-D-Y. It means 'simple happiness' in Gaelic."

"So, you're Scottish?"

I winced.

The girl shook her head, "No, Irish."

"Oh," was all my nephew could come up with. "Right."

An uncomfortable silence that couldn't have been more than a few seconds was mercifully broken by Tino's arrival in the driveway. Poi Dog broke into a hysterical fit as his master came up the short staircase, across the lanai, and into the house. He knelt, scratched the dog's belly, then crossed into the kitchen.

"Smells good arready," he said to Edita, then kissed her cheek.

"I got the barbecue going, and boiled the ribs for make 'em tender." It made me smile to hear Edita speak with her dad, how she'd slip into the pidgin dialect he'd used all his life.

Tino reached into the refrigerator, pulled out a bottle of root beer, offered one to each of the kids, then took one for himself. He hadn't taken a drink since his wife's murder. I knew it was part of his penance.

I flashed back to the last time I saw his wife, standing alone outside this same house, just returned from the market.

"It's been a long time, Ruby," I had said that day.

I hugged her gently, the bag of frozen food perched awkwardly between us. Stepping back, my hands moved to her upper arms, and I looked her squarely in the face, my own reflection coming back in the lenses of the dark glasses she wore.

I felt Ruby shudder as she broke free of me. She angled her head down and moved quickly to the house with out so much as a word. As she brushed past me, I noticed the lingering green and purple marks beneath her eyes.

"Howzit, Cady," Tino said then, taking a long pull from his soda bottle. "You staying for dinner?"

"Edita invited me, if it's okay."

"Got plenny grinds," he smiled. "I go wash up, den start to cook 'em up."

I grabbed a diet Coke from one of the bags we'd brought in, popped the top, and began unloading the rest. By the time we'd finished putting the potato-mac salad, bananas, papaya and sodas in the fridge, Tino was back in the kitchen. He picked up a tray of boiled short ribs and headed out to the barbecue in the backyard.

I started to follow, but Edita took hold of my arm. "I was hoping Uncle Mike could help me with the salad," she said to her dad. I caught the glance that shot between Edita and Cady.

Tino shrugged and turned to my nephew. "Hokay den. Miles can bring da sodas ousside. And grab up da kine from over there."

Miles looked at me blankly.

"He wants you to bring these," I said. I handed him the tongs, barbecue fork, and apron that sat on the counter beside the door. He took them and followed Tino outside.

Cady and Edita busied themselves tearing lettuce, slicing tomatoes, and exchanging furtive looks in agitated silence.

"Wanna tell me what's going on?" I finally asked.

Edita shrugged at her friend in a way that meant, *go on*. Cady set her jaw and gathered her resolve.

"Edita said you used to be a detective," she said in a rush.

My scalp bristled, tight against my skull. I didn't like where this was headed.

Edita glanced out the window at her dad and Miles at the barbecue, then back at Cady. "Tell him."

Cady sighed again, made her decision. "It's my sister. She's been missing since Sunday."

I felt my eyebrow twitch involuntarily.

"What's her name?" I asked.

"Ashley."

"How old is she?"

"Eighteen."

Outside, I saw Tino gesturing broadly as he talked with Miles. My nephew's expression of strained concentration told me he wasn't catching too much of my friend's pidgin slang.

"Does Ashley still live at home?"

"Yeah, she's a senior, a year ahead of Edita and me."

I nodded. "You think she might have just taken off with a friend, her boyfriend, maybe?"

Cady cut me off with a fierce shake of her head.

"You know, Cady," I said, "legally, your sister's an adult."

She was still shaking her head. "But she missed church."

I didn't get the point. "And?"

"And she knows my mom would have a cow if she missed church—which, like I said, she *did*—plus Ashley wasn't at school yesterday. Or today."

Two days gone.

A puff of gray smoke rose from the grill as Tino opened the lid. A few seconds later, the aroma of braised meat rolled in through the open window. Poi Dog made pitiful mewling sounds at the screen door, so I crossed over and let him out.

"Listen, Cady, if there is something wrong—and I'm not saying there is—it's really something for the police to handle. I have a friend—"

"No," she interrupted. "My mother would *freak*."

I was surprised by the alarm in her voice. "Your mother doesn't want to report Ashley missing?"

Cady's eyes slid to the floor.

"I don't understand," I said.

"She and my sister had a fight."

"What about?"

"Everything. Her boyfriend mostly."

"Well, there you go," I told her.

Cady stiffened, swallowing hard as she stared out the window into the dark. "You don't know my sister," she said softly.

I watched Edita put an arm around her friend's shoulders, then throw me an expression that cut me like a caneblade.

"I don't know what I can do," I said, catching Edita's eyes. "Her own mother doesn't even want to file a report."

Edita's face was hard, shot through with a teenager's righteous anger. "You haven't met her mother," was all she said.

                    *   *   *

We ate dinner at a picnic table on the outdoor lawn. A bright flood-light illuminated the mango tree that dominated Tino's backyard and cast irregular shadows against the house. A low rock wall, bordered by coconut palms and fruit trees, separated us from my family's old place next door. In the other direction was a thick snarl of untamed jungle, flowering vines, and philodendron.

Tino sensed the tension and tried to diffuse it with stories his old aunties had told him, but the girls weren't buying. Miles squirmed and tried to make idle conversation but got only grunts and monosyllabic answers to the questions he asked them. I could see his discomfort and the failure he felt in the sag of his shoulders.

"So that used to be our house?" Miles asked me in a final stalled attempt. The question hung there for a couple long seconds, answered only by the bark of a brown gecko from somewhere out in the trees.

"Your grandmother was raised there," I said finally. "We used to come here every summer."

"Why'd you sell it?"

From the corner of my eye, I caught the look that passed between Tino and Edita: a shared recollection of chaos, of flashing red lights, of spent shotgun casings and blood-spattered walls.

I remembered, too, the landing that led to the old front door. The initials I had scratched into the concrete a lifetime ago. *MTKV*. Mike Travis Kamahale-Van de Groot. My last two initials swept away by the flood of water under the bridge.

"Maybe some other time," I told him, and the night folded in around us all.

* * *

Tino and I settled into the wicker chairs on the lanai while Edita, Cady and Miles did the dishes. Tino blew absently at the steam that rose from the cup of coffee in his hand and watched Poi Dog turn circles at his feet, looking for a place to lie down. I rested my bare feet on the railing and heaved an involuntary sigh.

Muffled noises from the kitchen mingled with intermittent mumblings of conversation, and in my mind's eye, I replayed the look of heartbreak on Cady's face. The night grew darker when the light in the kitchen switched off.

Edita poked her head out the screen door and got her father's attention. "I'm gonna get my keys and take Cady home," she said.

Tino watched Miles move out onto the lanai as the girls' voices trailed away down the hall.

A few minutes later, Cady came out to say goodnight. Miles stood across from her, still tongue-tied, but managed a wave that earned him the smallest of smiles, her hand moving up to cover her crooked tooth.

I got up from my chair as Cady started toward Edita's car.

"You don't have to—"

"It's okay," I said. "I need to stretch my legs."

The night sky was still, ruffled only by the flight of fruit bats and the swells breaking on the reef. When we finally got to the car, I opened the passenger door and held it there for her.

Cady leaned inside, tossed her purse on the back seat as she glanced over my shoulder. Edita was at the far end of the turnaround, standing on the lanai saying something to Tino. She was rolling her car keys from one hand to the other as she spoke to her dad. Cady turned her gaze back to me.

"Please don't think I'm crazy," she said.

"I don't," I said. "I don't think you're crazy."

Her eyes slid from my face and looked out past the trees that rimmed the bay. "Edita says you were the one that found the people who killed her mom."

"Yeah," I nodded. "I was."

"She said you were the only one who believed her dad. You know, that it wasn't him."

I caught the scent of wild ginger in the soft breeze, and my eyes slid toward the reef.

"I'm scared for my sister, Mr. Travis," she said. She reached across and touched my arm. "Please."

I turned toward the sound of Edita stepping off the lanai, picking her way across the empty space.

"Please," she said again. "I know something's wrong."

I thrust my hands deep into my pockets and dropped my gaze to the sandy soil between my feet, momentarily lost inside my own head.

Of all the crimes I had seen in twenty years as a big-city cop, the ones that sickened me most were the ones that made children their victims. They say every generation has its wars and its warriors. I have come to believe that it's true. But I came of age in what was thought of as peacetime. The irony isn't lost on me. Though my war wasn't fought in the jungles of southeast Asia or the sand and dust of the Middle East, I waded hip-deep into an everyday kind of evil so appalling in its indifference it left you punch-drunk and broken, gasping for air. Some might think that's melodramatic. Fuck them. I fought my war on the streets of L.A.

I looked back at Cady's face, at the fear that shone in her eyes. "I'll see what I can do," I said finally.

Her lips parted slightly, and she fingered the tiny gold cross she wore around her neck.

"Swear," Cady said. Her voice was barely more than a whisper.

A gust of wind blew in from the bay and sounded like rain in the palm fronds.

"I swear," I said, barely able to look at the unguarded faith in Cady's expression.

"Goodnight, Mr. Travis," she breathed. "Thank you."

I turned toward my family's old house as the girls drove away. I moved toward it without thinking. I found myself looking for the small square of concrete where I'd placed my handprints and carved my initials as a child, but it was gone, lost among the other changes new owners had made.

I felt another door close silently behind me, another passage sealed off, like the jungle reclaiming something left too long inside it, abandoned. In a way, I was glad, and wondered again how Tino managed to remain here, in the very heart of the place where so much had died.

I moved off toward the shoreline and stood alone at the edge of the lagoon. In the distance, waves broke, exploded into white foam, and sent lambent ripples across the surface of the bay. The horizon was little more than a dull glow beneath the heavy overcast.

When I was a boy, I remember looking up at a clouded nighttime sky, watching the moonlight that reflected behind the haze. I used to think that the moon must grow angry at that—that it didn't have the strength to burn the clouds away and show itself like the sun could when it chose to.

That's how it was again that night, a dim halo around a half-moon whose light struggled vainly to touch the earth.

-12-

I got out of bed at four the next morning, unable to sleep for the disquiet that was eating away at the edges of my subconscious, feeding on an apprehension that had no name.

I threw on my usual uniform, a pair of surfer shorts and faded aloha shirt, and padded quietly up to the galley to heat the water for my tea. I stared out the window while I waited for it to come to a boil, watching the stars flicker and fade as the few remaining clouds skidded across the sky and disappeared behind the far horizon.

I filled my mug and took it up to the cool air on the transom and sat down with the yearbook and the list of names Edita had given me before I left her house the night before. A few had phone numbers beside them, a couple had addresses, but for the most part, it was the simple listing of Ashley's family and friends I had asked Edita for.

I flipped through the yearbook putting faces to names, sipped my Mango Ceylon, and did what I always did at the beginning of a case. As I gazed at those faces, the familiarity of it all stirred something of my own.

A sudden gust blew off the water, whipped the pennants that flew at the masthead, and raised gooseflesh on my arms. It was the start of a mean déjà vu.

*   *   *

At seven that morning, I drove Miles up to the plantation, then spent the next couple hours working through some supplier problems with Tino. The day was clear and warm, and the Soto brothers were unusually subdued as they worked the lower end of the fields alongside my nephew.

When we finished in the office, I climbed into the Jeep and drove south on the upper road, past the old donkey mill, until it merged with the highway just outside Kainaliu town. Parked cars lined the curb, and tourists strolled the boutiques and restaurants that took space in the procession of aged wooden buildings that had once been rooming houses for immigrant field labor. I caught a whiff of patchouli incense that drifted out of the bead shop on the corner as I stopped for a couple waiting at the crosswalk. I shifted back into gear and pressed on through the mercifully underdeveloped landscape that stretched all the way to Kealakekua. I used the time to try reaching Lani, but got only Rosalie's answering machine. Frustrated, I snapped the phone shut, knowing that another five miles would take me into a dead zone.

It was coming up on noon when I turned off the main road, into a rural subdivision called Nahele. Narrow residential streets branched off the main artery and wound through dense copses of fern, palm and ohia, down a slow rolling knoll that opened onto expansive views of Ki'ilae Bay.

I found the address I was looking for at the terminus of a road that dead-ended into a weed-strewn outcropping of lava. I parked the Jeep at the lip of the driveway, adjusted the windbreaker I wore to conceal the Beretta I carried, and carefully picked my way down the narrow stone staircase that led to the entry.

The house was two-stories, a simple post-and-pier design with a wide lanai that spanned the second floor, looking out toward the ocean. The front lawn was a spotty brown, mowed too short, revealing naked patches of dry soil. A ragged set of Italian Cypress flanked the front entry, looking sadly out of place. Out of habit, I placed my palm on the hood of a late-90's model Taurus parked out front. I could hear the engine ticking as it cooled.

I rang the doorbell and waited, watched a trail of ants make its way from the planter box into a crack in the landing. Inside, a dog barked, but nobody came to the door. I rang again.

It was finally answered by a man I took to be in his early forties, as thick around the belt as he was narrow in the chest. Curly brown hair was cropped close to his scalp, the first evidence of hair loss showing at the crown. He squinted at me through wire-rimmed glasses as he tucked loose tufts of his shirt back into his Dockers and moved to get between his barking white puff of a dog and the door.

"Can I help you?"

"Are you Mr. Logan?"

"That's right," he said, more curious than cautious. "I'm Frank Logan."

"Any chance you could come outside to talk?"

He squeezed through the opening in the doorway, careful not to let the dog out, and closed it behind him. "Sorry about that. He just goes nuts when the doorbell rings."

"My name's Mike Travis," I said. We shook hands. His grip was firmer than I expected.

"What can I do for you?"

I treaded carefully. "Mr. Logan, I'm here about your daughter—"

"Which daughter? Is it Cady?"

"No, no," I said calmly. "I'm here about Ashley."

"Is she in some kind of trouble? Has she done something wrong?"

An odd question, under the circumstances. "It's my understanding that she's been missing since Sunday."

"Missing?" He said, stiffening.

"Going on three days now, as I understand it."

His brow wrinkled in an expression of puzzlement. "I'm sorry, who did you say you were again?"

"Mike Travis. I sometimes work with the HPD." Which was true, as far as it went.

"I see," he said, and cleared his throat. "She's not been home for the last couple of days, but I don't know if I'd say she was missing."

"You're not concerned?"

Something else came into his eyes. "A parent is always concerned for his children. It's just that... I don't know how to put this."

I didn't wait for him to try again. "When I first asked about your daughter, you asked if she had done something wrong. Why would you think that?"

"Ashley's been more of a handful than usual for her mother lately," he sighed. "Acting differently. I don't know quite how to explain it."

"Can you give it a try?"

He puffed out his cheeks as he searched for the right words. "Rebellious? Argumentative? Yes, like that."

"Has Ashley ever been involved with drugs, Mr. Logan?"

I saw the skin pull tight at the corner of his eyes, the beginning of a protracted silence.

"Drugs, Mr. Logan?"

He looked offended. "We're a close-knit family, sir."

"I understand. Still, it doesn't always—"

"Our family is very committed to the Church. Ashley included. We're taught that sometimes even strong believers will stray. But it's those times when the rest of us have to band together, be strong, and not cotton to the lowest common denominator. We need to be an anchor of stability. We have to stand our ground, set an example."

"May I ask where you attend?" I thought I had a whiff of the answer already.

"Covenant Union."

Fundamentalism at its most dogmatic. I was not surprised.

The front door swung open, and a thick-set woman wearing a simple green shift stepped out on the landing.

"Frank!" The woman called. "Your lunch is getting cold."

"Over here, hon," he said. He shoved his hands in his pockets and rocked back on his heels.

The woman strode across the lawn to where we stood in the meager shade of a banana tree beside the driveway. She made a show of looking at the Timex on her wrist. "You're expected back at the office in forty-five minutes."

They stood side by side, but never touched, an invisible separation that told me it had been a long time since they had drawn any kind of tenderness from one another.

"I'm sorry," I said to Frank Logan. "I won't take much more of your time. What do you do, by the way?"

"I sell real estate. I'm with—"

"*Francis*," she interrupted. She spoke sternly, as if to a child. "Whatever this is, I'm sure it can wait for a more convenient time." She looked at me with hard blue-gray eyes. "Now come along," she said to her husband.

"I'm here about your daughter, Ashley, ma'am," I said. It stopped her in her tracks.

"Francis," she said again. Her voice was stone. She looked from me to her husband. "I'll handle this. You go on inside and finish your lunch."

Without another word, he did as he was told, never once looking back. He disappeared inside and closed the door behind him.

"I'm Sheila Logan," she said.

She had a heart-shaped face, a fair complexion dusted by freckles, and the premature crows' feet at the corners of her eyes and mouth that suggested a woman not given to laughter. Her hair had once been blonde, maybe strawberry, but there was little of her natural color left amid the gray. It was cut straight at the shoulders and held in place with simple plastic barrettes. Her look was shot through with an obdurate sternness.

"I'm Mike Travis."

She ignored the introduction. "What's this about Ashley?"

"I understand she's missing, Mrs. Logan."

Her expression showed no surprise, no anger, only wounded pride. "And what is that to you, Mr. Travis?"

"I already explained this to your husband."

"Explain it to me. Are you with the police?"

"I used to be."

"Cady put you up to this." Sheila Logan's face creased with annoyance, or something else, her profile etched against the glare off the ocean. "She did, didn't she?"

There was no point in lying. "She's worried about her sister."

Sheila Logan shook her head, color rising to her cheeks. "She should remember her place in this household, is what she should do. Do you have any children, Mr. Travis?"

"No, I don't."

"Then you have no idea what it's like raising young girls in a world like this one, do you?"

"Mrs. Logan, I think I have some—"

"Don't condescend me, Mr. Travis. This world is full of evil. You've seen it, I'm sure, if you were ever really a police officer. Alcohol, drugs, sex."

"Kids are exposed to more than we were at their ages. And I don't appreciate the inference, ma'am."

She chuffed a dry and brittle laugh. "This is what I'm talking about. There're no boundaries any more. Everything is just out there for everyone to see. There's no shame, no modesty. The language you hear at the movies, the nudity. And the MTV! It doesn't matter that young children—"

"With all respect, Ashley is eighteen. She's not a child any more. Not legally."

"You sound just like her," she said, fixing me with a self-righteous frown. "Rebelling against everything we stand for."

"May I ask what you mean?"

She squinted into the distance, then up into my face. "Not that it's any of your business, but you can start with that boyfriend of hers."

I thought back to the list Edita had given me. "Roland Delgado."

"Yes," she spat. "Why don't you go talk to him and see if you don't get an understanding of what I mean."

"You think he's a bad influence?"

"He's *Catholic*, for one thing." She held out her hand, palm up, and ticked off his shortcomings, one by one. "He's Mexican, or Portuguese, or something, I don't know. He's *poor*—"

I started to speak, but she cut me off.

"If she wanted to choose someone that was *guaranteed* to raise my hackles, she couldn't have chosen any better than Roland Delgado."

I waited to be sure she was finished. "Do you suspect he would hurt her in any way?"

She was incredulous. "*Hurt* her? Are you kidding? If I let her have her way, she'd probably be popping out little brown babies as we speak."

She took in the look on my face. "I've offended you," she said, matter-of-fact.

I didn't want to give her the satisfaction. "Is that where you think she's gone? With Roland Delgado?"

She ignored the question and asked one of her own instead. "Do you know what it means to be 'Equally Yoked,' Mr. Travis?"

The words rang back to my days in church with my mother. "From the Bible?"

"Yes. From the Bible."

"I'm not sure I understand your reference."

Her expression told me I'd just been categorized. "The Bible wants us to stay with our own kind, Mr. Travis."

"I'm not sure that's what—"

She rolled her eyes. "So, you're a former cop and a Bible scholar? How fortunate."

I'd heard it before, and it only got uglier from here. For reasons I never understood, the passage she was referring to had been misconstrued by I-don't-know-how-many small-minded groups to foster the idea that racism and bigotry was ordained by God Himself.

"Thank you for your time, Mrs. Logan," I said, and turned to walk away.

I was halfway up the steps to the Jeep when she called after me. "When you see Ashley, you remind her what the Bible says."

I turned. "And what is that, Mrs. Logan?"

She raised her chin defiantly. "It commands us to honor thy mother and father."

-13-

I let the jeep idle while I read from the sheet of notepaper I had written Roland Delgado's address on before I left the *Kehau*. With the phone number Edita and Cady had supplied me, it had taken only a few minutes on the Internet to come up with a corresponding address.

A glance at my Tag Heuer confirmed it was just past one o'clock, too early to catch Roland, but it was his parents I was more interested in speaking with. I ran through the route in my mind and set off for the main road. Fifteen minutes later, I pulled to a stop in the pea-gravel driveway of Roland Delgado's house.

It was a single-story rambler of no particular style, other than small and inexpensive, cut into an arid landscape of black lava and scrub jungle. The faded wood siding was dry and badly in need of paint, but the roof looked as if it had been recently replaced. Ripe papaya hung like orange globes from spindly limbs on the far side of the house, and bougainvillea burst from deep cracks in the lava, tangled with deep green leaves of philodendron. The nearest neighbor was a good half-mile away.

Along the side nearest me, a detached carport sat empty of everything but a tri-fin noserider, a workbench strewn with tools and oil stains, and an old Japanese pickup, red tape where taillights had once been, pitted with rust and age. As before, I placed my hand on the hood before I tried the doorbell. It was cool to the touch.

Red dirt and gravel crunched beneath my feet as I crossed to the front door, pulled open the screen, and knocked. A diamond-shaped pattern of green bottle-glass was set into a cracked and peeling wooden door and showed vague shapes of the furnishings inside. There was no answer after several tries.

I walked around back, into a yard that backed up onto acres of black rock, scrub brush, and thick stands of bamboo. In the distance, I saw a young man I took to be Roland, a .22 rifle at his shoulder, taking aim at a line of cans and bottles he'd set up along the ridge of an old stone wall. He turned as I came to a narrow ravine bridged by a pair of warped two-by-sixes. I felt them bow under my weight as I crossed.

"You Roland?" I called out.

He gave me his version of the empty teenage stare I'd been seeing so much of lately and turned back toward his makeshift targets. Without a word, he lifted the gun to his shoulder and took aim.

"Roland Delgado?" I tried again.

He didn't answer but firmed his stance and took a shot at a weather-faded silver Coors can. I saw a puff of dirt, then heard the delayed crack of the rifle. The beer can stood firm in its place on the wall.

"Delgado?"

Nothing.

It was hot, and my tolerance for bullshit had run out.

I opened my windbreaker, slipped the Beretta from the holster and racked the action. A double-tap on the trigger split the can he'd just missed into shards of shrapnel. I took aim at the two brown bottles beside it and burst them into dust, too. The reports were loud, their echoes rolling across the weed-strewn lava field as I dropped my shooting arm to my side.

Delgado flinched at the noise, then turned to me, eyes wide and staring.

"Shit," he said.

"Roland Delgado?"

"Yeah." His voice hinted at belligerence.

"I guess you didn't hear me the first three times I asked."

He was tall and lanky, and he stood with a slight hunch to his shoulders the way so many tall kids did. Deep brown eyes stared out of a narrow face, his dark complexion smooth and unmarked.

"Your mom or dad around?" I asked.

"Why?"

He was a handsome kid, but for eyes that carried a sullen, simmering hostility that I usually associated with runaways.

"Because I want to talk to them."

He tossed his shoulders in a loose-limbed expression of total indifference. "She's not here."

"Who isn't here?" I asked, wondering if he had just blown Ashley's cover.

"My mom."

"Where is she?"

"Work."

"How about your dad?"

A sudden gust of wind blew across the field, and a stand of dry bamboo rattled like bones. Delgado cut his eyes toward the noise.

"You just missed him," he said with a sarcastic smile. "By about six years." He started off toward the rock wall, the rifle dangling loosely in his hand. "Left me this twenty-two, though."

I holstered the Beretta and followed him across the field.

"I'm Mike Travis. I'm a friend of Edita Orlandella's." I offered a hand that he didn't shake.

"Yeah? So?"

"She calls you a friend, Roland."

He stooped to pick up an armful of rusty cans and reset a new line of targets. I bent down to help him.

"If you're a friend of hers, you're going to want to talk to me," I said.

"What about?"

"Ashley Logan."

The name stopped him dead in his tracks. He turned and faced me. "What about her?" There was something new in his tone.

"Why aren't you in school?"

"I got out early," he said. We both knew he was lying. "What about Ashley?"

"She's missing," I said and studied his eyes. I waited for the tell, for the involuntary stumble that didn't come.

"What?"

"When was the last time you saw her?"

He turned away from me, his concentration fixed on setting the cans along the top of the uneven wall.

"When did you see her last?" I repeated, losing my grip on patience again.

"Friday."

"Where?"

"At school."

"Bullshit, Roland."

He whirled around.

"I thought you were her boyfriend," I said.

"I am." His expression matched the inflection of his voice, a combination of hurt and annoyance that struck me as vain somehow.

"And you didn't see her all weekend?

"I told you," he said. " I saw her on Friday."

"At school."

"Yeah. At school." He was done talking.

So was I. Almost.

"Where does your mom work?"

"County Hospital."

"When does she get home?"

He shrugged again. "Who knows?"

"You've been a ton of help, Roland." I said, and started toward the house.

He muttered something at my retreating back that sounded a lot like fuck you.

-14-

South Kona County Hospital had the look of a place accustomed to making the most out of a little, a place far longer on intentions than resources.

I went in through the Emergency Room entrance, past a waiting room that smelled of antiseptic and desperation. The nurses behind the admitting desk looked beleaguered, overworked. I could imagine what the place looked like on a payday Friday night.

"Excuse me," I said to the nurse who stood facing away from me, beside a long row of chipped beige filing cabinets. When she turned, I saw she was on the phone.

She covered the mouthpiece and looked at me. "Be right with you," she said, and turned her back to me.

My mind slipped back to my first visit to this place, my arm pulsing blood from the shotgun wound put there by a tweaker who'd snuck aboard the *Kehau* and come within inches of punching my ticket. It was an irony I was still trying to resolve. I'd been in the islands for less than a month when it happened, retired from twenty years of solving other people's problems, a career's worth of seeing people at their foulest, their most violent, most evil. And I hadn't shrunk from it. Worse. I'd embraced it, used it as my fuel. But I knew every time it happened, a little of the stench clung to me. It seeped into the weave of my clothes, into my skin, my pores, my soul.

Sometimes the memories leaked out, unbidden, like the greasy sudation of an addict sweating out a three-balloon load. Like the junkie CI's vomit I hosed out of my unmarked car; the perp's reeking spittle I had to wash off my face; the jilted father who set his three-year-old kid on fire; the cuckold who put his wife's hand down the garbage disposal; the meth-whore who sold her twelve-year-old daughter to her dealers.

I scratched absently at the scars left on my shoulder by the pellets of that shotgun blast, then pulled my windbreaker a little higher, careful to hide the nine-mil.

The admitting nurse behind the counter hung up the phone. "Can I help you?"

"I need to speak with one of your staff: a nurse named Susan Delgado."

She looked at me dubiously. "You sure she's in ER?" The name on her uniform read *B. Gularte.*

"No, ma'am," I said. "I'm not sure what unit she's in, to tell you the truth."

Nurse Gularte gave me a quick once-over, picked up the phone, and punched in a three-digit number. She turned away from me, but I listened as she spoke in tones I couldn't quite catch, half expecting Security to burst through the swinging double doors and escort me out to the parking lot. But a few seconds later, she rang off and showed me a helpful smile. "Susan Delgado is upstairs in Pediatrics. You know where that is?"

"I'm sorry, I don't."

"Go out these glass doors," she pointed, "turn right, go up the stairs and into the main lobby. They can direct you from there."

As I pushed through the doors into the fresh air of daylight, I caught the approaching sound of an ambulance siren. I took the stairs two at a time toward the main entry, while the ER settled into the organized chaos that was its everyday routine.

*   *   *

I found Susan Delgado on the second floor, inside a wire-glass office cubicle, reading from a clipboard. She was a plain-looking woman of about forty or so, average height, medium build, with mousy brown hair shot through with flyaway strands of gray. There was a softness in her manner, though, that smoothed out her angular features and made her almost pretty.

"Ms. Delgado, I'm Mike Travis," I said. "I'd like to speak with you about your son."

"Is Roland in some kind of trouble?" she asked me, shaking my hand.

"No, ma'am," I said. "I didn't mean to give you that impression. I just have a couple of things I'd like to discuss with you."

She fixed me with a blue-eyed gaze that was both direct and strong. " I have a lunch break coming up. Why don't you meet me in the cafeteria in, say, fifteen minutes?"

I walked back out to the parking lot, took my cell phone from the glovebox in the Jeep, and checked my messages. Still nothing from Lani. Or Rosalie. I dialed Edita's cell number and it flipped over to voicemail after four rings.

"Edita, it's Uncle Mike," I said. "Any chance you can meet me at the Plantation around four this afternoon? I've got some questions for you regarding that matter we discussed last night," I said, opting for vagueness, not knowing who had access to her phone. "Call me if you can't make it."

The parking lot shimmered with heat waves, and a trickle of sweat ran down the middle of my back beneath the nylon windbreaker. I didn't trust leaving the Beretta in the Jeep's lock box, so continuing to carry it was my only option, despite the heat of the cloudless day. I pushed the jacket's elasticized sleeves up to my elbows and traded the air-conditioned odor of the hospital cafeteria for the clean, hot air of outdoors while I waited for Roland Delgado's mother.

*   *   *

She took the seat opposite me, her expression betraying a disquiet that hadn't been there when I had left her a few minutes before.

The cafeteria was nearly empty, only a scattering of hospital personnel and a few people in street clothes, visitors, eating flavorless food from Styrofoam plates on plastic trays. The steamy odor of overcooked vegetables drifted on the air, and the unctuous Muzak oozing from speakers embedded in the ceiling was the only camouflage for our conversation in a room otherwise occupied by quiet apprehension.

"I wanted to speak with you about Ashley Logan," I said.

"Oh?" The tension in Susan Delgado's features solidified.

"It may be nothing at all," I said.

She searched my face for deception, found none, then waved it away. "When you have teenagers, it seems like it's always something."

"I understand." I tried a smile. "Do you mind if I ask you a few questions?"

"No, it's fine," she answered, then cocked her head to one side. "I have to ask you, though, what this is all about. Are you a relative of hers?"

I took a deep breath, carefully measuring the answer I was about to give. "Ashley hasn't been seen in several days, and I have been asked to help locate her."

There was a short intake of breath. "Then, you're with the police?"

"Not at the moment," I said, letting all the omissions inside the white lie take hold in Susan Delgado's mind this time. I allowed her imagination to fill in the blanks I'd chosen to leave.

"So you're a private investigator," she said.

"Something like that."

She nodded, shifted her eyes from table to table, then back to me, waiting.

"Do you know Ashley very well, Ms. Delgado?"

"My son has been seeing her for a few months, now. They got together toward the end of their junior year, I think. Just before summer."

"And?"

"She seems like a nice girl. Very pretty. Polite."

"Personality? What is she like?"

"As I said, a nice girl. Innocent. Sheltered, even."

"Do they see much of one another, Ashley and Roland?"

"They're together all the time," she smiled. "Or on the phone."

"What is your sense of her home life?"

A puzzled look crossed her face. "I've told you. I think she's a charming young person."

"What I meant was, does she seem happy? Any trouble at school or with your son? Problems with her parents?"

She shifted in her seat, suddenly uncomfortable.

"I don't think I can..." Her eyes cut away from me, out to the corridor where a nurse pushed a rolling tray of meds toward the ward.

"Ms. Delgado, this is important."

Susan Delgado pursed her lips as she gazed down at the tabletop. Several seconds passed before she spoke. "A couple months ago Ashley was brought into E.R. It appeared she had tried to, ah…" She glanced around the room, taking stock of its occupants. "Tried to commit suicide." The word was like broken glass on her tongue.

"Did you see her?"

She nodded slowly. "After they treated her in E.R., she was brought up to Ped's. They thought it would be quieter there. I was the duty nurse. I changed the dressings. I saw what she'd tried to do."

"Wrists?"

She looked at me, eyes moist. "This way," she ran a forefinger sideways across her wrists. "Not too deep."

"Hesitation wounds."

"That's what Dr. Vogelzang called them."

"Psychologist?"

"Psychiatrist. Mandatory for suicide attempts." Susan Delgado sat straighter in her chair. There were private thoughts behind her eyes.

"Let me be frank, here," she said, paused, and weighed her words as carefully as I had earlier weighed my own. "Roland's father left us several years ago. One day he was there, the next…gone. I'm not bitter about it, not anymore, not really, but it hasn't been easy for either Roland or me.

"You see, I'm not as involved as I wish I could be in my son's life. I take every shift I can to pay the bills. Most days, I pull doubles—graveyard, swing, anything I can get. But it doesn't leave much time for me to be at home."

She looked up from the table and into my eyes, looking for condemnation.

"That's very commendable," I offered.

Susan Delgado looked away. "Roland has a part-time job of his own, too. Nights mostly, bussing tables at Los Amigos. You know the place?"

I nodded, but said nothing.

"He works hard, but the truth is, our hours don't exactly leave a lot of time for..." Her eyes glazed with a patina of tears.

She pulled a tissue from the pocket of her uniform and dabbed at the corners of her eyes. "I'm sorry," she whispered.

"Take your time."

"This is my son's senior year in high school. Such an important time for him, and I want him to have a future. I look at that girl, Ashley, and I think about what a good thing she could be for him."

"But?"

"But, obviously something's wrong. Roland won't talk with me about it."

"But you have a guess," I prompted.

She shook her head slowly, resigned. "I don't know."

"Take your time."

Her hand floated up and rubbed the base of her throat. "I think they're all feeling the pressures of things changing; of growing up, leaving school, maybe leaving the island.

"I know there are kids—maybe Ashley is one of them, I wouldn't know for sure—talking about SAT tests, applying for college." A cloud came over her and darkened her features again. "It's just that it seems as if he's doubting himself so much. It's as if he's starting to think he's not good enough."

"Not good enough for Ashley?"

Her shrug carried so much regret, I could almost touch it. "I don't know. I just can't help thinking it's my fault. That I haven't given him enough."

I thought of my nephew and his father who had everything, then looked at the woman sitting across from me.

"These things are so horrible. I've seen them snowball," she whispered. "Especially with teenage kids."

"Suicides."

The word seemed to hurt her. "My son is everything to me. Everything I have left."

I reached over and took Susan Delgado's hand in mine.

She looked at me through her tears. "Do you think he knows?"

I pictured the boy I had met only an hour before, recalling the bitter enmity that radiated off him.

"I don't see how he couldn't," I said, not knowing if my lie was a kindness or cruelty.

-15-

The wind in my face as I drove back that afternoon did little to clear my head of the sorrow and dispossession, resentment and self-righteousness in the words that echoed in my brain. Wherever Ashley Logan was, she'd left a mountain of other people's baggage behind her.

By the time I pulled to a stop in front of the shack that was the Plantation's office, I was ready for a long swim and a cold beer, not necessarily in that order. Instead, I went to the cooler and satisfied myself with a bottle of water and waited for Edita to arrive.

The Mule was gone, and so was the collection of burlap bags that had occupied the back half of the storage barn, so I knew Tino had taken Miles and the Soto brothers up to the drying shed at the northeast corner of the property. Before long, they'd be husking the pulp off the ripe cherry, separating and sorting the seed, and drying them in the sun.

The fields were quiet, but for the warm breeze that drifted up from the shoreline, weaved through the dense rows of coffee, and carried the smell of sea salt and moist soil. I took a seat in the shade of Edita's tree and listened to the far off clatter of parrots. I shielded my eyes from the sun and scanned the space between the clouds until they came into view—a flock of about fifty green birds that balanced briefly on the sky, made a long lazy circle, and landed in the macadamia grove that bordered the Plantation. It was said that the flock had begun with a single pair, abandoned by a resident forced into an unexpected return to the mainland. To naturalists like Rosalie, the birds represented everything that was wrong with man's interaction with the islands. I saw it differently. Like so much that had come here before, the alternatives were clear: adapt and survive, or die.

*   *   *

Edita arrived ten minutes later. I could see there was another girl in the car. I didn't need to guess who it was.

I caught the expression on Cady Logan's face from where I stood, even through the reflected glare of the windshield. It looked like hope, and I didn't like the way it made me feel. Too late to turn back, and too heavy to shrug off. I had said that I'd help her, and I was in it now, up to my neck.

Edita slammed her door and ran to me before Cady even had a chance to climb out. "Cady was with me when I got your message, Uncle Mike. I hope you're not mad."

"Don't worry about it," I said.

Cady came over and took a seat at the table, bright with expectation. "Did you find Ashley?" She wore a pair of faded low-rise jeans, a pink peasant blouse, and the same tiny cross around her neck she'd been wearing the night before.

"Not yet," I shook my head.

Hope melted from her face. "All right," she said softly.

"I went to see your parents today—"

Cady cut a worried glance at Edita.

"Don't worry," Edita told her. "Uncle Mike won't get you in trouble."

She wasn't comforted by the look on my face.

"They know you got me involved."

The color rose in her cheeks, but it was resignation that filled her eyes. "It's okay," she sighed. "They'd've found out sooner or later anyway. Were they mad?"

I wasn't going to lie to her. "Yes."

"That's typical." Her expression took the shape of embarrassment. "They're always mad about something. They're on us all the time."

"How so?"

In a way both familiar and without thought, Cady took the cross pendant between her fingers and stroked it gently.

"Her parents are pretty strict," Edita said.

"I got that impression," I said. "They don't seem to think too highly of Roland Delgado, either."

Cady shook her head, the first hint of anger tracing her features. "They don't like anybody who doesn't go to our church."

Something startled the parrots from the macadamia grove and sent them to the sky in an explosion of noise and flashing wings. I followed their track across the blue dome of sky until they disappeared into the sun.

"I talked with Roland's mother today," I said. "Roland, too."

"Has he seen her?" Cady asked. "Does he know where she is?"

"No," I said.

Edita rubbed her bare arms, shivering despite the afternoon heat. "This is starting to freak me out," she said.

I looked from Edita to Cady. "Was Roland at school today?"

"Yeah, he was there. His locker's right near Edita's and mine," Cady answered. "I see him every morning."

"And you haven't asked him about your sister?"

"Yeah," she said. "But I thought he might say something more to you."

"Doesn't he trust you?"

Embarrassment shaded her features again. "I doubt he trusts anybody in my family after what my mom did." There was a long, awkward pause before she continued. "My mom caught him and Ashley sort of, uh, making out. She totally screamed at him, told him to leave Ashley alone. Kicked him out of the house."

The girl looked away, tugging absently at the hem of her blouse. I waited for her to continue, but she didn't.

"And then what?" I said.

"My mom called Mrs. Delgado. Said all kinds of rude things to her."

"Roland's mom works at the hospital," Edita put in. "Works all the time. She's not around too much, and he doesn't have a dad."

I nodded. "Tell me about him."

"He's okay," Edita said with a toss of her shoulders. "Kind of quiet. He's a good guy, though. Nice."

"He talk to you much?"

"I guess," she shrugged. "But Roland holds a lot of stuff inside."

"Yeah," Cady agreed. "He kinda keeps to himself. Doesn't have too many friends. But I think he really likes Edita."

Edita's cheeks flushed as she began to protest.

"As a friend, I mean," Cady said.

"Does he have a temper? Get in fights, that sort of thing?"

"No, he's not like that. He's not the fighting type."

"Have he and Ashley been getting along lately? Any problems?"

Edita and Cady looked at one another, then back at me. "Just the usual stuff," Cady said. "Roland can get kinda jealous sometimes."

"Does Ashley get a lot of attention from other boys?"

Cady looked away. "Sometimes."

"Anybody in particular?"

Edita spoke first. "Kalani Pawai."

"What's his story?" I asked.

"Big guy, kinda good-looking in his own way." Edita began.

"He's a loudmouth," Cady finished. "A showoff."

Edita nodded. "That's true."

"Have Roland and Pawai had any problems you know about?"

Both girls shook their heads. "Not that I ever saw," Edita said. "But it wouldn't surprise me. Kalani can be a real asshole—oops, sorry, Uncle Mike, but he can be."

"And Kalani has an interest in Ashley?"

Cady averted her eyes again, her face dappled by sunlight that lingered behind the leaves. "Yeah," she said. "But I think a lot of guys like my sister."

"Either of you know where this guy lives?"

Cady shook her head, but a light crept into Edita's face. "I know where he works, though. The luau at the Shores."

I knew it well. The hotel was on the waterfront south of town. I often heard the drums, watched the flicker of bright lights and torch fires from the deck of the *Kehau*.

"How about your parents, Cady? Your mom said that Ashley'd been giving her some trouble."

Cady huffed a dry laugh and shook her head. "Did Mom tell you what she made us do?"

"No. Tell me."

"About two weeks ago, she comes back from work—it's not really work, she volunteers at the church Thrift Shop—anyway, while she's there, this other woman that works there? Mrs. Culkey? She gets my mom all worked up about Smack Daddy P—" Cady interrupted herself. "You know who that is?"

I nodded. "The rapper."

"Yeah," Cady said. "So Mrs. Culkey totally convinces Mom that all the music we've been listening to is from the devil. That it's all about sex and doing drugs. When she came home that day? She made us take all our CDs—all of 'em, not just Daddy P—and pile them in the back yard." Cady turned away, humiliated again.

I waited through a few seconds of silence, heard the distant squawk of mynahs in the mango trees. "And then what happened?"

"She smashed them with a shovel. Then she made us bury all the broken pieces."

I remembered the backlash against a single careless comment by John Lennon back in the sixties, the piles of burning Beatles records in the streets of small towns all across the South.

"And that upset your sister."

"That upset both of us."

"You couldn't talk to your mother about it?"

She chuffed that sad laugh again. "You don't talk to my mother. She talks to you."

It was all such a waste, such a sorry white-bread parental cliché. They want to control their little angel's every step but end up alienating the hell out of her instead. It was the same kind of sinkhole that was threatening to consume my brother and his son.

"Tell me something, Cady," I said. "When was the last time you saw your sister?"

"Saturday afternoon."

I watched her eyes grow dim. Her hand drifted to her throat again, and she gently caressed the pendant.

"At home?"

"Yeah." Her voice was hardly more than a whisper.

"Did something happen?"

Her chin began to quiver as she fought to control herself. A single tear traced a path along her cheek. She wiped it away with the back of her hand and nodded slowly. "We kind of had a fight."

"What about?"

The weak smile she showed me was heavy with regret. "I don't even know," she began, but her voice caught. "She was just being such a... such a bitch."

"And you don't know why?"

Cady shook her head as her tears began to fall freely. This time, she didn't try to wipe them away. "I think she might've snuck out of the house the night before."

"You're not sure?"

"Huh uh. We have our own rooms. I didn't really hear anything."

"So what makes you think she went out?"

"She was wearing makeup."

My face was blank.

"We're not allowed to wear makeup," Cady said. "Mom always says, 'You don't paint a rose.' I hate when she says that."

Edita edged closer to her friend, put a hand on her shoulder and rested it there. A cloud drifted across the sun and threw us into shadow.

"Cady," I began quietly. "Did you know your sister tried to kill herself?"

She dropped her gaze to the dirt between her feet, scratching absently at her wrist. "Yes," she breathed.

"Why?"

Cady Logan fixed me with a stare, her eyes hard and wet. "She didn't mean it. She wasn't really trying."

"You believe that?"

"I guess so." She looked away from me, her face lost in shadow. "I don't know."

"And your parents?"

A light in the girl's eyes shone with renewed hostility.

"They think Ashley did it just to spite them. Because she was mad. Because she was 'being rebellious.' They don't want to be embarrassed, you know, to look like bad parents. My dad's a church elder. Mom's trying to get him to run for County Council."

"And what do you think?"

Cady Logan didn't answer.

"Where would your sister go, Cady?"

She was silent for a long minute. "I don't know."

"No other family? No friends?"

"Not since Gran died. My only aunt is on the mainland. Ohio. And I don't think Ashley would go there. She's even more uptight than Mom is."

"Friends?"

"Maybe. But, still. I think I'd know."

"Nobody's talking at school? No gossip?"

She shook her head. "Nothing."

I looked at Edita.

"Nobody's saying anything, Uncle Mike."

"Don't you think that's kind of strange?" I asked.

She was silent as the cloud moved past, washing us all in pale afternoon light.

"I have no idea what's strange any more," Cady finally said.

*　　*　　*

I heard the Mule long before I saw it emerge from the trees and wind along the dirt trail that led down from the drying shed. Tino was driving, and all three boys rode in the back, arms locked onto the rail. Edita waved when she saw her dad, and he pulled to a stop beneath the tree where we sat. She stood, leaned in, and kissed her father's cheek.

"Whachoo doin' here onna school day?" Tino smiled.

"Came up to see Uncle Mike," she said.

Miles tossed the girls a self-conscious nod.

"Hey, Miles," I said. "I need a couple more minutes, here. How about you guys put those tools away, and I'll be up to get you."

"No worries," Tino said to me. He looked to his daughter and told her he'd see her at home.

When the Mule was out of earshot, I spoke directly to Cady.

"Can you think of anybody who would want to hurt Ashley? Anyone who's mad, or jealous enough to want to harm her?"

"Oh, God."

"Or your parents? Anybody you can think of that might want to hurt them?"

"What, like kidnapping?"

"I'm just talking possibilities."

"My parents don't have any money, really. We're not rich or anything."

I nodded. I didn't see the benefit in telling her they didn't have to be rich to be a target. I also left out the possibility that this could be the arbitrary act of a predator. A stranger. A random act of sexual violence.

"In a normal Missing Persons case, I'd want to get hold of anything that could tell me about Ashley's last movements. I'd want a diary, her cell phone, her computer. I'd want to get a look at her room."

Cady's face went dark. "Search it, you mean?"

"Yes."

"My parents would never go for it."

I watched the wheels turn behind her eyes, waited while she came to the solution herself. It needed to be her idea. It didn't take her long.

"You could meet me there when my mom's at the Thrift Store."

I nodded. "When does she work next?"

"I don't know. I'd have to check."

"Do it. Then call me. Better yet, call Edita, and have her pass it along."

The girls shared a conspiratorial glance and the first real smile I'd seen all day.

-16-

Lani returned my call as I was tying off the *Chingadera* to the stern cleat, lowering a pair of rubber bumpers, and paying out a little extra line to be sure the skiff didn't pound the *Kehau's* hull all night long. The trades were picking up and with them an increased possibility of scattered chop inside the bay.

Miles went below for a shower while I talked to Lani on the cell. She told me she was feeling a little weak, but had promised to go with Rosalie to a meeting at the Community Center. Heavy rains earlier in the week had caused a massive runoff of mud and chemicals from the new golf course being constructed a few miles south of town, and the toxic brown flume had nearly smothered the coral reef just offshore of the development. The Green community was outraged anew and wanted answers from the developer, Ogden Krupp, the carpetbagger from Nevada who had made his first fortune working the full-court schmooze on an American Indian tribe in order to build a high-priced golf resort much like the one he was attempting here.

Miles wanted to stay aboard the *Kehau*, and I had a pretty good idea why. So I told Lani I'd meet her at the Community Center, maybe take her to dinner afterward.

*   *   *

The old building smelled of mildew, sweat, and rotting wood—the ragged exterior long since yielding to unending exposure to salt air and rain. The meeting, though, was packed to capacity, leaving dozens of latecomers to stand at the rear. Lani waved me over to a front-row seat she and Rosalie had saved for me.

The developer was another three-namer like Gimball. Arndt Ogden Krupp, whose company identity itself—AOK Development—was a not-too-subtle jab in the eye of every town he barged into. Predictably, Krupp wasn't in attendance. Instead, he had a handful of hired minions, at least two of them lawyers, representing him. I recognized one of them from the day I testified in Mrs. Makahanui's civil suit. A podium stood at the center of the dais, flanked by expensive scale models and huge aerial photographs of the project.

What began as a fairly calm dialogue quickly degenerated into contentious derision after one of Krupp's attorneys tried to snow the local audience with that kind of lawyerly prevarication that was ethically bankrupting the profession: the kinds of comments that were so close to the truth, the truth could hide in its shadow. As usual, Rosalie was at the center of the fracas.

At one point, the chairwoman recognized me as a local waterman and asked for my opinion of the damage being done to the reef. I gave it to them straight. The developer's corner sat in stunned silence through the applause that followed my comments. For them, it was all downhill after that.

*   *   *

"Where's Miles?" Lani asked me as we took our seats at a two-top along the rail, beside the water. "I was looking forward to meeting him."

"He wanted to stay on the boat. Trying to reach his dad again."

She shook her head sadly. "Your brother hasn't called him back yet?"

"Nope."

"How long has it been? Three, four days?"

"He got here Sunday. This is Wednesday. The only call he got was from Hans."

"That's ridiculous. Shameful."

"Valden has no shame, Lani. I don't think he looks in the mirror when he shaves."

I watched her as she picked up her menu. She began reading it as I held mine, still closed, in my lap. The dim light played across her face, exaggerating her poor color. She caught me looking and suppressed a desire to recede into the shadows.

"You look beautiful," I said.

She turned away. "Nobody's beautiful when they're sick."

I reached across the table and gently touched the back of her hand with my fingertips. "You're wrong, of course."

She looked at me and smiled. "I'm not going to break."

"What did Dr. Russell say?"

"My blood pressure is a little high," she sighed. "He's doing some blood panels, too, but the results aren't back yet."

"How do you feel?"

"Tired, mostly."

"Still?"

She read the concern on my face. "I'm okay. Don't worry so much. It's probably nothing."

"You'll tell me when you hear back about the blood tests?"

"Of course." She showed me a smile that felt like warm water. "Let's talk about something else."

Lani went back to her menu, and I gazed out across the bay. A languorous breeze ruffled the flame of the torches that lined the waterfront and swirled thin wisps of smoke against the purple sky.

There is a rhythm in these islands, an abstraction, a seduction. I looked around the restaurant at the faces, amazed that so many seemed to be missing it. I suppose I shouldn't have been surprised. This place wasn't theirs. They were visitors. I pictured Lani on the beach, dancing for me that first time, so sensuous, that same firelight flickering on her brown skin, naked from the waist. When we finally made love, it was slow, lingering. She had taught me a new way to look at time and hadn't even known it.

When I turned back, she was studying my face.

"You haven't been sleeping again," she said.

I shook my head. "I've had a lot on my mind."

"Your nephew? The thing with Rosie's car?"

"Among other things," I said.

Our waiter came and took our orders. When he had written it all down, he asked, "Anything to begin? Wine? Cocktail?"

"Club soda," Lani answered.

"No wine tonight?"

She shook her head. "My stomach."

"I'll have the same," I said. "Club soda."

After he left, she turned her eyes on me. "What other things?"

I didn't follow.

"What other things are on your mind?" she said again.

I debated not telling her but knew she'd see right through me. Lani had felt me pull away once, not so long ago, and I had almost lost her. I wouldn't let that happen again.

"A friend of Edita's is missing. I'm trying to find her."

Deep vertical lines appeared between her dark eyes. "Isn't that something for the police?"

I ran a hand through my hair and rocked back in my seat.

"It's not that easy, Lani. She's only been gone a few days. The girl is eighteen. An adult. Legally, she can go wherever she pleases. If her parents don't report her, then there's not much the cops can do."

"Why you?"

I held her eyes with mine, saw the first stirrings of worry there. "Because I'm the only one Edita knows who's willing to try."

Lani knew the real reason, knew I was doing it because I needed to. I studied her face as she weighed her own thoughts. After a moment, she leaned toward me and whispered, "You're not responsible for everything that happens in her life, Mike. At that age, everything is a drama."

From the beginning, Lani had been cautious, never digging too deeply into my past, never once asking about the dog-eared card I still kept in the drawer beside my bed, that last pathetic valediction of a woman I'd once cared for, a young woman who'd been turned to ash by my last case in L.A. I had asked myself a thousand times since then if she had been ruined by some ineffectuality of my own, or simply caught in a current that could never have carried her home.

I looked at Lani and knew she had seen something buried in my eyes, but she left it alone as she most often did. I felt I should say something, wanted to, wanted to save her, too. But whatever words I might manage would only fall flat, or worse.

"There's something wrong," I said finally. "Something seriously messed up in that girl's life."

"Whose life?"

"Ashley Logan. The missing girl."

Lani reached for her glass. She took a slow sip as she looked at me over the rim, waiting for me to continue, perhaps not wanting me to.

"These goddamned people," I said. "These goddamned parents. Everywhere I look, there's nothing but collateral damage. Kids looking for something more from their parents. Parents expecting too much from their kids. Nobody talking. Nobody listening. I don't think I could stand it."

The crease in her brow disappeared, softened. "There are good parents, Mike. Good children, too."

I shook my head and looked back toward the sea. The *Kehau* was rocking gently on her moorings. "I've never seen one, Lani. Except maybe Edita."

"Sometimes you expect too much. You're too hard on people."

"The more tolerant I get, the more accepting I become, the less I find myself able to stand for something—or even stand against something." I turned to Lani, held her with my eyes. "I don't think that's who I want to be."

She took my hand in both of hers, stroked my palm with a tenderness that put a catch in my throat.

"You've spent your life thinking you could stop bad things from happening, Mike. But the truth is, that kind of power was never in your reach. And it didn't come with the badge."

There was something different in our parting that night, as I left her at Rosalie's door. Her lips were soft as they brushed my cheek, her skin too warm beneath my touch, a near corporeal sense of her slipping away.

-17-

I heard the music pounding even over the rumble of the twin Evinrude outboards affixed to the stern of the skiff.

Yellow light spilled from the *Kehau's* portholes, painted wavering lines across the blue-black surface of the bay as I levered the throttles into reverse and slowed the *Chingadera* to a glide. I took the painter in my hands and gingerly stepped to the bow, grabbed hold of the ladder that hung from the yacht's transom, and tied off the skiff for the second time that night.

"Eeeaaaughhh."

A primal scream so filled with agony, angst and anger that it slashed the night like a straight razor. Heavy-metal drum and bass lines pummeled the air, so loud, so thick, they physically hammered my chest.

Miles stood in the center of the salon, his back to me, head-banging violently to the rhythm of the music. Amber liquid slopped from the glass he held in his hand as he lost himself in a scalding guitar break. I stepped over to the stereo and twisted the volume down to zero.

The sudden silence created a vacuum like an unexpected drop in barometric pressure. Miles turned, startled. "Wha'thefuck—"

My eyes moved from the flush of his face to the glass in his hand. I didn't speak.

"Oh, hey. Shit," he slurred. "Sorry." His eyes were boozy, pink and wet. "I diddenknow i'was you."

"What's going on, Miles?"

He cracked a sloppy grin and raised his glass to me. "Just gettin' the party on." Miles made a move toward the stereo, but I headed him off and took the tumbler from his hand. I held it to my nose and sniffed at the contents.

"Bourbon," I said, stepping over to place it on the counter. My bare feet stepped in something wet, soggy. "You obviously got some of it in your mouth."

"Yeah, I think I mighta spilled a little. I was dancin'."

I took a rag from a drawer in the galley then stooped to sop the wet spot on the carpet. Miles watched me as if from a distance. "How about opening the windows, Miles. It's gonna smell like hell in here in the morning."

He crossed the short distance with exaggerated care and slid the windows open. A merciful breeze blew through the space and cooled the sweat that was already trickling down my back. My nephew's hair was wet, his forehead shining with perspiration. It was the kind of ending to the day that I should have seen coming.

I went to the refrigerator to grab an Asahi for myself, a bottle of water for Miles.

"I think you might be outta beer, dawg."

"Have a seat," I said, and went below to the dry-storage hatch, brought a warm six-pack back into the galley. I cracked the top off one, poured it over ice, then dissolved a couple of antacid tablets in a glass of water. I handed the fizzing glass to Miles, who had seated himself at the banquette against the bulkhead. "Drink this," I told him. "Slowly."

When he was finished, I stepped up the stairs and out into the night. I gestured for Miles to follow. He sank heavily into the captain's chair, and I leaned against the stern rail. I watched the reflection of dull light play across his face.

"Did you reach your dad?"

He took so long answering I thought he hadn't heard me.

"Yeah," he said finally.

A succession of waves slapped the hull in the long silence. I looked up into the rigging and watched the wind pick at the flag that draped from the mainmast.

"Wanna talk about it?" I asked.

The teak deck still held remnants of the afternoon sun. Miles lifted his bare feet from the wood, rested them unsteadily on the cool crossbars of the ship's wheel, and closed his eyes. "Do you remember me when I was a kid?" he asked me.

Images sputtered across time, imperfect, poorly formed.

A large room, tall ceiling. Heavy wood paneling and oversized leather chairs. Stoic faces surrounding a boardroom table. Silent flurries of snow outside the windows, descending all the way to the grimy street.

"Of course I do," I said. Valden had moved to New York when he graduated from college. I had remained in L.A.

"What was I like?"

"You were a good kid, Miles. Very polite. You used to tell me long stories that didn't have any point."

His smile was bruised, half-hearted. "Well, I remember you."

Thel Mishow, my father's attorney at the head of the conference table, a thick document in his hands. Valden in Armani pinstripes, staring straight at the wall, into nothing. His wife, LeeAnn, beside him, eyes rimmed in red from tears or lack of sleep, a little girl squirming, playing at her mother's feet on the thick carpet beside her.

"You gave me something that day in the boardroom," Miles said, his voice thick and hoarse. "That time after grandpa died."

Dark burlwood walls, the color of walnut, highly polished, reflected gray light from the windows. An oil portrait in a heavy gilt frame. My father's image staring down at what remained of his family as the will was read aloud.

"A police hat and toy badge," I said to my nephew. "You were only five, maybe six years old."

The silence was complete, but for the small noises of the little girl playing on the floor. Valden's son, Miles, dressed in khakis and blue blazer in the chair beside his father, hands in his lap. A razor-sharp part in short hair, wet with pomade, the likeness of a man in miniature. The meeting concludes, all provisions read, handshakes and condolences exchanged, a room gone quiet and cold. My father's entire estate has been divided in two.

"You don't deserve it," Valden says to me, his voice brittle with resentment. "You turned your back on him."

"My dad took them away from me," Miles said. "Threw them in a trash bin in the lobby, on the way out to the car. I cried all the way home."

LeeAnn follows her husband into the corridor, their daughter balanced on one hip, young Miles holding her free hand and walking at her side. She hesitates, lets the door close of its own volition, leaving her husband alone in the hall outside. Valden's wife stops, touches my arm, a lonely smile barely reaches her eyes. "He's upset, Mike," she says. "He didn't mean what he said."

I nod.

"Please forgive him," she says.

"He shouldn't have done that to you, Miles," I said. "I'm sorry."

"You know what my dad asked me on the phone tonight?" Miles said. "He wanted to know if I understood how it made him look. My running away. He's threatening to send me to military school."

Miles tilted his head to the sky, the way a man will do when he is denying his tears.

*   *   *

Miles was asleep even before I had a chance to shut his stateroom door. I could hear him snoring as I made my way back up to the salon.

Detective Moon's home number was on speed dial. I punched the code and waited. He picked up before the third ring.

"Sorry to call so late," I said.

"You really pissed in the Captain's soup, Travis."

"I need your help."

"I don't know anything more about the goddamned car bomb. It's not my case."

"It's not that. It's something else."

Back in L.A., I had contacts in damn near every utility, phone company, and credit card agency you could think of. I could have pulled phone records for the days preceding Ashley's disappearance, could have seen who she called, where she spent her money, followed those trails until they ran cold. But I hadn't had cause to develop those types of relationships in Kona. The only way I could consider trying was to go through Moon. Even though we were friends, I knew this was close to the line.

I gave him the thumbnail sketch on Ashley Logan, right down to her half-hearted suicide attempt. The line was quiet on his end, his two young boys asleep at that late hour.

"You want me to do what?"

"I need you to check the airline manifests for the past four days," I repeated. "I need to know if Ashley's name comes up."

"Without a warrant? Nobody's even filed a report on the kid."

"I know how it works, Moon. I know you have people you can call."

He sighed heavily. "Whattaya want it for? You know she's in the wind. You said it yourself."

"I need to be sure," I said. "I need to know where she went."

"And then what? Give her new address to her parents? She's eighteen for God's sake."

A long silence hummed down the line. He waited me out.

"I promised Ashley's sister I'd find her," I said finally. "I promised Edita, too. I need to know if she's okay. That's all I want. If she's not on the manifests, I'll keep looking on the island."

"You're a pushover," he said, but his tone told me he'd do it. "Anything else?"

"No, thanks."

"Gimme a day or two."

I should have rested easy that night. I should have slept like the dead.

-18-

1973. Mid-October.

I'm sitting on the knoll overlooking the practice field, my jacket is the blanket I sit on. It is late afternoon and the varsity squad is being punished for something, probably their loss last weekend to Roosevelt. My freshman team has already finished and showered. On the track directly below me, the cheerleaders work through routines, conscious of the eyes that fall on them, liking it. Stacy Thorne glances up and catches me staring, lets a smile briefly touch her lips before she looks away.

I feel someone walk up behind me and take a seat on the grass.

"Need a ride?" It's Tom Delamico. Tommy D. In addition to being the freshman starting wide receiver, I'm pretty sure he deals dope. He knows I'm not a customer. "My mom's coming in a few minutes."

I shake my head. "No, thanks. I'm waiting for Valden. He's driving me home."

Tommy D stands to leave, scans the lot for his mother and sits back down. "Nice view," he says.

"Yeah."

"Didn't your brother used to go out with her?" Tommy inclines his head toward Stacy.

I nod.

"She's such a fox. I swear, I'd give anything—"

"Nice girl, too," I interrupt. *I don't know what anybody's heard about the party.*

Tommy smiles. "What the hell happened? I mean, why would he ever break up with somebody like that?"

I shrug. "Ask Valden."

"What a dick, man," he says, shaking his head.

I don't disagree.

The varsity coaches blow their whistles. The sound is carried toward me by the cold wind that comes down off the low, brown hills. The team is running lines now, practice almost over. It's always the last drill before they hit the showers.

Three long-haired guys slouch beside a trash can on the steps that lead to the Administration building. They're smoking cigarettes. One of them is tall and skinny. I can see the shadows of a bad complexion from where I'm sitting with Tommy D. It's the guy from Valden's party.

"You know those guys?" I ask him.

Tommy follows my gaze, locking onto the three smokers. He squints, nods. "Yeah. Two of 'em, anyway."

"The tall one?"

Tommy nods. "Jake Dillard. Real asshole. Why?"

"No reason." I don't ask how he knows them.

Tommy D shrugs, like, what's it to him.

Below, the cheerleaders are gathering their belongings; some break off into twos and threes and head for the parking lot. Stacy glances up at the knoll and catches my eye again. We have barely spoken a word since the night of the party. Only nods in the hallway, a mumbled "hi" a couple of times.

A car horn honks. Tommy turns and looks back toward the gym. His mother's station wagon is idling there in the yellow zone where the buses usually park.

"Sure you don't want a ride?"

"Yeah, I'm sure. Thanks."

Tommy D picks up his books and trots back to where his mother waits for him. I stand, brush dry grass from my jacket and the back of my pants. I pick my way down the slope. Stacy is still there, talking to one of the other girls. The tall one with the jet-black hair and blue eyes. Ginger, so inappropriately named, I think. Ginger sees me coming and makes an unsubtle departure. I don't know if I'm grateful or ashamed.

"Stacy," I say.

"Hey, Mike," she says. Her eyes slip from my face to the grainy dirt of the track between her tennis shoes.

"You're looking good," I say, then realize my mistake. I feel my face go red. "The pep squad, I mean. Your routines are looking good."

"Thanks." She smiles at me. "I knew what you meant."

I haven't got anything else to say. Words hang in my mind, but they all sound ridiculous to me. "Well. Anyway…" I say as I turn to leave.

Stacy puts a hand to her lips. In her eyes I see the smile she's trying to hide. "Anyway…" she mimics, teasing me.

"I didn't know what else to say," I explain.

Her fingers brush through her hair.

"I'm just kidding you, Mike. You're sweet."

My ears feel hot in the chill wind. I don't know what to do with my hands. "I gotta go," I say.

"I never got to—" She cuts herself short. Her eyes drift away and focus on a place behind me. Before I can turn to look, I hear football cleats scratch the dirt track. Valden sauntering off the field.

"Tadpole," my brother says, tossing his helmet at me. I catch it before it hits me in the face.

My brother turns to Stacy. "This fella botherin' you little lady?" he drawls, smiling. It's the first time I've seen him speak to her in at least two weeks. Since the party. Since the breakup.

Stacy's cheeks are pink. Not from the cold, I think. I watch her face and wait for the anger he deserves. Anger that never comes. I hand Valden's helmet back to him.

"See you back at the car," I say.

Valden nods. He never takes his eyes off Stacy as I walk away.

*   ✳   ✳   ✳*

The Sunday matinee lets out at four-thirty.

My buddies and I take our time walking to Mitchell's Liquor. I buy a soda for the rest of the way home. By quarter after five, I'm pressing the button on the speaker box that hangs from a steel pole at the entrance to our driveway. Mrs. Waldron answers and buzzes me in. A minute later, I'm walking through the tall wrought-iron gates to our house. Our Estate.

The back door is open, and I enter through the kitchen. Mrs. Waldron is stirring something in an iron pot. Steam rises as she turns to tell me that our dinner will be ready in an hour. I say okay and continue on toward the staircase. In an hour, the table will be set for two: Valden and me. The Waldrons never eat in the main house, but in their apartment over the garage. I don't give this a second thought.

I pass Valden's room. I hear music on the other side of the door. Pink Floyd. I don't knock. It's my album. I want it back.

I twist the knob, push the door open. There is no time to hide.

Stacy Thorne straddles my brother. Her breasts are white, the outline of the bikini she wore all summer still stenciled on her skin. The sheets are pulled up around her thighs, a thin sheen of sweat glows on her back. Her eyes are round with surprise, and something else.

For reasons I don't understand, I feel dizzy, sick. I feel as though I've taken a blow to the head.

Stacy stares at me for a long second. She falls across my brother's chest, tugging at the sheets to cover herself.

Valden turns to face me, slow, lazy, like an afterthought. "I borrowed your record." His smile is reptilian. "I hope you don't mind."

I back away, out into the hall.

"Hey, Tadpole," he calls.

I step up to the doorway, turn my head, try to avert my eyes.

"Close the door, for Chrissakes."

-19-

I t was dead dark when I awoke.

I brewed my tea and took it to the aft deck, the corrosive remnants of my dream burning like a festering wound. I dropped down and did my hundred pushups, rolled over and did an equal number of sit-ups. When I was finished, I sat on the cool teak, felt the sweat run down my chest, and filled my hungry lungs with clean morning air. But my spirit felt no clearer for the effort.

Miles awoke on his own as the first flush of false dawn glowed behind the gentle slope of Hualalai Volcano, and the stars still blinked overhead. He stepped out on deck, shirtless, wearing only the pair of shorts I had bought him. The farmer's tan he'd acquired in the coffee fields accentuated his narrow shoulders, his thin, wiry frame.

"How you feeling?" I asked, knowing full well exactly how he felt.

"Not the best." His eyes were red-rimmed, watery.

I got him a couple aspirin and a Sprite from the galley. "This'll help."

The morning came softly, quiet but for the groan of stretching ropes and wind in the rigging. We sat in silence, watching the stars flicker and fade into the pastel light of day.

"Listen. I'm sorry about—"

"You wanna stay aboard today?" I interrupted. There wasn't anything for him to apologize for. "There're some things you could do for me here. I can let Tino know you're working for me."

"No." Miles shook his head, not wanting to accept my charity. "I'll work in the fields."

The air was still and clear; the outline of the mountain cut sharp against the brightening sky. Along the shore, a pair of white heron glided above the thick tangle of palms and wild vines, wings outstretched, smooth and silent.

"Thanks." His voice was bare, raw.

"For what?"

He shrugged eloquently.

"Forget it," I said, smiling inwardly. "Breakfast then?"

His face lost its color as his stomach turned over. "Oh, God," was all he could manage.

*   *   *

The call came as I returned from dropping Miles at the Plantation.

"Uncle Mike?" It was Edita. "I talked to Cady this morning."

"So, what's the deal?"

"Her mom's working today. At the Thrift Shop." There was a smile in her tone. "We can meet you at lunch."

"'We' who?"

"Cady isn't allowed to drive. I told her I'd take her."

I gave it a couple seconds' thought.

"C'mon, it's no problem," she said. "We have fifty minutes for lunch. I can get from school to her house in ten minutes."

"No problem leaving?"

She laughed. "We have an open campus."

"Okay. What time?"

I heard the excitement of intrigue in her tone. "We're out at eleven-forty. I can be there a little before twelve."

*   *   *

It was five minutes before noon when I arrived at the Logan's house. Edita's car was already parked in the driveway.

The front door was open, so I stepped into the foyer and called out for the girls.

"We're in here," Cady answered from a room toward the back of the house. I followed the sound of her voice past a sparsely furnished family room and into the kitchen. Cady perched on the counter beside the sink, sipping from a can of soda, feet swinging, heels grazing the cabinets beneath her. The Logan family dog napped contentedly in Edita's lap. She was sitting at the kitchen table, scratching its neck.

"We don't have much time," I said. "Let's get going."

Cady jumped down from the counter and led the way upstairs to Ashley's room. In the hall, framed family photos flanked a sizable wooden cross that occupied the center of the wall. The photos were mostly black-and-white portraits of unsmiling, severe faces that spoke of proscription and inflexibility. The place smelled of lemon oil and dust, and a pall of something damp.

"It's this one," Cady said. She pushed open a door painted the same listless off-white as the rest of the house.

What I saw inside shouldn't have surprised me: a room done up in pink and white, stuffed animals, and lace pillows. Framed prints of horses and unicorns decorated the walls where there should have been posters of rock bands or movie stars, or a collage of photos and phrases cut from teen magazines. A small desk sat beneath a window that looked out over the driveway below. The window was framed by gauzy white curtains with pink gingham tie-backs. The desktop was cluttered with schoolbooks and a candle in the shape of an ice cream sundae, a gift from a friend I was sure. It was the room of a little girl, or someone made to live like one.

"Jesus," I breathed.

"What?" She'd lived with it so long she didn't even notice.

"Nothing," I said. "Cady, do you notice anything of Ashley's that might be missing?"

"Like what?"

"A cell phone, a laptop, anything like that?"

Cady shook her head even as her eyes scanned the room. "We're not allowed to have cell phones."

"Computer, then? I'd like to see her email."

"Mom keeps the computer locked in Dad's study. It's password protected, and she only lets us use it if one of them is there to supervise. They don't like us out on the Internet if they're not around."

"Do you have email accounts?"

Cady's eyes slid sideways, catching Edita's before they slipped to the floor. There was shame in her face. "No."

"How about a backpack, or a purse, anything she likes to keep with her?"

Cady went to the closet, opened the door, and examined the upper shelf. The floor was cluttered with shoes and boxes. "Her purse is gone." She looked at me hopefully. "Is that good?"

"It's something. Did Ashley have a car?" I asked, knowing the answer.

Cady rolled her eyes. "She has her license, but..."

"But she's not allowed to have a car of her own," I finished for her. Cady nodded. I glanced at my watch. Ten minutes were already gone. "Give me a minute, let me poke around. That okay with you?"

She glanced at Edita, then me. "Sure."

I went to the desk first, and opened the top drawer. Pens, pencils, note cards, rubber bands, and an address book. I thumbed through the pages—a sparse collection of names and numbers that I didn't have time to examine thoroughly. That would have to wait for later.

"May I?" I asked.

"Sure," she said as I pocketed the little book.

I returned my attention to the next drawer. It held a ream of lined notebook paper, a three-ring binder, a box of paperclips, and a handful of highlighters. Nothing. I quickly leafed through the binder, found only class notes and the doodling of a bored student. I slid it shut and went for the bottom drawer. There was a black leather Bible, Ashley's name stamped in gold on the cover. Beneath it, a stack of pamphlets, study guides from a church group, and a couple of brochures from colleges in California.

"UC Davis," I said. I held up the brochures for Cady to see. "Chico State. Sonoma State. Your sister was applying to college?"

"She wanted to go somewhere near Gran. But she died."

"Your grandmother?"

Cady nodded, looked out the window.

"I'm sorry."

"It's okay."

"They were close, your grandmother and Ashley?"

The fondness in the girl's eyes told me everything. "Oh, yeah."

"And college? Is she still planning to go?"

"Who knows?"

I turned back to the bottom drawer again, still on my knees. I studied it from the outside this time, and noticed a gap between it and the floor. I pulled the drawer all the way out, slid it off the runners and placed it on the carpet beside me. It was there. The hiding place. A stack of well-worn magazines, Seventeen and Glamour, sure to be contraband in this house. I looked up at Cady.

"She have any other secret places like this?"

Her eyes were wide with surprise. "I didn't know about that one."

"Goddammit," I breathed. I shoved the drawer back onto the runners, back into place. Ashley's secret safely tucked away again. "You gotta help me here, Cady. Does Ashley keep a diary? A journal? Anything like that?"

I saw her mind working, still surprised by her sister's cleverness. She nodded. "She writes in a notebook sometimes. One of those spiral kinds. Bright orange."

"Where does she keep it?"

Her eyes moved to the nightstand beside the bed.

I rifled through it quickly, found nothing, only hairpins, an orthodontic retainer, elastic bands, and a tattered paperback by Taylor Caldwell.

"Nothing. You sure this is where she keeps it?"

Cady nodded, vaguely guilty.

"You've read it," I said. "Anything in it you haven't already told me."

"No, sir," she said softly. "I don't think so."

"Have you seen it since Ashley's been missing?"

"No."

"Then she must have taken it with her."

"Why?"

"So it wouldn't be found," I said.

I glanced at the drawer where the secret stash of magazines had been hidden, crossed over, and removed it again. I went through them one by one, subscription postcards fluttering loosely onto the floor, hoping I might have missed the journal my first time through.

I moved to the closet, eyeing everything, allowing my instincts to process the scene in the little time I had left.

"What are you looking for in there?" It was Edita. She'd never seen me act like a cop, maybe never really thought of me as one.

"I'll know when I find it."

On the floor, among the shoeboxes and dirty laundry was an overnight bag. I pulled it out and opened it. I slipped my hand inside, felt around the lining and came across a zippered compartment heavy with something. I slid it open, removing a plastic sandwich bag. It was filled with makeup. Eyeliner, shadow, a compact and some pencils of various shades. More Logan family contraband. I placed it all back into the bag.

I looked at my watch again.

I crossed over to the bed and felt the space between the mattress and box spring. The old standby. Nothing. Ashley Logan would be too smart to believe anything would remain unnoticed there for long. My guess was that their mother conducted searches like mine on a routine basis.

"Where's the bathroom?"

Edita and Cady exchanged a curious glance.

"We're running out of time," I said.

Without a word, she turned and led me down a short hall.

The air in the small space was closed, hot, and smelled of mildew and dampness. A wet towel hung from a curtain rod above the tub.

For a moment, I imagined a frightened young girl, a razor blade held tightly in thin, shaking hands, the first tentative incisions through flesh. In my mind's eye, I saw her avert her eyes before she tried again, deeper this time, until bright drops of blood stained the white porcelain.

"Uncle Mike?"

"Wait out in the hallway," I said.

I rummaged through the medicine chest and then the small drawers in the vanity beside the sink. Curling iron, acne cream, tampons. Brushes and combs. Washcloths, damp towels. Shampoo, conditioner. A safety razor. A box of blades. I stood, glanced back at the empty white tub and wondered how many times Ashley's mother had scrubbed it, bleached it, trying to wash away every trace, every last vestige of her failure.

I turned away, felt behind the toilet tank and lifted the lid. Nothing.

None of us heard the car pull into the driveway, didn't hear the front door open, never heard the squeal of footfalls on loose stair risers.

-20-

"Cady! Edita! What in—"

I stepped from the bathroom out into the hall. Sheila Logan's face was blotched with red, barely able to contain her fury. The family dog barked excitedly and circled the woman's feet.

"*You*," she accused, crossing her arms across her chest as if she'd been caught naked. Her eyes glowed insanely for a second before she turned on her heels. "I'm calling the police."

"Mom—"

"Do it," I said to her. "Ask for Detective Moon."

Sheila Logan stopped in her tracks, then turned slowly to face me.

"Pardon me?"

"I said, '*Do it*,' Mrs. Logan. Your daughter's been missing since Sunday. For God's sake, do it. Call the police."

She gave me a once-over, looking as if she smelled something unpleasant. "You're trespassing."

"*Mom*—" Cady pleaded.

The dog kept up its tirade, adding to the confusion. Sheila Logan shoved it roughly aside with her foot. The dog squealed and crawled down the stairs on its belly, ears pinned back against its head.

She pointed at Cady, nearly put her stiff forefinger in the girl's chest. "You get back to school *this instant*, young lady."

Cady stood her ground. "Mom, I *invited* Mr. Travis."

Sheila pinned Edita with a glare. "You, too. Go. *Now.*"

Both girls looked to me. I nodded. "It's okay."

Edita and Cady retreated. They slid past Cady's mother, not wanting to touch her, involuntarily brushing her shoulder in the narrow hall.

Sheila Logan waited until the girls were out of earshot. "It is *far* from 'okay,' Mr. Travis."

"Mrs. Logan, no one has seen Ashley for four days. She could be kidnapped, injured, or maybe something worse—"

Her mouth hardened, familiar frown lines showed themselves on her lips, and between her eyes.

"My daughter is none of your concern. I've told you that before. If my husband and I felt we had cause for worry, we'd call the authorities. But we don't."

This arrogant runaround was pissing me off. She heard it in my voice.

"Your highly developed sense of denial doesn't change the facts, Mrs. Logan. I suggest you pull your head out of your ass."

She stepped back as if I had slapped her.

"I want to know what you were doing in my house with a seventeen-year-old girl?"

My eyes were cold. "I don't care for the implication, ma'am. Cady's worried about her sister, and she asked me to help. I'm helping."

"Cady is a teenage girl."

"It doesn't make her wrong."

"Excuse me?"

"You heard me."

We stared at one another for several seconds. I'd had practice. I had been mad-dogged by every brand of slimebag and degenerate Los Angeles had to offer. The notion that a rancorous middle-aged housewife thought she could back me down nearly made me laugh out loud.

"Something funny, Mr. Travis?"

I shook my head and showed her a smile that held no hint of real humor. "Yes, I think something's funny. I think something's funny as hell. I think I'm gonna find out what it is."

"Get out."

I moved past her, down the stairs. The dog resumed barking as soon as my feet hit the landing. Sheila Logan was right on my heels.

I stopped abruptly as I reached the front door, then turned to face her. She nearly ran into me, took two steps back, eyes wide.

"You lied to me, Mrs. Logan. You never told me the truth about your daughter. That she tried to kill herself."

She hesitated, but only for a moment. Her eyes were cold.

"You're absolutely wrong about Ashley," she said. "She's a *good* girl. Raised in the *Church*. She's going through a rough patch. Rebelling against our rules. Nothing more."

Church. Capital C. Sheila had returned to speaking in italics and capitals, a woman grown sanctimonious and smug, lacking even enough humility or awareness to recognize it was her intent, not Ashley's, that I had called into question.

"Ashley is not with Roland Delgado, Mrs. Logan."

She shook her head sadly, sorry for me.

"This family trusts in the mercy of God, Mr. Travis. Who, might I ask, do you answer to?"

This woman had no idea of the things I had seen, the things that could be done to a young girl out there alone. This woman's faith, I now saw, was placed not so much in God, but in the belief that she had the capacity to control her world.

"I answer to a different set of angels," I said, and left her standing at the front door, gaping at my retreating back.

*   *   *

Once I had returned to the *Kehau*, I pulled Ashley's address book from my pocket and examined every page. Not many names: an entry for 'Gran,' with an address in Sacramento; Roland Delgado's number, no address; a local movie theatre, a hair salon, and a notation for 'H.G.' accompanied by a local number. I made a note of it so I could run it through the reverse directory, then moved on. I leafed through page after page, searching for erasures, notes, anything. The remainder of the book was blank but for a single entry under 'P.' Kalani Pawai. A familiar name. This was the kid Cady and Edita had mentioned, the one who made Roland Delgado jealous. Again, I made a note, though I already knew where to find Pawai.

I needed some time alone, time to think.

I loaded my scuba gear into the *Chingadera* and headed north. I pushed the throttles until the twin Evinrudes sliced through every swell and roller between my mooring and the dive spot the locals call Turtle Heaven.

The girl's disappearance had me running in circles and beginning to wonder if the whole thing was smoke. I had seen the way the Logans lived, got a solid impression of what their teenage daughters' lives must be like. Clearly, it was enough to drive any eighteen-year-old with even the slightest sense of independence to run. It was the simplest, most logical explanation, and experience taught me that the simplest explanation was also the most likely. Occam's Razor. Still, Ashley's slashed wrists put a different spin on things. Where would she go? Her grandmother was dead, which meant Ashley was likely still on the island, unless she'd made a more desperate move, but that seemed out of character. It didn't feel right. A run for the mainland with nowhere to go seemed too big a leap for such a sheltered girl. But I had seen the faces of the runaways the chicken hawks cruised in bus stations and teen shelters. In a couple of days, Moon's contacts with the airlines would answer at least that part of it.

Despite my inclination toward the simplest solution, my gut kept dogging me, and it was my habit to pay attention to it. Perhaps I had seen too much as a cop. Maybe it was obscuring my judgment. But as I had closed that address book, locked it in my nav desk drawer, it was Ashley's face that had stuck in my head.

I tied off to a mooring at Turtle Heaven, a hundred yards off the rocky coastline that ran the length of the western shore. The white flame of Hawaiian sun burned in a cobalt sky that was dusted with thin wisps of cloud. Flinty spikes of light bounced hard off the surface of the sea and trailed all the way to the horizon. The heat felt good on my skin, clean and constant.

I pumped some air into my BC, held my mask and mouthpiece to my face, and stepped off the transom, into the turquoise water. I checked the dive computer attached to my regulator, adjusted the bezel on my watch, and began a slow descent, equalizing the pressure every fifteen feet or so until I reached bottom. The visibility was well over a hundred and fifty feet, water temp nearly eighty, despite the depth, and the only sound I could hear was that of my own breathing.

The images of the last few days spun down into my subconscious, and I let the sensation of weightlessness overtake me.

I glided over a cluster of coral heads teeming with reef fish. Schools of momo and yellow tang were suspended in silence as I watched them pluck at slender fingers of jagged rock. A bit farther on, to the northwest, a sharp lava pinnacle rose from the seabed and came within a few feet of the surface. A clutch of green sea turtles rested in nooks along its base, alien eyes open, watchful, even as smaller fish picked at their carapaces, stripping them of the algae that had grown there. Behind me, a trail of crystalline bubbles caught the sun, shimmered briefly, and disappeared.

This was the silence I craved. Here, in these depths, where no human voice could intrude, was where I could sort out what I knew about the disappearance of Ashley Logan. Her mother's words, that selfish faith, lost meaning here. So did Roland Delgado's sentient rage.

Mine was a Zen calm. I was here, surrounded by life and death struggles carried out without words, without sound, without warning.

I drifted back toward an old bull turtle laying in the sand beneath a bloom of bleach-white coral. A school of blue damselfish circled his head as I looked into his eyes. "Try not to be an asshole," he seemed to say to me. "We're all in this together."

*   *   *

It was late afternoon when I took my seat at Snyder's.

The après golf crowd had something playing on the jukebox; some kind of Vegasy Rat-Pack riff that floated on the thin haze of smoke swirling around the ceiling fans. The music sounded like it was winking at me, at some secret we shared. Or should.

Lolly was busy with a table in back, so I crossed over to where Snyder stood at the bar. Two fat men in loud pants, the jukebox's sponsors I was sure, leaned against the wall, their backs to me. I realized too late one of them was Addison Gimball.

"A killer drive, a beautiful approach shot. I'm telling you—" he was saying.

I tuned them out as I caught Snyder's eye.

"Hey, Mike," Snyder said. "Asahi and ice?"

The two men looked up from their conversation.

"Thanks," I answered, and started back for my table.

"Excuse me," a voice behind me said.

I turned.

"Mike Travis?" It was the guy standing with Gimball. The one I didn't recognize.

"That's right," I said.

His eyes were glazed and slightly out of focus. "I hear you've been saying some indelicate things about The Estates."

"Do I know you?"

His grin had nothing to do with humor.

"Arndt Ogden Krupp. AOK Development." He didn't offer his hand.

I looked him over. Round face, loud pants, sweat-wrinkled golf shirt and sunburned skin. It was easy to see that Arndt Ogden Krupp was a man of singular energy, an extrovert whose behavior was as mercurial as the weather. He bristled and popped from every pore, and like a rogue weather system, had the ability to alter the course of your entire day. He was like a typhoon stuffed into an ugly pair of golf slacks.

I was not in the mood.

I turned my eyes to Gimball. "It's hard to tell which one of you has got worse taste in friends."

Gimball reddened as Krupp's thin smile slid off his face.

"You'd do well to keep to your own business, Mr. Travis," Krupp told me. "Steer yourself clear of these local political dust-ups."

"That's a good one, Krupp," I said. "I like the irony. Where did you say you're from again?"

He fixed me with a well-practiced boardroom glare. It was becoming a big day for stare-downs.

Snyder watched us closely, the muscles in his jaw throbbing with tension.

"You're a big fellow, Travis," Krupp said. His eyes filled with black light, his voice tight with Glenlivet and a rush of testosterone. "But you'd be wise to be more careful who you take on."

My vision wheeled down to a pinpoint. It was a much too familiar sensation that presaged violence. "I think you misunderstand me, sir," I said. "I consider hubris a serious character defect."

Krupp's pupils dilated, a vein in his forehead pulsed hotly.

"You had best watch yourself, Mr. Travis."

I hooked a finger at Krupp.

Snyder's jaw began to twitch. He shot me a glance, shook his head slightly. I kept my eyes on the fat developer, crooked my finger at him again.

Krupp took a step and leaned in toward me.

I spoke softly into his ear. "You think you can walk into this town and wipe your feet on people's lives? Think again." Krupp straightened, holding my gaze. "I've got pieces of people a lot richer and tougher than you in my stool," I said.

The fat man recoiled. I got another good look at his eyes before he caught himself, trying to recover his composure.

"Nice to meet you, Travis," he said. "I'm sure we'll see one another again."

"Count on it, Bubba." I winked, showed him a broad smile, and walked back to my seat.

A minute later, Lolly brought my Asahi and a glass of ice. She put them on the table in front of me as I waited for Tino to drop my nephew off. "Long day?"

"You can tell?"

"Read you like a book, Mike Travis." There were threads of hesitation in her smile. She hooked a thumb over her shoulder. "So what was all that about?"

"You know what Erich Fromm said? He said, 'Greed is a bottomless pit which exhausts a person in an endless effort to satisfy the need without ever reaching satisfaction.'"

She cocked her head, appraising me.

"Lolly!" Snyder called from over the bar.

"Be right back," she sighed.

I poured my beer slowly, watching the foam envelop the ice and reach for the rim of the slim pilsner glass. When I tilted it to my lips, I felt the coolness reach my stomach lining as the fading light outside cut through the slats of Snyder's saloon doors. Golden bars of sun and smoke floated on the air, and the jukebox mercifully cued up some old Dave Mason.

Lolly came up behind me and propped a paper bag into the seat across from mine. "Your mail."

"Thanks," I said, rubbing my temples.

"You okay?"

"Headache."

Her eyes cut across to Gimball and Krupp. "I know what you mean."

"I came in for some adult conversation," I said. "But I'm surrounded by fucking kids everywhere I turn."

"How's your nephew doing?"

"He's fine," I said, knowing she could read my lie. I was sorry I'd said it. I didn't want to hurt her but knew she would leave it alone. "Tino should be bringing him by pretty soon," I offered instead.

"You never had children, did you?"

"No."

"Brothers? Sisters?"

I pulled at my Asahi.

"I had a brother," I said. "A long time ago."

Her face was beautiful, open. I saw her take something from me. "We're all just grown-up children, Mike."

My mind flickered back to my first year in Sex Crimes, interviewing a nine-year-old girl who thought she was her daddy's wife. I felt like I was sleepwalking, disassociated from my own life.

I looked at Lolly again and wondered what she saw, sure that it wasn't me. I'm capable of shooting, killing, acting with vicious force; capable of survival, even protection, but had somehow come to believe I was damned. I asked myself if I'd lost my humanity, and heard no answer.

She paused, turned something over in her mind, then leaned across the table. Her breath was warm against my ear.

"Everyone needs an angel sometime," she said softly.

-21-

The sun was down by the time I left Snyder's, tucked safely behind the razor thin horizon line that marked off the boundary to my end of the earth.

I left Miles with a burger, fries, and a coke, sitting at a table in the back where he had a good view of the game on TV. I knew Lolly would keep an eye on him while I was away. I told them I wouldn't be long.

Across the street at the King Kamehameha Hotel, men in pressed white slacks touched flame to the wicks of bamboo cressets that peppered the street with pools of orange light. The night air was dense with humidity and the smell of sea salt, frangipani, and jasmine.

I left the Jeep in Snyder's lot and walked the length of Alii Drive. The moon was coming up over the rooftops by the time I reached the seawall. Waves broke hard against the stone, burst into rooster tails of silver spray, and filled the air with condensation. A half block later, the hotel came into view.

The Coral Shores was a five-story concrete remnant of the early-70s, perched on a ragged point of black rock that jutted out into the south end of the bay. Tall stands of coconut palms, fire-tipped torches, and fragrant plumeria broke from an emerald lawn that encircled the grounds.

The luau had begun well before sunset, the pounding of tribal drums echoing through the lobby. Clusters of bright lights stood atop tall poles and shone between the branches of a thick hibiscus hedge that bordered the luau grounds. There was a rich, smoky aroma of imu-cooked pork drifting on the wind. Inside, long tables lined with tourists drank bucket-sized mai-tais and ate copiously from a buffet of laulau, poke, and poi, as they stared at the stage, enraptured.

I stood at the open end of the enclosure and eyed the stage. A line of beautiful young women and muscular, shirtless men moved in unison, rich green vines of ti leaves and maile encircling necks and ankles, blood red flowers tucked into thick black hair. These could be the sons and daughters of the Alii, princes and princesses of an alternate history.

"Can I help you?" the girl at the entrance asked. She wore a deep blue lavalava around her slender hips and a matching bikini bra, a white tiare flower behind her ear.

I pointed to the stage. "Isn't that Kalani Pawai?" I recognized the square-jawed face from the yearbook Edita had loaned me.

The hostess turned and scanned the faces in the colored lights. She nodded. "The big one," she said. "Third from the left."

"That's what I thought," I said. "What time does the show end?"

She looked at me with mild curiosity, then at the watch on her wrist. Her skin was marbled with firelight. "About another half-hour, I think."

I thanked her and walked out to the parking lot. I found the roped-off section reserved for employees, the pavement a purple carpet of fallen jacaranda blossoms that pulped wetly beneath my feet. I leaned against the trunk of a shower tree, deep in the shadows cast by sodium lights. The air was heavy and moist, the overhead lamps awash in a golden glow.

I gazed off through the grove of trees, toward the shoreline, and watched far off curtains of rain fall uselessly into the sea.

*   *   *

Kalani Pawai was among the last of the performers to emerge from the dressing room.

Up close, he was even bigger than he looked on stage, like somebody had ripped the hind legs off a wild boar and smacked them onto a side-of-beef biker body. He had a barrel chest that strained at the seams of a gray tank shirt, a heavy gold chain around his corded neck. In stark contrast to the graceful dance I'd seen earlier, his looked like a body built for violence.

Two other young men walked with him to his car, a chopped down rice-burner with oversized custom rims and an expensive paint job. I couldn't understand the words being spoken over the background noise made by waves and growling bullfrogs, but I knew a drug deal when I saw one. Without thinking, I touched the butt of the Beretta, watched the men as they laughed, saw them exchange something poorly concealed in a complicated handshake. The two walked off toward the street as Pawai turned to unlock his car door.

I stepped out of the trees, the night air still rich with the smell of the imu oven, night jasmine, and wet grass.

"Kalani Pawai?"

He turned, eyes narrow, the flat planes of his face deep in shadow.

"I don't know you, dawg. Go fuck yourself."

"Mike Travis," I said. "I need to talk to you."

Pawai looked at me like something his cat coughed up. "I told you to fuck off, bitch." He twisted the key in the door lock.

"And I said, 'I need to talk to you.'" I peeled back my windbreaker, let him see that I was carrying. "Step away from the car."

"You five-oh?" He made no move to raise his hands, just held my stare, vibing me hard.

"I told you to step away from the car," I said. "I'm not dicking around."

He kept his eyes locked on mine as I approached. I was close enough to see the pulse in the veins of his temples. His arms were braided with muscles that coiled like steel cable beneath his dark skin.

Pawai took a step back, turned, feinted left, then ducked right. He took a full stride toward me, cocked his fist, and let fly. He was big, but I was quicker, saw it coming, and juked sideways enough to catch only the outer arc of his swing. The keys he held sliced neatly through my brow, barely missing my eye. As his roundhouse continued its arc, I stepped inside of it, used his momentum against him and shoved him against the side of his car. I took hold of one thick wrist, slammed the keys from his hand and brought it up high between his shoulder blades. With my free hand, I grabbed his neck, slammed his face into the trunk. Blood coursed from his nose and down his chin. He struggled, tried to use his legs to push against me, but the leverage I had on his arm kept him down.

"Chill, asshole," I said, breathing hard from the adrenaline rush, the first trickle of my own warm blood sliding down my cheek.

"The fuck?" he mumbled, his jaw jammed forcefully against his paint job.

"I asked if you were Kalani Pawai."

"I heard you."

"Then answer me."

"Okay. Yeah."

"Got anything in your pockets that's gonna cut me?"

He shook his head.

I pulled his wrist a little higher between the shoulder blades, started to pat him down.

"Get your motherfuckin' hands off me, bitch."

I brought my heel down brutally on his instep. His throat whistled with a sharp intake of breath.

"Do not make me pull my piece," I said. Thick sweat was beginning to run down my back, my shirt clinging to my clammy skin.

"Hokay, okay. Be cool," he panted.

I took his wallet from his back pocket. I found his license, memorized the address printed there, then tossed it on the trunk beside his face. "Now I know where you live. Understand what I'm telling you?"

He nodded.

I reached around in front of him, felt a bulge inside his right pocket. I reached in and withdrew a clear plastic sandwich bag. I held it up in the dim light. In it were several dozen pastel-colored pills—blue, pink, and yellow—embossed with some kind of design. I felt his body tense, trying to make another move on me. Before he could, I delivered a vicious blow to his kidney. A rasping cry escaped his throat, and I felt his knees go weak.

"How long you wanna be pissing blood?" I said. "This is the last time I'm gonna tell you. Hold still." I took a closer look at the baggie. The design stamped on the pills was a butterfly.

"How long you been dealing Ecstasy, Pawai?"

"It ain't mine," he said. His breath came in short, shallow bursts.

"Good one," I said. "A classic."

"I'm holdin' for this other dude, I swear."

"Who the fuck you think you're talking to?" I said, pocketing the bag.

The rest of his pockets were empty, except for a small roll of cash wrapped in a rubber band, and the five twenties he'd received a few minutes earlier. I tossed the cash onto his car seat.

"You know Ashley Logan?" I asked him.

"I don't gotta talk to you. You not a cop."

"Is that right?" I said. "You sure? You really want to go down that road? I already got you dealing, shitbird. I got your stash right here in my jacket."

"Whatchoo wan' from me?"

"Answer my question."

I felt the tension leach out of his muscles. "Turn me loose first."

"When I let you loose, Pawai, turn around slow," I said. "You move on me, I'll drop you. You believe me?"

He nodded again.

I took a step back, and let go of his arm.

"Turn around," I said. "Do it slow."

Pawai did as I asked, turned slowly, and leaned against his car. A dark stain ringed the wide collar of his tank shirt; his face was shiny with blood and sweat.

"Whachoo wanna ask me?"

"Ashley Logan. You know her?"

"Naw, dawg. Never heard of her."

"Don't fuck with me. Your name is in her address book."

A nasty light came into his eyes. He nodded deliberately, licked his lips. "You mean Ashley Logan? *Haole* chick, fine ass, sweet little titties?" He showed me an unctuous smirk that raised a familiar buzzing in my head. "I guess I'd let her suck my dick, if she ask me real nice."

He never saw me coming. The knee to his groin doubled him over. I waited while he caught his breath. "Next time, I'll kick you so hard you'll be pissing out your asshole. We back on the same page?"

He nodded, his face drained of color, and looked like he might throw up.

"You heard from her recently? Seen her?"

"Like how?" he grunted.

"Are we speaking English here?"

"Naw, dawg, I ain't heard from her."

"Sell her some X maybe?"

"Naw, man. I tole you. Tha' shit don' belong to me."

"Fuck you, Pawai. Turn around. I'm hooking you up," I bluffed. "We're done here."

"Wait, wait, wait."

"When did you last see Ashley Logan?"

"Last week. Friday, maybe."

"Friday. You're sure."

"Yeah. Friday."

"Where?"

He tossed off a give-a-shit shrug. "I don't remember."

"Try harder."

"School, I guess." His eyes skittered off my face and out toward the vine-covered chain link that hid the parking lot from the street.

"You yankin' me, Pawai?"

"Naw. I ain't fuckin' wit' you. It was Friday."

"You better not be lying."

The unmistakable rumble of a Harley Davidson rolled past, on the other side of the fence, and disappeared up the road.

I stepped away from him and started making my way back to Snyder's.

"What you say your name was?" he called after me.

"Mike Travis," I smiled, tapping the side of my head. "And I got your address right here, brah."

-22-

A heavy rain came in from the northeast and brought a chill wind off the slopes of Mauna Kea. Thick drops pummeled the deck of the *Kehau* and washed the thin sheen of salt from the teak and brightwork. But by noon, the storm had blown over, scrubbed the sky of vog and haze, and left six inches of snow on the peak of the dormant volcano.

It took me two hours with the reverse directory on the Internet, and I still couldn't find a matching address to go with the 'H.G.' written in Ashley's book. When I dialed the number, it had been disconnected.

I went to the galley and fixed myself a tomato and onion sandwich. I washed it down with a diet cola while I sat on the transom and watched the shore boats deliver passengers from the cruise ship that was anchored in the bay and deposit them on the pier. The wharf was lined with tour buses and taxis waiting to make the trek down south to the fresh flow of lava that was spilling from the Pu'u O'o vent.

I turned my face to the afternoon sun and closed my eyes as the *Kehau* rolled gently beneath me, incongruously thinking of Kalani Pawai. As I stood to go below and wash the dishes, my cell phone rang.

"Mr. Travis, this is Susan Delgado. Roland got your number from Edita."

In the background, I heard the disembodied sound of a doctor being paged over the hospital's public address system. She interrupted me before I could speak.

"I wanted you to know that my son was beaten up this morning by a young man named Kalani Pawai. I think he broke Roland's nose."

"Mrs. Delgado—"

"I took you for a nice man, Mr. Travis. I now know I was wrong to confide in you." There was a chaotic rumble of conversation as a pair of nurses pushed a gurney through the corridor where Susan Delgado stood. She waited until they passed before she finished with me. "I want you to stay away from what's left of my family."

I went below for a shower, taking my time under the hot spray. When I dried myself off, I looked into the mirror over the sink, at the stubble on my chin, the new scar above my eye. The slash from Pawai's keys had scabbed over cleanly, but my whiskers were beginning to show a new hint of gray.

My phone rang again as I shaved. I put down the razor, tied a towel around my waist as I went up the stairs to the salon to pick it up. This time it was Moon.

"You got something for me?" I asked.

"Not yet, Big City. But that girl you're looking for? You got a picture?"

I almost asked him why, but thought better of it. "From her high school yearbook."

"Can you get me a copy?"

"When and where?"

"Four o'clock. You know the picnic area down by the boat harbor?"

I said I did.

"Meet me there. Bring the picture."

*   *   *

I parked the Jeep in the lot beside the Kona brewery. The air was leaden with the burnt and bitter odor of hops and grain.

I took Edita's yearbook into the copy shop, had Ashley Logan and Roland Delgado's school photos enlarged and several duplicates made. The cashier gave me a look reserved for lechers and perverts, but took my cash and made change without comment. I told her to have a nice day, and she answered me with a roll of her eyes.

There was still over an hour before I was due to meet Moon, so I tucked the yearbook and the new copies into the Jeep's lockbox and drove to County Hospital.

Roland Delgado occupied the bed closest to the window in a three-patient room in the Pediatric wing. The bed in the middle was unoccupied, so I drew the curtains behind me as I crossed to the far end of the room. The back of Delgado's bed was elevated to offer a better view of the television affixed to the wall. Some sort of Judge-Deciding-Bullshit-Civil-Cases show was on with the sound turned down low. He didn't turn his head when I stepped up beside him.

Green and purple half-moons underscored both of his eyes, a livid mouse, the size of a golf ball, stretched the skin of his forehead. A deep red gash ran from the corner of his mouth to a place just beneath his nose. An IV bag dripped colorless fluid into a tube that terminated into a shunt in his right wrist, the pump beeping intermittently as he ignored me.

"Roland? You all right?"

He kept his eyes glued on Judge Judy, or whoever. "I look all right to you?"

"Kalani Pawai do that?"

Roland turned his head, looking at me for the first time. His eyes glowed red from deeply bruised sockets. "Your name came up."

"Does this have anything to do with him dealing X?"

Roland Delgado rubbed gingerly at the place where the IV needle entered his wrist and winced. "He said you took him off for his stash. He thinks I put you onto him."

"Why would he think that?"

He shrugged and turned his attention back to the television. "My mom know you're here?"

He had no sooner said the words when I heard the whisper of rubber soles on linoleum. His mother pulled the curtain back with a forceful tug and fixed me with a hard stare.

"I told you to stay away from my son," she hissed.

"Mrs. Delgado, there's something wrong—"

"There most certainly is, Mr. Travis. I didn't see it before, but you carry something bad around with you. I think you're a dangerous man."

"Roland," I said. "Who's H.G.?"

He turned his face toward the muted light of the curtained window. "I don't know what you're talking about."

"It was in Ashley's address book. 'H.G.' There was no working phone number. Who is it?"

"Don't make me call Security, Mr. Travis," Roland's mother said.

I took one of my cards from my shirt pocket, the version with only my name and cell number, and tossed it on the bed. It landed face-up on Roland's chest.

"I believe he knows more than he's saying."

"You stay away from here," she repeated. The skin on Susan Delgado's face stitched an angry crease between her eyes. "You've done quite enough already."

"I'm sorry for what happened," I said, turning back to Roland. "I can help you, son. But you need to talk to me. And you need to do it soon."

*   *   *

I found Moon sitting on a bench at the end of a dirt road that terminated at the mouth of the Honokohau boat basin. He was tossing pieces of bread into the clear water at the foot of the breakwater, feeding a school of Moorish idols that picked at the crumbs with delicate pecks of their slender snouts. Across the narrow channel, a sportfishing boat was backed up to the fuel dock, a good-sized blue marlin being hoisted from its transom on a thick metal hook.

"Whaddaya think, Big City? Six, seven hundred pounds?" he asked me.

I looked across the narrow throat of the harbor, taking stock of the fish that hung from the scale, blood dripping from its bill and the gash near its dorsal where it had been gaffed. "Five bucks says no less than seven-fifty."

"You're on," he said. He pushed the torn loaf of bread back into its sack.

The sun glinted sharply on the turquoise surface of the harbor, and the air was sweet with the smell of drying seagrass. Below us, the brown and heavily-scaled head of a sea turtle broke the surface. Its eyes seemed to lock on mine for a long moment before it took a breath and dove for the bottom.

"When I was a kid, you couldn't walk down the beach without tripping over one of those things sleeping on the sand," Moon said.

"That was before golf courses and jet-skis."

He followed the turtle's progress beneath the surface. "They're making a comeback."

"Slowly," I agreed.

Another fishing boat entered the harbor, cutting back on the throttles and sending a wake toward the rocks below where we sat. A white cloud of exhaust followed on the wind, and I turned away as it passed over us.

"How're my airline manifests coming?" I asked.

"Making progress."

"Tomorrow?"

"Probably." He rubbed his hands on his pants, drying his palms. Moon seemed distracted and more taciturn than usual.

"Everything copacetic with your boys?"

He swiveled on the edge of the bench to face me. I couldn't see his eyes behind his dark glasses. "It just makes you think, that's all."

I took a plastic bag out of my pocket, handed it to Moon. He unrolled it and looked at the contents.

"Where'd you get this?"

"Took it off a kid named Kalani Pawai last night."

I saw his eyebrows arch above the thick frames of his shades. "Took it off him? That how you got that scratch on your face?"

"Not important."

"What do you want me to do with it?"

"I don't know," I shrugged. "Lock it up somewhere, see if it becomes useful down the line."

Moon rolled the bag into a bulky tube and stuffed it in his pocket. "You got the picture I asked for?"

I handed him two copies. He studied Ashley Logan's face as the wind picked at the edges of the paper. "Pretty girl."

"You look like you could use a cold one."

Moon shook his head and handed me the crumpled bag with the bread inside it. "I gotta get back."

He turned and walked across the sand toward his Bronco, his black cowboy boots kicking fine clouds of dust in the air. I took his place on the bench and finished feeding the fish. I heard him drive out of the lot as a group of tourists took photos beside the dead blue marlin that hung upside down from a rope on the far side of the basin. A viscous pool of black blood was already congealing on the concrete beneath its pointed bill.

*   *   *

An hour later I was back at the substation. The uniformed officer named Pahoa was still manning the reception desk.

"Detective Moon here?"

The officer shook his head. "Left half an hour ago."

I took a five-dollar bill from my wallet, gave it to Pahoa. "Tell him the marlin went six-seventy-three."

He looked at me as he had before, but this time I saw a light come into his eyes. "You the guy from that house down in Honaunau. The guy who found—"

"I don't know what you're talking about," I lied.

Pahoa eyed the bill I'd handed him. "Six-seventy-three?"

"Yeah," I said. "Just tell him. He'll know."

*   *   *

"Uncle Mike, did you hear about Roland Delgado?"

I told Edita I had.

"He said it was Kalani Pawai who did it."

There was an annoying delay on my cell connection, probably from the satellite. I heard the echo of my own voice before she spoke.

"Yeah, it was."

"Did you see it happen?"

"I was in class. But I heard."

"Is there anything about Pawai you haven't told me? Or about Roland?"

She was silent for a few seconds. "Like what?"

"I don't know," I said. "Anything." I didn't want to get into the Ecstasy thing with her just yet. Another rumor would only clutter things up, confuse whatever I might be able to learn from the high school grapevine.

"I don't think so," she said. "Why?"

"Forget it."

She was smart, and knew there was something I wasn't telling her. Nevertheless, she changed the subject. "I'm going to take Roland some cookies. They're letting him go home tonight."

"I'm sure he'll appreciate it."

"Okay then," she said. "I just wanted you to know what happened."

"Thanks, kiddo. You did the right thing."

"Will I see you tomorrow?"

"Tomorrow?"

"At the Plantation. Tomorrow's Saturday."

"Sure, sure," I said, and felt the fatigue of the whole long damn week sink to the marrow of my bones.

-23-

The sea was a flat pewter mirror, dully reflecting the shelf of low clouds that ranged out over the coastline. The flag at the *Kehau's* masthead lay limp in the still morning air.

I was eating breakfast with Miles in the galley when my cell phone rang. I had told him he could take the day off, but he refused my offer. Something told me his desire to come along with me had more to do with Edita working Saturdays than anything else.

I went to the nav desk, picked up the phone, and flipped it open.

"Wake you up?" Hans asked me.

"It's almost seven already. What do you think?"

Traffic noise hummed in the background of Hans' silence. "Valden wants Miles to come home. His school starts in a week."

My nephew glanced at me curiously as he sliced off a generous chunk of white pineapple and put it on his plate.

"Anything else?" I said.

"Mike, listen, this is ridiculous—"

"This is ridiculous, Hans. You gotta ask yourself, is this your phone call to make?"

"I told you—"

"Take it easy, pard," I said, and rang off.

*   *   *

I slammed on the brakes as I approached the Plantation road, narrowly missing an old pickup half-hidden in the tall weeds beside the gate. I killed the ignition, climbed down from the Jeep, and cursed the asshole who had abandoned the truck as I twisted the key in the padlock on the chain that barricaded the dirt road. The morning was quiet but for the sounds of cattle grazing along the rocky pasture that bordered the Plantation, and the far-off barking of dogs. I looped the chain around the stanchion and jumped back in the Jeep.

"Whose truck?" Miles asked.

"I don't know." It looked like a thousand others on the island. "But if it's still there at the end of the day, I'm having it impounded."

The concrete floor of the shed radiated a morning chill as I passed through the doorway. I lifted a pair of small wood-handled sickles off a hook on the wall and carried it back outside. Miles followed me down to the row of coffee trees that ran beside the spool table, the leaves of a monkeypod flittering in the wind like a million green butterflies. I knelt beside one of the plants, and pulled one of the lower branches aside to reveal the spindly trunk.

"We're trimming today," I said. "I'll show you how."

My nephew watched closely as we went through a couple of trees together until I was convinced Miles knew which stems to cut and which ones to leave alone. "Just be careful. These sickles are sharp as hell."

He nodded. "What do I do with the branches?"

"Leave the cuttings in a pile. When you're finished, Tino'll bring the Mule through, and you'll pick them all up."

"When's that gonna be?"

"He's meeting with the guy who does our roasting, should be back by noon."

A look of undisguised disappointment crossed his face.

"Edita'll be here any minute," I said.

His disappointment turned to embarrassment as I walked back to the office.

* * *

I was sitting at the desk, going over our cash flow projections, when I heard Edita drive up. I was about to go out and greet her, but the muted sound of Miles' and her conversation floated up the hill toward me, and stopped me before I got to the door. I smiled to myself and took my seat, turning my attention back to the spreadsheet I had been studying.

Thirty seconds later, I heard her scream. It was the kind that makes your blood run cold.

The papers on the desk skittered to the floor as I ran from the office, the door slamming behind me as it rocked back on its hinges. I followed the sound of Edita's panic, slipped in the loose dirt at the top of the rise, and slid down the slope where I'd left Miles a few minutes earlier.

My eyes locked on Edita's face as I got to my feet. Her hands were folded into fists that covered her mouth in a scream that had gone silent. She stood unmoving, feet pinned to the ground, looking up into the branches of the tree she called her favorite.

Beyond her, I could just make out the silhouette of a body dangling at the end of a rope, twisting, kicking at the empty air beneath it. Less than a second later, she had her arms wrapped around the boy's legs, trying to lift him, to relieve the pressure of the rope that was biting into his throat.

Miles had jumped up on the spool table, had one hand on the rope that stretched tightly from the overhead branch, and had the other sawing viciously with the sickle he had been using to trim the coffee. Before I could reach them, my nephew's knife sliced through the last threads of brown cord and dropped the dangling body to the dirt. It lay there for a long moment, inert inside a cloud of red dust, as Edita knelt down, cradled the boy's head in her arms.

My nephew pulled at the sloppy noose, as Edita melted to tears. She was whispering words I couldn't make out.

I felt for a pulse as Miles unfastened the knot, an angry red rut in the skin around Roland Delgado's neck that now matched the damage Kalani Pawai had done to his face. Roland's pulse was weak, but his neck was unbroken, so I left him with Miles and Edita as I ran back to the office and called for an ambulance. Ten minutes later, I heard the siren down on Hualalai Road, as the ambulance made the final turn onto the Plantation.

*   *   *

Dust from the departed emergency vehicles still hung in the air, shooting it through with white bars of light as the sun seeped down between the limbs. Edita sat on the spool table, oblivious to the frayed length of rope that still hung from the branch above her head, her face mud-smeared and pained. We sat together in silence and watched a pair of wild canaries pick at the meat of an overripe papaya that had fallen to the ground and broken open, soft and viscous as a ruptured organ.

I heard Miles' footsteps in the gravel as he came down the slope. Without a word, he took a seat at the table beside Edita, handed her a damp towel and a bottle of water, and watched her wipe the dirt from her cheeks.

I left them there and walked back to the office. I tried to reach Tino on his cell phone, but there was no answer. I dialed Detective Moon.

"Ashley Logan's boyfriend just tried to kill himself," I told him.

"When?"

"About twenty minutes ago. Edita found him at the end of a rope."

"How is he?"

"Okay. I called for a bus. They took him away just a couple minutes ago."

He sighed heavily, and I heard the sound of ringing phones in the background. "Edita all right?"

"Like you'd expect," I said. "You got those manifests yet?"

"No."

"God *damn* it. This is seriously fucked up, Moon."

We both felt the same way about coincidence.

*   *   *

I climbed up into the branches, crawling out along the heavy arm that Roland Delgado had sat upon and laid in wait for Edita to drive up, so he could drop his burdens into her life. I unwrapped the rope from the thick limb, felt a wave of fury wash over me, and thought about what Delgado had tried to do to Edita, the guilt he was prepared to let her carry, the image he'd burned into her mind. Then I looked down at my nephew, his arm around Edita's shoulders, her head buried in the crook of his neck as her tears darkened the collar of his shirt.

-24-

I told Miles to take Edita's car and drive her home.

I tacked a note for Tino on the office door and drove down to the entrance of the Plantation, parking in the weeds beside the abandoned pickup. I tried the door, but it was locked. Everything about the Delgado kid was beginning to piss me off. I had given him my number, told him to call, told him I could help. But instead, he had come to my coffee farm and tried to shit all over Edita's life, tried to off himself right before her eyes.

I smashed the drivers' side window with a rock and reached in and unlocked the door. The inside was strewn with fast food rubbish and smelled of mold and stale perspiration. A St. Christopher medal and a dried flower lei dangled from the rearview and reminded me again of Sheila Logan's prejudice.

I spent the next hour inside that filthy truck going through every slip of paper, every castoff piece of garbage, looking for the note I hoped would explain what he'd done, but found nothing, only worked up a sweat and a new dislike for drive-through Mexican food. I tossed all the trash back inside Delgado's pickup and slammed the door.

* * *

Los Amigos occupied the second story of a retail building that ran a full block along Alii Drive, with a balcony that offered a peek-a-boo view of the ocean between the buildings on the opposite side of the street. It was the kind of place that was heavily decorated with sombreros and piñatas but hadn't had an actual Mexican in the kitchen since the Carter administration. The saying among the locals went, "the drinks are lousy, but at least they're overpriced."

"Table for one?" The girl at the podium asked.

"I'd like to see the manager," I said.

A look of concern crossed her face. I hadn't even eaten yet. "Sir?"

"The manager? Is he in?"

"Just a moment," she said, and disappeared into the kitchen.

Two minutes later the hostess was back, a pink-faced, heavy-set, blonde man in his late-forties in her wake. The name on his badge read Pablo. He looked as much like a Pablo as I looked like Bjorn Borg.

"Can I help you?" Pablo asked.

"Are you the manager?"

He stood a little straighter. "I am."

"Can we talk outside?"

He led me out onto a small patio just out of earshot of the front door, and turned to me with an expression that hinted at impatience. "How may I help you?"

"Do you have an employee by the name of Roland Delgado?"

Pablo pursed his lips and looked out toward the parking lot. "What's this about? Has there been some kind of trouble?"

"Why would you ask me that?"

He took a half step back, eyeing me in a way that told me he'd made me for a cop. In my experience, there were only two kinds of people who did that. "Because you don't look like a guy who brings good news."

"Delgado," I said. "Does he work here or not?"

Pablo ran a swollen pink tongue across his lips. "He should be here right now. He's on eleven-to-four. But he didn't show."

"He didn't call in?"

The manager huffed a sarcastic wheeze. "Right."

"Your employees have lockers?"

He turned to me, eyes locked on mine. "What?"

"I want to see his locker."

"I don't think so," he said, and started back toward the dining room.

I grabbed his arm. It was soft, unmuscled, and doughy in my hand. "*Pablo*," I said. "This can take five minutes now, or a long, long time later on. *Comprende?*"

He looked at his arm where my hand squeezed his flesh, then back at me. I recognized it then, an expression I'd seen a thousand times. It's one of the ironies of working with snitches: you rely on them, but you end up hating them just the same.

"Follow me," he said.

*   *   *

True to my word to Pablo, I was back in the Jeep ten minutes later.

There was nothing worth a shit to me in Delgado's locker, so I headed down south, hoping to catch Kalani Pawai at home on a Saturday afternoon. I turned left off the main road and followed a quiet residential street past an assortment of tract houses that I guessed had been built during the late-1980s boom. Though not exactly upscale, the hibiscus hedges were well-tended, the trees were trimmed, and there weren't any cars propped on cinderblocks on front lawns. It was the kind of neighborhood where both parents worked to pay the mortgage while they left the kids at home to raise themselves.

I pulled to a stop in front of a single-story neo-Polynesian-style place with a peaked shingle roof and a garage that faced the street. Kalani Pawai was in the driveway, his shirtless back to me, a bucket of soapy water on the pavement beside his bare feet. He paid no attention to my arrival, the muscles in his arms and back flexing in the sun as he ran the chamois over the car's shiny chrome rims. Both car doors were open; the stereo inside hammered some kind of gangsta rap into the quiet afternoon.

"Nice ride," I said.

He got to his feet, stood straight, and turned to me. He looked me full in the face but said nothing.

I circled around the back of his car, eyed the tags, and dragged a finger along the paint job as I walked from the rear quarter panel all the way to the hood. Pawai watched me, squeezing the wet chamois in his meaty hands until his knuckles went white.

"Remember me?" I smiled, hopped up on the hood and sat.

"Get off my car."

"What is this thing, anyway? Toyota? Acura?"

Pawai snapped the chamois, tossed it over his shoulder and let the water drip down his bare chest. "Acura."

I ran my hand across the hood beside me. "Momo rims, xenon head-lights. The X business must be booming."

There was a twitch at the corner of his eye, and he didn't know what to do with his hands. "Get off my car."

"Nice paint job, too. Flames and shit. Very cool," I smiled. "Wanna hear a joke?"

Pawai glanced over my shoulder, toward the front door. I knew then that at least one of his parents was home. He didn't answer.

"This elephant is walking through the jungle and falls in a big hole. He's trapped, can't get out no matter how hard he tries. He hollers and yells, but nobody comes to help him. Finally, along comes this mouse, walks to the edge of the hole, looks down and sees the elephant… You heard this one before?"

Pawai watched me silently, peeling my skin off with his eyes.

"Guess not," I said. "So the mouse tells the elephant he'll help him out of the hole. The mouse runs off, and a few minutes later, drives back to where the elephant is trapped. The mouse is driving this rice-burning hot rod. A lot like yours, now that I think about it, Kalani."

I paused and took in his twitching, anxious agitation. He was wrapped tight and seemed to be boiling from the inside.

"Anyway, the mouse takes a rope, ties it to his fancy-ass car, and the elephant ties the other end to himself. Sure as hell, a couple minutes later, the mouse revs the engine, drops it into gear, and drags the elephant out of the trap to safety. Of course the elephant is grateful and promises to help the mouse if he ever needs it.

"You still with me, Pawai? You need me to turn down your stereo?"

A young neighbor kid, maybe ten or so, pedaled by on a bike. "Hey Kalani!" he hollered.

Without turning, Pawai raised a hand and acknowledged the kid. He never took his eye off me.

"Well, not too many days later, the mouse falls in that same damned hole and can't get out. Can you believe it? He yells and hollers, and after awhile, along comes that elephant. He recognizes the mouse from before and has to think for a minute in order to figure out how he's going to rescue the mouse. See, the elephant doesn't have a fancy car like the mouse does. Then he comes up with the plan: he turns toward the big hole, leans over, and drops his big, long elephant dick all the way down to the mouse. The mouse grabs hold, and the elephant reels him back to the top and rescues him."

"What the fuck you want?" Pawai asked me.

"Wanna know the moral of the story, Kalani? It's this: If you've got a big enough dick, you don't need a fancy ride." I watched him watch me laugh.

He took a step toward me, and I slid off the hood to face him. Any hint of humor fell from my eyes.

"Why'd you fuck up Roland Delgado?" I asked.

"'Cause he's a punked-out pussy."

"So you busted his nose."

"Yeah."

"Nothing to do with drugs."

"No."

"Nothing to do with Ashley Logan."

"That's right."

I looked up into the trees and watched a pair of Java sparrows chatter noisily for a few seconds then fly off. A sudden gust pulled hard at the branches.

"Roland Delgado tried to kill himself today," I said. "I start connecting the dots, who do you think they'll lead me to?"

His eyes cut sideways. "Got nothing to do wit' me, brah."

"You're a fucking liar." I said. I began walking back to my Jeep.

The front door of the house opened as I climbed in and snapped on my seatbelt. A male voice called over to Pawai.

"Everything all right out here?"

"Just giving this guy some directions," Kalani answered.

I returned the man's half-hearted wave and watched him step back inside the house. He gave his son a quick once-over before he slammed the door.

"Catch you later, Pawai," I said. "Count on it."

*   *   *

On my way back into town, I stopped at the hospital to check on Roland Delgado.

His mother was sitting in a chair beside his bed, her back to the door. A thin white tube snaked from his shattered nose and across his chest, terminating in an oxygen bottle strapped to a rolling cart on the floor. An IV tree dripped clear liquid into his veins, and a heart monitor traced soundless, rhythmic lines across a lighted screen. Susan Delgado held his hand in both of hers, and gazed toward the window, at the curtains drawn tight against the late afternoon sun. The room was dim and still, heavy with inconsolable defeat.

"Mrs. Delgado?"

She was so deep inside herself, she didn't even start at the sound of my voice. "Don't expect me to thank you, Mr. Travis."

I stepped into the darkness and moved closer to the bed.

"Please don't," she said.

I stopped halfway into the room. "How is he?"

She turned in her chair, never letting go of her son's hand. The glow from the monitor cast one side of her face in shadow. Even in the gray half-light, I could see the exhaustion there. "Sedated. He comes in and out." Her voice was toneless, dead.

"He's going to be all right, Mrs. Delgado."

She studied my face for a long moment, nodded, and turned back toward the bed.

"My son tried to kill himself," she whispered. She wasn't speaking to me.

Susan Delgado shook her head and began to cry. The tears slid silently down her face, her chest heaving as she fought for control.

It was the loneliest sound I have ever heard.

-25-

I finally got through to Tino at home. He told me Edita had filled him in about Roland's suicide attempt, then had taken a walk with my nephew out to the lagoon.

"Your boy Miles done good, brah," he said.

"He's not such a bad kid."

"Maybe he come bettah than either of us think."

The sky was turning a deeper shade of blue, bouncing the last hard rays of the day's sunshine off my windshield. I squinted against the glare as I drove back toward town.

"I'll come by and pick him up," I said. "I'm only about ten minutes away."

"No bother, brah," Tino said. "The kids is doin' fine. Let Miles stay 'da night. Onna couch, yeah?"

"You sure?"

"You don' end up with Ruby, but maybe your nephew come marry my daughter one day."

"Jesus, man."

Tino laughed. He had a way of skinning things all the way to the bone.

"No worries, Mikey. I tell Miles to call you later."

*   *   *

Not long after I hung up with Tino, I was brought to a halt by an unexpected snarl of traffic. After nearly five full minutes, I hadn't moved more than a few yards, so I pulled off the road, onto the unpaved shoulder, and killed the ignition.

I crossed to the *makai* side of the road and walked in the direction of the blockage. I didn't have to go more than the length of a football field to find the cause.

At first, I couldn't understand the words, but the unmistakable sound of a chanting crowd carried up the rise toward me. A huge D-9 earthmover seemed to be the center of attention, ringed by marchers carrying signs, and blocking the entrance to Arndt Ogden Krupp's development, Nalu Nakolo Estates. A tall man in a khaki safari vest hefted a professional video rig on his shoulder and took in the scene through his viewfinder, with a half-dozen more still photographers beside him.

I circled around behind the cameras and got my first look at the handful of protesters who had chained themselves to the blade of the D-9. They were dressed in native Hawaiian robes and the crimson and gold crescent headdresses of the Ali'i.

Car horns honked, and drivers began to wave and flash outstretched thumb-and-pinky shakas of support, creating a new wave of pandemonium. I watched the marchers slowly circle the stranded bulldozer, carrying signs that said things like *Stop the Desecration* and *This Land is OUR Land.*

Traffic had come to a complete halt in both directions, and drivers piled out of their cars, joining the scene as news cameras consumed every angle. I was just about ready to head back to the Jeep to try squeezing by traffic along the shoulder, when I saw Lani and Rosalie come around from behind the heavy metal treads of the huge machine. The confusion was so pervasive, they didn't see me until I was in lockstep beside them.

"What happened to you?" Lani asked me. She nearly had to shout to be heard over the honking horns and chanting crowd. Even so, there was something in her tone. "Your eye," she said, pointing to her own for emphasis. "What happened?"

I had already forgotten about the slice Kalani Pawai had taken out of my eyebrow with his car keys.

"Nothing," I said. "An accident." We both knew she didn't believe me, and I felt the divide grow wider.

"Pick up a sign," Rosalie hollered to me. "Get in line."

I shook my head. "I don't think so." As it was, I had to march beside them in order to talk.

"You of all people should get behind this thing," Rosalie said. "These are your people in the ground out here."

I ignored the jab and turned to Lani. "Let's go home."

She bit the corner of her lip. "We need to talk."

I've never liked the sound of those four words. Nothing good ever follows them. "Let's go," I said.

"I promised Rosie I'd march."

I glanced back at Rosalie. She shrugged, like, what could she do?

"Tomorrow, then," I said.

"I'm working."

"Christ."

"What's happening with that girl, Mike?" she asked, changing the subject. "Have you found her?"

I was overtaken by a kind of bone-wearying exhaustion that made me realize I had completely lost control of my own life. "I've gotta go."

Lani kissed me on the side of the mouth, and I stopped in my tracks. She brushed the length of my arm with her hand as she turned her head away, moving on for another pass around the D-9.

I stepped back from the picket line and started for the road. I sensed somebody's eyes on me, and looked up into the tractor's cab. Arndt Ogden Krupp stood beside the operator, leaning heavily on the roll cage, arms folded in front of his chest. He made a pistol with his fingers, pointed it at me and winked.

I had seen that move before.

*   *   *

"I thought I might find you here," Moon said.

"You're a hell of a detective."

"You look like you got a few dents in your fenders."

"'Shock and Awe'," I said, knocking back a shot of Makers Mark and chasing it with Asahi.

Moon took the seat across from me.

"I've been having bad thoughts," I said. "I'm conducting a surgical strike on the miscreant brain cells."

Snyder came out from behind the bar and took Moon's order, then walked away without a word to me. The detective lit a cigarette, exhaling a long stream of smoke through his nostrils. "She's not on the manifests, Big City."

I nodded like I already knew.

"I don't know how you stand it," I said.

"Stand what?"

Snyder brought Moon's beer and another round for me. He set them on the table and took his place back on the duckboards.

"Teenage kid tried to kill himself today," I said after Snyder had walked away. "Waited in a tree with a rope around his neck until Edita showed up."

Moon snuffed his cigarette and took a pull straight from the bottle. The slow rotation of the ceiling fans roiled smoke up from the ashtray.

"The kid doesn't even know how fucked life can really be yet," I said. "What the hell are you supposed to do with that?"

"You said Edita's all right?"

I nodded. "How old are your kids, Moon?"

Moon picked up his bottle, tore at the label with his thumbnail. He sighed then, his face hard with something like concern. "And Lani?"

"I don't know," I said. I took another taste of bourbon.

He set his beer on the table with exaggerated care. He didn't look at me when he spoke. "This thing with Ashley Logan, I think you need to let it go."

I turned to face him, but his eyes were locked on the bottle he twisted between his thick fingers.

"Then what?"

"I don't know," he said. There was a long pause before he spoke again. "Mike, her parents won't even file a report. She took off. Let it go."

Somebody slipped a dollar in the jukebox, and a slow, sixteen-bar blues drifted on the haze inside the place. I shook my head and felt like I was falling.

"I don't think I can," I said.

Moon drank half his beer with one long pull, slipped his cigarettes back in his pocket. He stood and pushed his chair under the table.

"You can't save everybody," he said as he stepped away from the table. "Not even if you promise."

"I know." I couldn't look at him when I answered. "I've been getting that a lot lately."

He put a hand on my shoulder and squeezed. I don't know if it was sympathy or understanding. Maybe it was absolution.

-26-

1973. Early November.

The house is warm and smells like autumn and wood smoke from the fire Mrs. Waldron has lit in the living room fireplace. I look up from my home-work as I sit at the desk in my bedroom, watching the wind pluck the last few leaves from the limbs of the coral tree outside my window. Bright lights illuminate the grounds that encircle the estate and begin to throw shadows across the rolling lawn that extends all the way to the entry gates, closed tight against a deepening twilight.

"Hey, Mike," my brother says, breaks into my thoughts, startles me.

I turn in my chair, see him standing in my doorway, outlined in yellow light that spills in from the hall. The indistinct murmur of Mr. and Mrs. Waldron's voices drifts up from the kitchen, the rich smell of cooked vegetables and roasting meat heavy in the air.

"I didn't mean to startle you," Valden says with uncharacteristic civility. I know he wants something.

"What is it?"

He steps into the darkened room; only the light from my desk lamp illu-minates his face and the envelope he holds in his hand. "You going to school tomorrow?"

"Yeah. Aren't you?"

"I got a dentist appointment in the morning." His eyes cut away from me for a moment, and I know he's lying. I let it pass.

"How'm I getting to school?"

My brother shrugs, "Mrs. Waldron can drive you."

"Did you ask her?"

A brief flush of annoyance crosses his face, then disappears, temporarily outmatched by his need of whatever he's come in here for. "I'll take care of it," he says.

"Whatever," I reply as I turn back to the books spread out on my desk. The sky outside has grown dark, and I see my brother's reflection in the window tapping an envelope against the heel of his hand.

"Can you do me a favor?" he asks.

"What?"

He purses his lips and takes another step toward me. "You know Jake Dillard?"

The name gets my attention. It's the skinny guy with bad skin from Valden's party, the guy even Tommy D says is an asshole. "Yeah."

Valden held the envelope out to me, something like uncertainty in his eyes. "I need you to give this to him."

"What's in it?"

My brother shakes his head, losing his patience. "For Chrissakes, Mike, I just need you to give this to him."

"Then what?" I ask, waiting for the other shoe to drop.

"Then nothing."

"Just give him the envelope," I repeat, taking it from Valden's outstretched hand.

"Yeah. Meet him by the bleachers. At the ticket booth. Before first period."

"You in trouble, Valden?"

"Gimme a break." He laughs, but it sounds forced and hollow. "Who are you, Joe Friday?"

*   *   *

A cold wind picks trash from the garbage cans that stand unemptied along the sidewalk that leads up to the school, blows across the mostly vacant parking lot. A gray cloud of exhaust condensation roils out of the tailpipe of Mrs. Waldron's station wagon as she idles there, waiting for me to gather my books off the backseat. I thank her for the ride and shut the door. I watch her drive away toward the exit.

I wait until she's turned on to the main road, until her taillights disappear, before I take my algebra book from by book bag and slip the envelope from between the pages. It feels heavy in my hands now that I am alone, like a secret, like guilt. I zip my jacket all the way to my throat, a trenchant morning wind biting into my skin.

Jake Dillard is standing beside the ticket booth at the entrance to the football field, his face obscured by a cloud of cigarette smoke and condensed breath. He tears off the end of his cig, drops the cherry on the concrete, and snuffs it with the toe of his ratty sneakers. He tucks the unsmoked remainder behind his ear.

He shows me an unctuous smile as I approach, and I toss an uneasy glance over my shoulder. We move around the back of the booth, out of the wind that tosses long locks of hair across his ravaged skin, before he speaks.

"You got something for me?"

I slide the white envelope from my back pocket and hand it to him without a word. I start to walk away, but he makes a grab for my arm, catches only a handful of the jacket I wear. "Hang on, slick."

I shrug his hand off me, and turn to leave.

"Valden'll be pissed, you don't give him what he paid for." He clutches a second white envelope, the kind you'd use to mail a letter, between his fingers. Even over the hum of wind in my ears, I hear the dry rattle of something inside. It sounds like loose grains of sand.

*   *   *

I see Valden across the quad, eating lunch with a bunch of guys from the team. He says something to them that makes them laugh, then crosses the dry, brown grass to where I'm standing.

"Hey, Tadpole, you get the—"

I reach into my book bag for the thing I've been carrying all morning, afraid to leave it unattended in my locker. Valden makes a quick glance over both shoulders. The look on his face makes me nervous.

"Not here," he hisses. He grabs my elbow and pulls me between two rows of metal lockers.

My brother snatches the envelope from my hand, tells me to wait right there, then disappears around the corner where I know his locker is. I step into a patch of diffused sunlight that almost warms my face, and lean against the wall with my book bag at my feet. I close my eyes and hear the discordant sound of the marching band floating on the noontime breeze, mingling with the noise of a thousand secrets being shared, confidences betrayed, between bites of food drawn from brown paper sacks.

I look up when I hear Valden's feet scuff the concrete as he returns to that space between the lockers. He crooks a finger and calls me over. He hands me another envelope. This one has Stacy Thorne's name written on it in my brother's uneven hand.

"Give this to Stacy for me."

I shake my head. "Do it yourself."

"C'mon, Mike," he says. *"Don't be a dick."*

"Forget it."

His eyes go hard, the familiar Valden returning. I find it oddly comforting. *"You ever want another ride to school, you'll give her the goddamn thing,"* he *says as he stuffs it into my jacket and walks away.*

*   *   *

My hair is still wet from my after-practice shower as I emerge into the feeble afternoon light. The cheerleaders are working through the last of their routines while the varsity team runs plays on the upper field. The girls kick and bounce to the tinny sound of taped music that stutters from a boombox on a bench in front of them. I take a seat on the block wall that lines the far end of the track and watch Stacy Thorne from a distance.

"Picking out a date for Homecoming?" Tommy D says as the locker room door swings shut behind him.

"Right."

"You all right?" he asks. "You look like you just got drafted."

"I'm okay."

He nods, though he doesn't believe me. "Going to Dan's party on Friday?"

"Yeah, probably."

He shrugs into his backpack and slaps me on the shoulder. "Take it easy, Mike."

"I'll take it any way I can get it," I say automatically, our standard joke. The words sound cheap and threadbare in my ears.

I wait for what seems a long time, until Stacy is alone, before I walk over. She's kneeling before a zippered canvas bag she's filling with props and equipment. Her eyes turn wary when she sees me approach, and I know right away she can read me.

"I was expecting Valden," she says.

"I figured."

An unexpected gust kicks up a dust devil that disappears in the lee of the bleachers.

"Has he said anything to you?" She looks away from me even as she asks the question.

"About what?"

She shakes a fine cloud of dirt from a pair of pompons on the ground beside her, stuffs them into the canvas bag. "Never mind."

I am washed by an unwonted sense of shame as I reach into my jacket and pull out the envelope with her name written on it. I am a participant in something cruel, and I don't know what it is.

"Valden told me to give this to you." I hold it at arm's length, as though the dry rattle inside was that of a snake.

When she turns to me, there is fear in her eyes.

I want to shove the thing back in my pocket. I want to pretend it never happened. "I'm sorry," is all I can think of to say.

At first her face holds no expression, then her lip begins to tremble, and a single crystal bead slips from the corner of her eye. She makes no move to wipe it away as we stand together in the brittle November wind.

-27-

The bleating of my cell phone ripped me from a tangled sleep. Some time during the night, the sky had opened up, unleashing a torrential downpour that hammered the deck of the *Kehau*, reminding me again of that night in Avalon. That kind of rain always would.

I reached for my phone on the nightstand, but found I was on the far side of the bed, Lani's side. Only the faintest trace of her scent remained on the pillow in which I had buried my head.

"Travis? Moon here."

My brain was a viscous fog, my tongue lined with cotton. "What time is it?"

"Six fifteen."

"Fuck."

"I think we found Ashley Logan."

I sat bolt upright, my legs caught in a confusion of twisted sheets.

"Meet me at County as soon as you can," was all he said.

*   *   *

"Some shore fisherman found her about three hours ago," Moon said as our footfalls echoed off the hard tile and empty walls of the long corridor. The odor of antiseptic and heavy disinfectants lacerated the air. "She was caught in the rocks just north of the State Park."

We pushed through a pair of swinging doors, nearly running down a young orderly wearing faded green scrubs.

"Where's the doc?"

"In there," the kid said. He hooked a thumb toward another pair of swinging doors. "But it's a restricted—"

Moon badged him without missing a step.

The room was small, cold, and damp, and reeked of alcohol, dry-rot, and industrial cleanser. A tall, thin man in a surgical gown stood beside the room's single metal table, the bloated and battered body of a young woman laid out on it, her clothing neatly placed on an adjacent tile counter.

"I'm Detective Moon, this is Mike Travis." Moon's voice echoed off the tile walls.

"Doctor Preston," he said, his voice clipped, terse. He extracted a pair of rubber gloves from a dispenser, tossed them to Moon, then did the same for me. "This is your case, I take it. You know who the victim is?"

Moon slipped the photo I had given him from his pocket, moved around to the head of the table.

"Yeah," Moon said. "Gimme a sec."

It was clear she had spent some time in the ocean before she'd been found, her skin loose, waxy, and scarred by the effects of shoreline rocks and sea animals. Her eyes held a wide-open stare that, to me, appeared to hold more penitence than fear.

I blew into the open end of the surgical gloves, inflating them in a way that more easily accommodated my hands, then gently took her right wrist between my thumb and forefinger. It felt light, nearly weightless, as I carefully turned it over. I saw the scars of those first hesitant strokes of the razor.

I looked at Moon, nodded.

"Ashley Logan," I said to the doctor.

"Age?"

"Eighteen."

Preston gazed down at her face, an alien and lifeless gray, her lips tinted blue from lack of oxygen. My eyes roved the confines of the room, and my mind reached back to my rookie year as an L.A. cop, recalled the doctor walking between long rows of steel tables, the tours he gave to young med students. *Drawer Tours*, he'd call them, and smile.

"Looks like she drowned," I said. "See the froth cone?" He gestured toward the mushroom-shaped cone of foam in her nose and mouth.

Dr. Preston looked at me from under a heavy brow, then turned away, carefully examined her eyes. "There is petechial hemorrhaging in the conjunctivae," he said. "Here on the lower lids."

Moon and I craned our necks.

"Bear in mind that drowning is not a diagnostic conclusion," Preston said. "I'm going to have to rule out any other possibilities in order to render a final opinion."

"Check for sexual assault," I said.

"The hospital may be small," the doctor said. He eyed me with something just short of condescension. "But this is not the first autopsy I've done."

"And a tox screen," I said. I didn't need the arrogance. "All the recreationals: pot, coke, Special K, ice, Ecstasy, the works. You with me?"

"Anything else?" Preston asked. He removed a scalpel from the tray beside the operating table. "Perhaps you'd like to do this yourself?"

I looked at Moon and shook my head.

"Call me as soon as you're finished, please," Moon said, and placed his card on the tray.

*   *   *

The rain had ebbed to a fine mist as I followed Moon's Bronco back to the substation. I followed him inside, through the glass doors and into the squad room. A young-looking uniformed patrolman sat in front of a typewriter filling the blanks on some kind of report form. Moon tapped him on the shoulder and pointed to an interview room in the back.

"Sandoval," Moon said when the patrol officer came in the room. "This is Mike Travis. He's with me."

Sandoval nodded his understanding. He shook my hand with a firm, dry grip. "I remember you."

Sandoval shut the door and took a seat at the end of the table, then proceeded to give us chapter and verse on the 9-1-1 call-out he'd taken just after three that morning. Almost an hour later, Moon and me interrupting his narrative intermittently for questions or clarifications, we had the story. And, unfortunately, it was a simple one that didn't cast much light on how Ashley Logan had come to lay in a refrigerated drawer.

Two fisherman, a father and son, had spent most of the previous night fishing from the low rock cliffs, where the island shelf ran to deep water and brought night-hunting game fish in search of food along the current line. The moon had risen late, and it wasn't until it hovered above the far horizon that it cast its silver light across the black water and illuminated something that seemed to be caught on the rocks. At first, they thought it was an injured sea mammal, a monk seal or dolphin. But as they hauled in their lines to investigate, it didn't take them long to see what it was.

Ashley Logan had been floating face down, caught in an eddy of white water that pressed her into a shallow V cut into the sharp lava. She had been wearing only board shorts and a bikini top. As the elder fisherman waited beside her body, the son ran to their truck and dialed 9-1-1 on his cell.

Sandoval responded to the scene and promptly called for a coroner's bus. It was difficult to tell, he said, how or when her injuries had been sustained. Moon thanked him, and we followed him out the door into the squad room.

Captain Cerillo was standing in the doorway of his office, beckoning us over with a wave.

"Terrible thing," Cerillo said to me. "She turn out to be your girl?"

"Yeah."

The Captain sighed. "Detective Moon can handle the notification."

"We'll both do it," I said.

Cerillo smoothed his mustache, taking his time with a private thought. He looked as if he was going to turn away, then decided against it.

"Why is it that wherever you are, dead people turn up?" he asked me. "If I didn't believe you were a decent man, you'd scare the hell out of me."

Ever since my first year in L.A. Homicide, I'd been labeled a maverick, an iconoclast, a pain in the ass. Cerillo's assessment hardly registered on my dials.

"Detective Riley making any headway on that car bomb, Captain?" I asked.

"Believe it or not, Travis, I want to like you," he said as he turned away. "But you sure as hell don't make it easy."

We walked out the glass doors, across the wet pavement of the parking lot to Moon's truck. The rain had stopped, but the sky was still ribbed with strips of gray clouds. Moon slid behind the wheel and lit a cigarette before firing the ignition. "I fucking hate these things," he said.

*   *   *

On the way to the Logan's house, we stopped off at County hospital.

"Despite her appearance," Dr. Preston said, as we sat across from him at his desk. "I was able to collect some very good samples. Bacteria grows fastest in fresh, stagnant water."

"And?" I asked.

He looked up from the chart in his hands and drew a breath that sounded as though I was exhausting his endless supply of patience. "I drew a fluid sample from the vitreous humor of the eye, as well as blood and urine. All three tested positive for alcohol, traces of ketamine hydrochloride and amphetamine."

Ketamine. Special-K. A veterinary anesthetic with some heavy dissociative properties that produced not only hallucinations, but actually separated the mind from the body. It's a particular favorite among date-rapists.

"What kind of amphetamine?" I asked.

Preston leafed through the pages of the report he read from and found what he was looking for. "Methylenedioxymethamphetamine."

"MDMA," I said, looking at Moon. "Ecstasy."

The doctor nodded. "But no trace of semen."

I felt a lancing pain behind my eyes, like someone had wrapped my head in razor wire.

"She wasn't raped, then?" Moon asked.

"Difficult to tell. There was some apparent trauma, but not what I normally associate with rape. And there were no other signs of struggle."

"There wouldn't be if she'd been dosed with ketamine, now would there?" I said, my voice laced with a blistering rage that had no outlet.

"I'm only the messenger."

I wanted to grab the doctor by the collar and drag him across the desk, slap some compassion into him. I stood and headed for the door. "You need to reverse-engineer the Ecstasy for specific chemistry. And check for DNA. From under her nails or anywhere else you can think of," I said. "Get it."

"DNA tests are sent to the mainland," he said with a shake of his head. "Those results will likely take several weeks."

"Well, take your fucking time, doctor," I said. "I can see how busy you are."

*   *   *

"Smooth," Moon said as he caught up to me in the hospital lot.

"Fuck him."

He unlocked the Bronco and we both climbed in. The interior was close and hot and smelled of stale tobacco.

"I want to make one more stop before we go down south," I said, and gave him Kalani Pawai's address.

Moon checked his rearview and pulled out of the stall without a word.

-28-

There was no sign of Kalani Pawai's car when we arrived at his house. Moon pulled to the curb, and I told him to wait while I went to the door.

The tousle-haired woman who opened the door looked as if I had just woken her up, despite the late morning hour. She pulled close the loose collar of her worn housecoat as she examined me through red-rimmed eyes, sizing up my intentions.

"I'm looking for Kalani," I said. "Would you get him for me, please?"

"He's fishing," she told me. "It's Sunday." Her tone said I should have known.

"Do you know where?"

Deep lines creased her forehead, and she tossed off an elaborate shrug. "Lyman's? Maybe down by Hale Halawai? I dunno."

I slipped a card from my pocket and handed it to her. It was the one with my name and cell number. "If I miss him, please have him call me, ma'am."

An expression of distrust crowded her heavy features. "Does my son know you?"

I smiled. "Absolutely." I hoped it didn't look too cruel.

* * *

We found him just south of the surf spot called Lyman's, on Ali'i Drive between the three- and four-mile markers.

The sun had burned through the cloud cover and turned the sky a brilliant blue. Kalani Pawai stood out on a point of black rock that jutted into La'aloa Bay, tossing a circular net into the turquoise water just beyond the break line. He was shirtless and bare-footed, his well-muscled arms and back shining with sweat. Under any other set of circumstances, it would have been a postcard.

"Better if you stay put," I said.

Moon eyed me for several long seconds before he nodded.

A tall stand of coconut palms lined the rocky shore, arcing gracefully into the breeze. A week ago, I had been surfing with Snyder at this very spot. It seemed more like a year.

I watched Pawai haul in the net he had tossed, saw it come up empty. He didn't see me step up behind him as he carefully re-folded it, readying it for his next throw.

"How's fishing?"

He turned his head and fixed me with an empty glare.

"Ashley Logan's body washed up on the beach this morning," I said. "She was full of Ecstasy, Ket, and alcohol. Anything you want to get off your chest?"

"I tol' you before, man. Ain't got nothin' to do wit' me."

"You need to hear me on this: X is notoriously unreliable in content. It's full of caffeine, ephedrine, MDE, all kinds of crap. Of course, you probably know that. Point is, the shit I got off you has a distinctive chemistry, Pawai. Unique. If it matches what we found in Ashley's system, there won't be a safe place for you anywhere on this planet. Best thing you can do is talk to me. You watch TV, you know how it works. The first guy who talks, walks."

His eyes cut away from me.

"I gave my card to your mother," I said.

"Say what?"

"Don't wait too long. When all those tests come back—DNA, drug chemistry—you'll need a surgeon to extract all the warrants that'll get shoved up your ass."

I left him standing there on the shoreline, the wind tossing his thick, black hair, a fine white mist from the breakers catching the sun like shards of broken glass.

*   *   *

Cady Logan was surprised to see me at her door, the noisy white puff of a dog circling her feet. She glanced at Moon a few paces behind me, and my throat went dry when I saw the hope in her eyes.

"Did you find Ashley?"

"Are your mom and dad home?"

She scowled at my evasion. "They're at church. There's a carnival today. I was just getting ready to go there myself."

"Carnival?"

"A fund raiser. They do it every year."

I couldn't stay there any longer, the weight of what felt like my failure threatened to turn me to stone.

"Enjoy your day, Cady."

"What about my sister?" she called after me.

I had already turned away.

*   *   *

Covenant Union occupied four prime acres at the top of a slope that looked down on Na'ala Bay, the church building itself a sprawling monstrosity of concrete and stained glass that couldn't have looked more out of place if it had been rimmed in flashing neon. The pastor was a notorious huckster and self-styled prophet who shamelessly drove a bright yellow Hummer. He parked it every Sunday in the same lot as parishioners who couldn't pay both its gas and insurance bills in the same month.

A chain-link fence ran the perimeter of a generous expanse of grass that served as the playground for pre-K day care and was now crowded with game booths and food tents for their annual carnival. A fragrant cloud of smoke bloomed from a wood-fired barbeque at the far corner, where whole roasted chickens turned slowly on a spit above a brazier of ribs and tri-tip and corn-on-the-cob.

Moon and I stood at the gate as I searched the crowd for Sheila and Frank Logan, our ears assaulted by screaming children and music that blared from loudspeakers affixed to tall wooden poles strung with colored lights. Not far off, a clown in a puffed and polka-dotted suit dispensed helium balloons to a clutch of tiny, grasping hands. The wide red smile that was slashed across his face looked like an open wound.

"I think I see him," I said.

"Which one?"

"The pasty guy in the ring-toss booth."

Moon shook his head. "This is fucked-up," I heard him mutter as I led the way across the wide, green lawn. I don't know if it was my imagination, or if the crowd actually parted before me, responding in some primal, feral manner to our presence.

We waited at the back of the line as Frank Logan took tickets from childrens' hands and exchanged them for colored rings. He smiled, offering encouragement to the youngest ones, as they took careful aim at the row of long-necked soda bottles arranged along the wooden table behind him. I felt sick to my stomach as we stood there in the meager shade, waiting to get his attention. These would be his final unknowing seconds before his world came down around his narrow shoulders.

From the corner of my eye I caught an eddy of color and turned to see the clown cutting a diagonal path across the playing field, toward us. A trail of anxious children followed in his path, calling out for more balloons.

"Too bad, good try," Frank Logan said as he ruffled the hair of a small boy who appeared to be on the verge of tears. "Okay, who's—" he said as he lifted his eyes, looking directly into mine.

"Mr. Logan," I began. "I think you—"

I was interrupted by the clown who suddenly appeared at my side.

"Frank," the clown said. "What is this?"

Her husband's expression was empty, his eyes roved from me to Moon, then rested on his wife. Sheila Logan peered angrily from behind the stark makeup, the wide outline of an incongruous grin painted on her face. The troop of young kids she had outrun caught up to her, and tugged at her baggy pants.

"Stop it!" she hissed. "Not now!" They flinched and backed away like frightened animals.

Moon crouched down on his haunches. "There'll be balloons enough for everybody," he told the kids. "We just need a minute, okay?"

They looked at him suspiciously and melted slowly into the crowd. I waited until they were well away.

"Is there somewhere we can talk?" I asked.

Frank Logan turned as if to come out from the booth.

"You stay where you are, Francis." To me, she said, "This is hardly the place, Mr. Travis. Please leave."

I looked at her husband, ignoring his wife's venom. "This is Detective Moon from the HPD. We need to talk," I said quietly. "All four of us."

Without a word, Frank Logan went out back, under the canvas awning and gestured to a man standing nearby. "You mind taking over for a few minutes?" he asked the man.

He came to meet us a few seconds later, inclining his head toward a tree just beyond the gates. When he glanced at his wife, her eyes were flinty, incensed at his insubordination.

The carnival music receded as we neared the church building and stepped beneath the outstretched arms of a jacaranda. Sheila Logan stopped short, standing fast in the sunlight. The garish colored balloons she gripped so tightly glowed hot, insulting the pastel of blossoms that fell from the branches like rain.

"Mr. and Mrs. Logan, there's no easy way to tell you this," I said. "Your daughter Ashley was found early this morning. I'm afraid she's dead. I'm very sorry."

Sheila Logan's free hand went to her face, smearing the smile that was painted there. She looked as if she might stop breathing.

Her husband stood his ground, the vacant light returning to his face. Time seemed to halt in that horrible moment, infused with a profound isolation and defeat that defied description. As I watched these two begin to digest their grief, I was struck again by the distance between this husband and wife, at the absence of comfort to be sustained, one from the other. They were together only in that they stood side by side.

"How?" Frank Logan whispered.

"We're not completely sure," Moon said. "It appears she might have drowned."

"No," Sheila said as she stood there in the hot sun, her face disfigured by smeared makeup and rage. She took a step toward me and slapped me hard across the face.

I made no move at all, my cheek aflame with hot needles. She seemed lost, stuck inside her thoughts, then suddenly turned loose of the grip she held on the balloons and rushed me. Her throat was choked and clotted with tears as she pummeled me on the chest and face with her fists until she collapsed in my arms.

We stood like that for several minutes, amid the fallen petals at our feet, my arms enfolding a sobbing clown as her tears stained my shirt a deep, bloody red.

Moon offered to drive them home, but Frank Logan refused. He collapsed at the base of the tree, leaned his back against the trunk, and laid his face in his hands, a man completely alone.

As we walked to Moon's truck, I looked up at the sky, to the heaven I wished for Ashley Logan, and saw the tiny outline of a child's balloon drifting silently between the earth and the hard, white sun.

-29-

The next morning, I did what I almost never do. I slept late.

My head was full of spiders, and nothing I could tell myself would rid me of the corrosive storm of remorse and condemnation that had gathered in my brain. I needed to get as far from the Logan case as I could, retreat to the only place I thought I might find ablution. As far as I was concerned, it was over. Moon had the Ecstasy samples, and he knew all about Kalani Pawai. If there was a connection, it was his to make, not mine. My promise was fulfilled, and I'd had enough.

I told Miles he needed to skip work at the Plantation to help me, which was a load of crap, but I wanted to talk to him about his future. The bitter ends of his life needed splicing. And so did mine.

When I came topside, the sun was pouring bright light on the lee slope of Hualalai, tinting the treetops and the torn wisps of clouds with white gold. I called Snyder as I sat on the *Kehau's* fantail, a hot mug of Mango Ceylon in my hand, my bare feet resting on the wheel.

"You need to get out on the water," I told him. "Every time I see you, you're in a bar."

"It's Monday, Travis. I gotta work."

"That's why God made employees. I'm taking *Kehau* up to Makalawena. I could use another pair of hands on deck."

"I don't think so," Snyder said without resolve.

"I'll have you back by two."

He thought it over as I listened to the high whistle of cardinals nesting in the orchid trees outside his house. "I'll make a couple calls, see if Daniel or Bridget can open up for me."

"I'll pick you up at the pier in an hour."

*   *   *

An hour and a half later, we were pressing through a modest swell coming down out of the northwest. Silver beads of spray caught the wind and blew across the deck as we rounded Kaiwi Point.

"Stay this course and keep running across the wind," I said as I turned the helm over to Miles. The sea was deep blue, dotted with whitecaps and bright flashes of sun glare.

He took the wheel and looked at me vacantly, his stiff-legged stance wide for balance. I caught Snyder's grin out of the corner of my eye.

"You understand what I want you to do?" I asked Miles.

He shook his head. "No idea."

I gestured toward the bow. "Head the pointy end toward that island in the distance, and keep the sails full and tight."

My nephew's face had tanned a healthy brown in the week he'd been here, his skin and eyes more clear.

"What happened to your hair, son?" Snyder asked him. "You don't look like a goddamned vampire anymore."

Miles' eyes slid off toward the beach, something wistful there. "Edita helped me wash the dye out of it."

"Ah," Snyder said. He arched his eyebrows knowingly. "Women."

Miles fought the smile that pulled at the corners of his mouth, feigned concentration on the far horizon.

Snyder stood, slapped my nephew on the shoulder as he crossed behind him, and made his way up the gunwale to the bow. Once he was out of earshot, I took up a place beside Miles at the helm, and leaned against the bulkhead.

Along the shoreline, crystal blue waves rumbled against the rocks. Great geysers of foam shot into the air and left a ghostlike mist hanging on the sky.

"I never got the chance to tell you, Miles. That was a good thing you did for Roland Delgado," I said. "And Edita."

He made a noise that could have been a laugh, but sounded more like the bark of a sleeping dog. After a moment, Miles pulled his gaze from the hazy outline of Maui in the distance, and I saw my own distorted reflection in the polarized lenses of his shades.

"What happened to your face?" he asked.

I touched the scab along my brow, but only felt the dull ache from Sheila Logan's fists on my chest from the day before. "Guy took a swing at me."

"What for?"

Dense stands of coconut palms and scrub pine traced the crescents of white sand beaches that dotted the ragged coast.

"I made him see who he really is. He didn't appreciate it."

I felt the *Kehau* stutter as the mainsail lost the wind, luffed, and snapped sharply. Miles watched me curiously as I leaned over and hauled in the line.

"Your school starts in a week," I said. "Your dad's not going to abide you hiding out here forever."

"He's not gonna make it easy. Going back, I mean."

"You can't put it off much longer, Miles. You've got to make your stand, or you'll never be able to look at your own reflection."

He studied the slow roll of the compass for a long moment. "I know," he said finally, his voice carried off on the breeze.

"There's this old song by a guy named Graham Nash. I don't know if you've heard of him," I said. "There's a lyric that says, 'a man's a man who looks a man right between the eyes.'"

His expression betrayed something brittle behind the façade he was trying hard to maintain.

"You with me, Miles?"

I think I saw him nod slightly before I left him to his own thoughts, his knuckles going white from the grip he had on the wheel. I ducked under the yardarm as I went forward, and took a seat with Snyder on the bow. He was sitting on the warm wooden deck, his feet dangling into the blowback of white water that churned off the bow.

"Big change in that kid," he said.

"He's raising himself. His father's a fucking phantom."

Snyder studied the whitecaps in the channel. The air was bright with the smell of sunshine and salt. "You know, Mike, he thinks the only reason you don't walk on water is that you don't like wet shoes."

They were words I didn't deserve, didn't even want to hear.

"You mind if I ask you something personal?" Snyder asked me.

I didn't answer. Off in the distance, a heavy line of clouds was following a low-pressure system that appeared to be pushing toward the island.

He asked his question anyway. "What are you doing out here, man? I mean, I've always had you figured like a mosquito in a nudist colony—you got a lot of choices."

Like a flicker of dry lightning, a face floated unbidden into my memory: Tyrese Ganney, a mid-level dealer I had turned into a snitch after I collared him and his sister bagging three keys of Mexican Brown in the kitchen of a small apartment in Silverlake. His sister had a two-year-old child who I swore I'd put in the system if they didn't testify against their upstream connection, an asshole I'd been after for months.

Three months later, Christmas Eve, I got a call. I found Tyrese and his sister handcuffed to a wall heater, shot up with battery acid. The needle was still jammed in his vein. There was no sign of the baby.

"This is the most remote island chain on the planet," I said to Snyder, but I was still thinking about Tyrese.

One week later, New Year's Eve, they found Tyrese's connection under a railroad bridge, on a dried-out slab of concrete in the L.A. River. He'd bled out from a nine-mil through-and-through that tore off his manhood and ripped a fatal gash in his femoral artery. That one never did get solved. Nobody I knew tried all that hard.

"There's nowhere you can go that's further from everywhere else," I finished.

I could see Snyder was about to say something when Miles called out to me. "Uncle Mike," he hollered over the sound of the wind. "Somebody's trying to call you."

"Hell with 'em," I said. "I'm off the clock."

Miles shook his head. "It's the third time the thing's gone off."

I went back to the transom, pissed off at myself for not disconnecting my cell after I'd called Snyder that morning. I dialed my access code and heard Moon's message on my voicemail. When it was finished, I played it again, just to be sure I'd heard it right.

I dropped the phone back on the nav desk, a hot seed of anger burning a hole in my stomach. I stepped out into the light, cupped my hands around my mouth, and called out to Snyder. "Prepare to come about," I said. "We gotta go back to town."

I took the helm from Miles, and Snyder worked the rigging as I brought the *Kehau* around. The day took on a strange quiet as we ran before the wind, a lacy drift of rain hanging like Spanish moss from that line of distant clouds, like images of angels in the atmosphere. No one said a word.

-30-

Captain Max Cerillo stood at the crest of a grassy slope, looking down on the scene. Even from a distance, I could see his high forehead was beaded with sweat. I watched Cerillo anxiously stroke his mustache as he spoke with Detective Moon.

The Captain waved me through when he saw I had been stopped at the yellow tape by a patrolman in a heavy, dark blue uniform. I felt the young cop's eyes on me as I climbed the short rise to where they stood, Moon turning his back to the wind as he attempted to light a cigarette.

"I will not have this shit on my island," Cerillo said to me, as though I had been the cause. He pointed a thick finger down the hill to where a half-dozen uniformed cops milled and stooped and photographed the body still lying at the base of the stairs that led from the entrance to Kaimalono High School. "I got one kid dead, and another one bleeding out in an ambulance on the way to Kona Community."

"What the hell happened?" I asked.

"According to witnesses, they'd just let out for lunch, and the shooter opened up from somewhere over there," Moon said. He indicated a spot just beyond where we stood, a thick tangle of bamboo, monstera and tall grass. "We've got uniforms looking for casings, cigarette butts, all that shit."

The sun was still high in the sky, but the bottom of the gully was engulfed in shadow. A trickle of water ran in the nearly dry bed, and the warm odor of horses drifted over from the corral on the far side of the embankment.

"Kalani Pawai?" I asked.

Moon nodded, blew dual streams of smoke from his nostrils. "One in the throat, and one that looks like a heart shot. Died before they could even call it in."

"It was a girl took the other two," Cerillo added. "Here and here." He gestured to the ball of his shoulder and just off-center of his chest.

I looked down the hill toward the entrance to the parking lot. A man and woman were climbing out of the back of a van while the driver was being told to turn around and park in the street. I recognized the man as the photographer from the demonstration on the street outside the Estates.

"Shit," Cerillo muttered. "I gotta go handle this."

Before he left, the Captain turned to me, his face a mask of agitation. He leaned close and spoke so softly I could barely hear it over the dry rattle of leaves overhead. "In about twenty seconds, I'm going to walk down this hill." Cerillo eyed the photographer as he lined up a shot of the school grounds. "I just wanted you to know that what Detective Moon is about to tell you? It comes straight from me."

He shook his head as if to clear it, sighed, and ran a hand through his thick black hair. "I will not have this shit on my island," he said again, and carefully sidestepped his way down the incline.

"Come with me," Moon said.

I followed him down a short rise, behind the berm of the gully, out of sight of the school. I could smell the mud and dampness coming up off the streambed. He drew a thick envelope from his hip pocket and handed it to me.

I slipped my finger under the flap and carefully tore it open. It took a moment to register.

"This is a PI card," I said. "I didn't ask for this."

"Doesn't matter. You got it now."

"I don't want it," I said, handing it back. I didn't look at the rest of the contents.

Moon took a long, thoughtful drag off the butt he held between his fingers and looked off into the trees. "The Captain thought you might say that. I was told to remind you that your permit to carry that Beretta exists exclusively at his pleasure."

I felt the heat rise on the back of my neck.

Some guys take a bullet, and it turns them off of handguns for good; they flinch at the sound of a backfire for the rest of their lives. Me? A tweeker nearly took off my head with a shotgun, and now it's a rare day when I don't want my weapon duct taped to my hand. If it's them or me, it ain't gonna be me.

"Don't they call that blackmail?" I said.

"Commerce."

"I don't get it."

"Read on," Moon said, pointing at the envelope I still held in my hand. I pulled out a three-page document, a contract for services with my name at the top.

"Who's Herb Kinoshita?" I asked.

"Former HPD Captain. Retired. He's got a daughter attending this school. He's hiring you to investigate for a possible civil suit. She's very upset by it."

Keeping it in the family. The story was complete bullshit, but I took another look at the contract. "He's generous with the County's money."

"The Captain believes you get what you pay for."

"Which Captain?"

"Both," he said. "But you'll work through me."

"Do I need to ask why this is happening?"

"No," Moon said. He dropped the butt and crushed it into the moist dirt with the toe of his boot. "Consider it a compliment."

"I get paid in cash, of course."

"Retainer's in the envelope. Anything else?"

I shook my head. "If I refuse?"

Moon looked me dead in the eyes. "The door swings both ways, Big City. I'm telling you that as a friend."

* * *

The students had been ushered into the gymnasium, well apart from the hive of activity humming around Pawai's body. A plain-clothes detective stood at the door, amid a knot of teachers and school staff, a clipboard in his hand. I gave him my name as I walked in, and he ran his finger down a long list until he found the match I knew Cerillo would have already arranged for.

Edita ran across the hardwood as soon as she saw me, her expression suffused with disbelief. She threw her arms around me and buried her face against my chest.

"You all right?" I asked. "Have you called your dad?"

"My phone's in my locker," she said as she pulled away from me. "They won't let us leave."

I nodded. "They're going to want to take statements."

"I want to get out of here. I want to go home."

I pulled her close and whispered in her ear. "I'll get you out as soon as I can."

"I want to go home," she repeated, looking like she was about to lose it.

"Did you see anything, Edita?"

"I was just coming out of class," she said. "On the whole other side of campus." Her voice was shaking, letting go now that I was there to lean on. "It didn't sound like a gun. It didn't sound like much of anything."

Gunshots never sound like they do on television. I looked around at the crowd of students. "What about Cady? Where's she?"

"She didn't come to school today. She's pretty upset about Ashley. We all are. I can't believe this is happening."

"I'll call your dad and get you out of here as soon as I can," I said. "You hang in there, all right?"

She looked at me as if she hadn't heard me right, as if I were insane. I made a decision.

I took hold of her elbow and pulled her gently toward the far exit. I waited until the officer at the main door turned his back to me, then opened it just enough for her to squeeze out into daylight, and followed her outside. I quietly shut the door behind me and slipped my cell phone from my pocket.

"Take this and call your dad. Now. Make it fast. Tell him to meet you down the road, by Takagawa Store. You know the place?"

Edita nodded.

"Go the long way around that building," I said, indicating the squat wooden structure at the far side of the campus. "Then follow the gully all the way down to the road. Cross under the bridge to the other side before you head south to Takagawa's, okay?"

She made the call, tears flooding her eyes when she heard her father's voice. When she finished, her earlier look of bewilderment had turned to real fear.

"If you don't go now, Edita, I don't know how long you'll be stuck here." I put my arms around her one last time. "Now, go."

She had been through enough.

*   *   *

I caught up with Moon as he was being ushered into a small corner office in the main Administration Building. I followed him through a wooden door with a frosted-glass window—the words ROGER McGEE and PRINCIPAL hand-lettered upon it—and took a seat in one of the guest chairs on the opposite side of a gray steel desk. Outside, Kalani Pawai's body was being shunted onto a gurney, covered with a white sheet, and slid into the back of an idling coroner's van. The principal stood at the window, his tie pulled loose around the unbuttoned collar of his shirt, his hands buried in his pockets. I could tell the man wasn't listening as Moon gave him our names.

"We'd like to begin taking statements of everybody who was a witness to the shootings, Mr. McGee. The sooner the better. I'm also going to want access to the victims' lockers, their academic records, and any—"

McGee was a tall man, ruddy-faced and thick across the chest, looked more like a football coach than a principal. He rolled up his sleeves as Moon was speaking, then heaved a tired sigh as he turned away from the window, the skin around his eyes drawn tight.

"I've been advised by the attorney for the school district not to allow any statements to be made by our students without the specific authorization of their parents," he interrupted.

"You can see—"

McGee showed us the palm of his hand, a vaguely condescending gesture he surely used often on his charges. "And, as for access to lockers, I'm afraid I'm going to have to ask that you obtain a warrant."

"This is a murder investigation, Mr. McGee," Moon said.

The principal nodded and took his seat behind the desk. "Your frustration is understandable. But these days, we have to be careful with respect to the violation of anyone's rights."

"'Rights,' my ass," I said. "You're concerned about lawsuits."

There was resignation in his shrug. "The district is unwilling to take on any unnecessary liability."

"Beyond having two students shot a hundred feet from your office window? How about you, Mr. McGee?" I asked. "What did you see?"

"I can't be sure. I was on the phone when I heard the shots. And it was over before I even knew what was happening. But I might have seen smoke coming from those bushes up there on the rise."

Moon leaned forward in his chair, following the direction of the principal's gesture. "Up there, where those two officers are standing?"

"That's correct."

"How many shots?"

McGee placed his elbows on his desk, rested his chin on steepled fingers. "Four? Five?"

"How close together?"

"Close. A few seconds, tops."

Moon and I shared a sidelong glance.

"You ever in the military, Mr. McGee?" Moon asked.

"I'm afraid not."

"Then you wouldn't be able to say whether it sounded like an automatic weapon?"

He shook his head. "I'm afraid not."

"Could you give me the name of the female victim?"

"I already gave it—"

"Will you give him the goddamn name, please?" I said. "Your school just turned into a free-fire zone."

"Claudia Garibay," he said, and spelled the last name.

"We'll need to see her academic records. Kalani Pawai's, as well," Moon said calmly, firmly establishing my bad-cop cred.

"As I said, you'll have to get—"

"A warrant," I finished for him.

"That's right."

"Actually, that's wrong," I smiled. "Those records belong to the State of Hawaii. What's theirs is ours."

"What is it you're looking for?" he asked, momentarily off-balance.

"We'd like any records from their counselors, as well," I added.

He shook his head. "You'll have to see Ms. Castle for that."

Moon spread his hands out before him, palms up.

"Our school counselor," McGee provided.

The principal left us alone in his office while he retrieved what he had on Garibay and Pawai. I turned to Moon and said, "While you're arranging for the warrant on the lockers, include Ashley Logan and Roland Delgado."

"Wait here. I'll make the call."

Roger McGee returned a few minutes later. He handed me a pair of manila folders with obvious displeasure. His eyes scanned the room for Moon.

"He's making a phone call," I said.

"Is there anything else?"

"Has anyone asked you for a list of witnesses? Anyone you saw in the immediate area of the shootings?"

"The first detective has it," he said. "I believe he's in the gymnasium."

McGee's eyes moved toward his window as the coroner's van pulled away from the curb. "May we clean the blood off the stairway now?" he asked.

"The officers will let you know when they're finished processing the scene."

The room seemed to grow smaller as we stood together in silence.

"We appreciate your help, sir," I offered.

He slid his hands into his pockets and dropped his eyes to the floor. Whatever strength that had been propping him up was beginning to drain from his system.

"For what it's worth, Mr. McGee, you're handling this as well as anyone could be expected to."

He nodded slightly, then took his seat, losing what remained of his composure. I saw him drop his head into his hands as I closed the door behind me. He was glad to see me go.

Moon was in the outer corridor finishing his call as I approached. "Logan and Delgado are a no-go," he said. "Ashley Logan is the victim of an unrelated incident, and there's no probable cause for Delgado."

"We'll see," I said as I began to walk away.

"Where're you going?"

"Hospital," I said, my footfalls echoing off the walls of the long corridor.

*   *   *

THE LATE afternoon sun reflected off the glass doors of the Emergency Room like a blood-red ball. Behind the reception desk was the same nurse I'd met on my first visit, a telephone receiver wedged between her cheek and shoulder as before. She held up a finger, informing me I should wait. Her brow was creased deeply in concentration as she listened to whoever was on the line.

I looked around the small room and noticed a teenage girl sitting alone in the corner. She was dark-skinned and pretty, her slender face marred only by a fine dusting of acne scars that pitted her well-defined cheekbones. She fidgeted anxiously as her eyes darted across the pages of the magazine she held, turning the pages too quickly to be taking anything in.

"May I help you now?" the nurse named B. Gularte asked me.

"A young girl was just brought in, a gunshot?"

"Are you family?"

"Police," I said, hoping she wouldn't ask for ID. I didn't think I looked much like a cop anymore, but nurse Gularte seemed to believe otherwise.

"She's in O.R."

"Any word on her condition?"

She shook her head wearily. "You'll have to speak with Dr. Chun when he comes out."

It was a familiar name. He was the one who'd dug the shotgun pellets out of my shoulder.

"That's her friend over there, though," she said. She indicated the girl with the magazine. "She came in right behind the EMTs."

I took a seat in a hard plastic chair beside the girl and offered my hand. "I'm Mike Travis," I said. "How's Claudia doing?"

Her eyes glazed momentarily. She looked confused as she took my hand in hers. "I don't know, exactly."

"What's your name?"

"Crescenciano," she said softly. "Crescenciano Perreira. People call me 'Sweet.'"

"Were you with her when it happened?"

She dropped the magazine in an empty chair beside her. "Yeah."

"Did you see who did it?"

Her expression took on that familiar blankness common among victims of sudden violence. "No. You think she's going to be okay?"

"I don't know," I said. She seemed grateful for a shred of honesty.

"We were coming down the steps to go to lunch. There's this noise, and the next thing I know, Kalani's on the ground. There was blood coming out of his throat..." Her eyes went out of focus.

"They shot him first? Before Claudia?"

She nodded. "I started to run away," she said, her voice shot through with shame.

"Did you talk to the police?"

The girl called Sweet shook her head. A lock of dark hair fell across her face. She made no attempt to brush it away. "I was holding her keys. She hated carrying a purse. I followed the ambulance in her car."

"How many shots, Sweet?"

"Four."

"You're sure?"

She hooked the loose strands of hair behind her ears and looked me squarely in the eye. "I'll never forget."

*   *   *

I strode past the nurse's station in the Pediatric ward. There was no sign of Susan Delgado. Without another thought, I moved down the short hall and stepped into the room where I had last seen her son. The curtains were drawn as before, rimmed by the last light of the day, the only sound coming from the voices on the television he watched.

"You been here all day, Roland?"

He lifted his arm, eyeing the IV needle taped to his hand. The clear plastic tube trailed away into the bag that hung on the pole beside the bed. "Where am I gonna go?"

"Kalani Pawai took a pair of bullets this afternoon. He died."

He turned his head away, looking toward the dull glow from the window.

"You don't appear too shaken up about it."

"I'm crying," he said. "It's a real fucking tragedy."

"I'd be careful who you say that kind of thing to."

"Or what? Go to jail for not giving a shit?"

"You know Claudia Garibay?"

A smile touched the corners of his blackened eyes. "Yeah."

"She took two to the chest. She's downstairs in E.R. as we speak."

"Sucks to be her."

"What's this about, Roland?"

"You'd better go now, Mr. Travis." He touched the call button beside his bed. "My mom's gonna be pissed you were here."

-31-

The night was dark and speckled with flickering stars, the moon a razor-thin waxing crescent in the eastern sky.

My headlights sliced through the blackness as I pulled into the dirt turnaround in front of Tino's house and cut the ignition. As I climbed down from the Jeep, Poi Dog came around from the backyard, barking and kicking up a cloud of sand and dust. Tino stepped out on the lanai and squinted into the dark.

"It's only me," I called to him. "It's Mike."

"Jesus Christ. Some kinda goddamn day, brah."

His face was lined and tired, heavily shadowed in the dull yellow glow from the light beside the screen door. On the wall behind him, a pale brown gecko silently stalked a moth.

"I need a favor, Tino."

"You don' look so good," he said as I came into the light. "How 'bout some beef stew an' rice? Edita and me, we're just finishing up."

The smell of home cooking floated on the still, humid air. He held the screen open as I climbed the worn wooden stairs. Edita stood at the sink, her arms immersed in a sink full of soap bubbles. She looked up as I came in with her dad.

"How is she, Uncle Mike?"

"I stopped by the hospital, but no word yet. I'm sorry."

Edita looked through the window above the sink, her vacant reflection slightly warped in the rippling glass. She brushed her forehead with the back of her hand, exhausted and confused.

"I need a favor," I said to her.

Tino stepped to the counter and scooped up a helping of steamed white rice, topped it with a ladle of thick broth, his back turned to me as she nodded.

"Sure," she said. "Anything."

"I need to borrow your car," I said. "Just for a couple hours."

A frown creased her brow. "Sure, but—"

"I'd rather not go into it."

Tino placed the steaming bowl on the small table, took a spoon and a paper napkin from the drawer beside Edita.

"Bettah you eat something, brah," he said.

I took a seat facing into the kitchen. Tino pulled up a chair opposite me, rocked it back on two legs and leaned against the wall.

"Cady called me this afternoon," Edita said softly. Her tone was leaden, shot through with defeat. "Ashley's funeral is on Friday."

"How is she?"

Edita stared into the gray dishwater. I saw Tino watching me from the corner of my eye.

"It's not your fault," I said.

"I know." Her voice said otherwise. "Will you be there?"

A few seconds lapsed before I answered. "I'm not sure that's the best idea."

Poi Dog nudged the screen door and padded across the hardwood floor, sniffing around my ankles before curling up at Tino's feet. The room was thick with silence, not a breath of wind or waves against the shoreline.

"I need something else, Edita. I need you to tell me where to find Ashley and Roland's school lockers."

"What?"

"You've got to promise me this will go no further."

"Okay," she said. "I'll show you."

I shook my head. "You know their locker numbers?"

She looked at a thought inside her head. "No, not exactly."

I slid a pad of notepaper and a pen off the desk beside the telephone. "Can you draw me a map?"

I ate appreciatively as she dried her hands on a dishtowel then did what I asked. I realized only then that I hadn't eaten since early that morning. When she was finished, she turned the pad around so I could see it. She used her pen as a pointer.

"This is the gym, where I saw you this afternoon," she said. "You go around this building here, and make a right. It'll lead you straight into the quad. All the lockers are along this wall, or in rows along the center area here."

I nodded.

"Roland and Ashley are seniors, so their lockers are mostly in this area. They're blue, I think. Anyway, Roland's is about here. Second from the top. And Ashley's is right next to it. On the right."

"You're sure?"

Her chocolate brown eyes were clear and serious. "I told you before. Mine is right by Roland's. You can't miss it. It's got a big white A'ama Surf Company sticker on it."

Everybody in town knew the logo. I had one on the bumper of my Jeep.

"What kind of locks?"

"We bring our own. Some people use the kind with little keys. You know, like for a bike."

That was good. For what I had in mind, at least. I tore off the top page of the note pad and slipped it into my shirt pocket. Edita stood, lifted her car keys from the hook beside the door and set them on the table beside my empty bowl.

"One more thing?" I said.

"Okay."

"I need you to write down the names of everybody Kalani Pawai hung out with. His close friends. Claudia's, too."

"Who's Claudia?"

"Claudia Garibay," I said, unintentionally allowing frustration to creep into my tone. It had been a long day, growing longer.

"Oh. Honey Girl."

"What?"

"Everybody called her Honey Girl," she said.

My heart skipped a beat. "Was she a friend of Ashley Logan's?"

Edita slowly shook her head. "I doubt it. Honey Girl was kind of, uh, wild," she said finally, shooting a furtive glance at Tino. He was still leaning against the wall, arms folded across his thick chest. "But I guess you never know."

*   *   *

I parked Edita's car in front of Takagawa's, a dilapidated two-story neighborhood grocery from the early 1900s, the kind the locals called a Cracked Seed Store.

I sat there for several long minutes, scanning the darkened street, thinking. I have never shrunk from taking matters into my own hands, but for a moment I wondered if it was only a remnant conceit from my years as a detective. It was a thought I left behind as I reached into the backseat. I picked up the bolt cutters I had removed from the Jeep's lockbox before I left Tino's, and quietly got out of the car.

I glanced skyward as I crossed the deserted road. The dim white shadow of the Milky Way spilled across the purple sky, as I melted into the thick copse of philodendron and ginger that lined the unpaved shoulder. I followed a shallow gully all the way to the bridge and crossed under as I had told Edita to do just a few hours earlier. It was slow going in the moonless black, but fifteen minutes later, I climbed the embankment across from the school gym. I felt my way along the walls until I entered the open quad.

I scanned the area as best I could, my eyes having adjusted somewhat to the night, but there was no sign of roving security, no cops left behind to watch the crime scene.

It didn't take much time to find the lockers, and even less to find out that someone else had been there before me.

* * *

When I got back to Tino's, the porch light was still burning, besieged by flying insects, but there was no sign of motion inside.

Edita had done what I had asked and left the list folded and tucked into my windshield visor. As quietly as I could, I replaced the bolt cutters in the Jeep's lockbox, and slid Edita's keys behind the bleached white coral stone that stood at their doorway.

I didn't turn on my headlights until I was well up the dirt road beyond their house.

*　　*　　*

The tide was only a whisper on the small delta of sand at the foot of the pier, the rippling surface of the bay reflecting the streetlights and a fringe of white foam.

I took a seat on the Jeep's warm hood and leaned my back against the windscreen. In the near distance, I watched *Kehau* rock on her mooring, the fine motion of light at her bow and mainmast. But inside, I felt vaguely soiled, and told myself again that ours is not a justice system, it is a legal system. And there were times when somebody had to balance the two.

I slid my cell phone from my pocket, not bothering to check the time, not caring. I punched in a number I knew by heart.

"I had no right to talk to you that way," I said when Hans answered.

"What the hell time is it?"

"I don't know."

"You all right?"

"Not really. I just wanted to tell you: I'm no different than you."

"What are we talking about?"

A breath of cool wind blew in off the water, tugging at my hair and the loose tails of my shirt.

"I don't know," I said. "I just thought I should tell you."

"Forget it, pard. You had a point."

"Take it easy."

"You, too," he said. "Get some sleep."

I leaned back and traced my eyes across the constellations, and saw Orion falling headlong into the sea.

-32-

1973. Mid-November.

The sky is a blanket of cold gray clouds. It's been threatening rain for three days, but the storm we've been told to expect still hasn't appeared. My eyes slide past the window, and I gaze out beyond the bare tree limbs, across the brown lawn toward the tall light stanchions that border the empty football field. The end of a losing season.

In the back of my head, I hear my algebra teacher's droning, but from my seat in the back of the class, it's nothing but a monotonous hum. I am the last one to leave the room when the bell finally rings, reluctant to enter the crowded hallway. My mind is somewhere else, sealed away in a place of my own making; a place it has remained since I heard that Stacy Thorne had been rushed to the hospital.

Tommy D catches up to me as I push my way through the stream of kids heading for the buses. He's got a book bag flung over his shoulder. "Where you been, man? I haven't seen you all day."

"I've been around."

"You hear about Stacy Thorne? They say she's pretty bad off."

I nod.

"Bummer," he says. He shakes his head as if to clear it. I wish it was that easy. "Hey, you know what you're doing for Thanksgiving yet?"

"I'll find out when my dad gets back from New York."

He looks at me strangely, even though he knows that it's always the same. "When's that?"

I have to think about it. "Friday, maybe. Saturday. I don't remember." Even in my own ears, it sounds empty, and I realize it doesn't really matter.

My friend glances at his watch, hitches his backpack up on his shoulder. "I gotta catch the bus, man. Take it easy," he says. He waits for the standard response that doesn't come.

I watch him blend into the crowd that is moving slowly toward the parking lot.

It is quieter as I head to my locker. Only the older kids, the ones with cars, remain behind. I see my brother standing at the far end of the corridor with a group of his friends. I turn away before we can make eye contact.

He comes up behind me as I put my books in my locker. I ignore him.

"I'm leaving in five minutes," he says. "Don't be late, or I'll take off without you."

"I don't need a ride."

"What are you gonna do? Walk home?"

"Forget about it."

"I asked you a question, Tadpole."

I slam my locker door and walk away without another look. I can feel his eyes on my back as I step between a small clot of onlookers. I look into their faces as I pass, but they avert their eyes as if they're embarrassed— for me or my brother or themselves. I don't know.

It is a dim, diffused sunlight that wavers behind the clouds, weak and out of focus. There is only the faintest trace of shadow as I walk along the sidewalk.

He pulls up beside me as I stand waiting at the curb. A brisk wind pulls at the flaps of my jacket.

"Get in," he says, a cloud across his face.

"I'm waiting for Mrs. Waldron."

"What for?"

"None of your business."

"Get in the damn car."

I stand my ground, finding I no longer care what my brother thinks of me. It is a strange and liberating feeling. I start to walk off, but Valden throws his door open and walks around to the front of the car. He stands there, and it looks for a moment like he's going to kick the car's grill. Instead, he turns away, gets back in his Beemer. He leaves a trail of burn marks on the pavement and a cloud of acrid smoke in the air. A trio of faces stare out from the rear window of the last bus in line. I ignore them, too.

*   *   *

Mrs. Waldron drops me at the hospital entrance. She tells me she'll wait for me in the lobby.

The flowers in the gift shop look shoddy and cheap. Instead, I choose a stuffed animal from the shelf, and a card that says Get Well Soon. I write a brief note on the inside, then pull a twenty from my wallet and hand it to the blue-haired lady at the counter. She shows me a smile that says How Cute, and I feel my eyes begin to swell and have to look away.

The volunteer at the desk tells me where to go, and I follow the maze of intersecting corridors to Stacy's room. It is noisy and too warm, and the air seems heavy with the odor of disinfectant and suffering; pitiful noises leak from open doors.

The entrance to Stacy's room is half open, a privacy curtain is drawn in such a way that I can't see in. I knock softly on the doorframe and step inside. A woman, Stacy's mother, steps into the open, her face mostly in shadow.

"I'm Mike Van de Groot," I tell her.

She nods. "You're a friend of Stacy's," she says. Her soft voice is little more than a sigh. "From school."

"Yes, ma'am."

The high shelves along the walls are lined with small vases of flowers. A smile forms on the woman's lips. She is an older version of Stacy herself.

"Here," she says, "let me take those," and I hand her the gift I have brought. She opens the card and turns to her daughter. She reads the card aloud, though it is clear she's unable to hear a word.

Stacy is lying on her back, still as death, her skin glowing with fever. An oxygen tube snakes from her nostrils, held in place with an elastic band that confines her blond hair. I know she would be humiliated to be seen this way, and I cast my eyes to the floor.

Mrs. Thorne places my card on the table beside the bed and arranges the stuffed bear so that it faces her. "You're Valden Van de Groot's brother?"

"Yes, ma'am."

Her eyes shine with moisture as she looks at me. "She thinks very highly of you boys."

When she says this, I feel as though I want to be sick.

"How is she?" I ask.

Her face goes out of focus as she looks at thoughts inside her head. "Stacy's been like this for almost two days..."

I wait as her voice trails away, but she is no longer speaking to me. She places her hand on Stacy's cheek. "Wake up, sweet girl," she whispers. "Please, baby, wake up."

*   *   *

The rain finally came on the day that Stacy died.

I am sitting in my second period English class when the announcement comes over the loudspeaker. The room is dead silent at first, then a murmur of muffled sobs and sibilant whispers covers the dull throb of rain against the window.

I don't know how I get to the bathroom, but I am on the cold tile floor, emptying my stomach into the dirty bowl, my arms wrapped around it like a mother. Tears sting my eyes as I heave my guts hollow. I am pounding my fists bloody on the metal stall dividers when they find me, the filthy drawings etched there now smeared with my blood.

I don't say a word to Mrs. Waldron when she comes to take me home.

-33-

I slipped naked from the bed, my breath still coming in ragged bursts, my heart pounding inside my chest. I doused my face with cold water from the sink, but it wasn't enough. Not by a long fucking shot. I was sick to my stomach, sick in my heart, needed to touch something real. I needed to touch Lani, to feel her skin on mine. I needed to strip myself of everything, my clothes, my guns, most especially my past, dive bare and unprotected into the sea. I needed a baptism.

Miles was still sleeping aboard the *Kehau* as I piloted the skiff across the early-morning smoothness of the bay to meet Moon for breakfast at the Ocean View Inn. He was seated at a scuffed Formica table by the window, sipping coffee and reading the paper when I arrived.

"You seen this?" Moon showed me the front page, a photo of Captain Cerillo and a lot of yellow crime scene tape outside the high school.

"You get those warrants?"

He folded the paper and dropped it on the empty chair beside him. "Yeah. Gonna serve 'em first thing after breakfast."

A tired-looking waitress took our orders. When she ambled away, I handed him the list Edita had made for me.

"We need to talk to those guys. They're Kalani Pawai's running buddies."

Moon took the paper without looking. He slipped it into his shirt pocket while he studied my face. "You all right?"

"Within acceptable limits."

"Looks like you're strung a little tight, Big City."

I waved it off and leaned back in my chair. "Ashley and Roland's lockers are empty. Somebody cleaned them out."

Moon cut his eyes out the window, puffed his cheeks as he heaved a deep sigh. "I don't want to know how you know that."

"Don't give me that crap. This is exactly what you wanted from me. No badge, no rules."

He scanned the room before leaning across the table. I could smell the sharp scent of whatever he used to slick back his hair. "Somebody oughtta post a warning label on your forehead."

"I still have the County's cash in the drawer beside my bed. You want it back, say the word."

He picked up a spoon, spun it slowly with his thumb and forefinger. He spoke to me without looking up. "I heard back from the lab last night. The X in Ashley Logan's bloodstream was a match with the stuff you took off Pawai."

I nodded, watching the boat from Jake's Dive Locker take its place at the pier. I couldn't tell if Yosemite was at the helm. "What about ballistics?"

"Seven mil," he said. "Belted mag."

"Deer rifle."

We stopped talking when our waitress stepped up behind the detective, placed his plate in front of him. I put my teabag in a small pot of hot water and watched Moon pour salt all over his fried Spam and eggs.

"You're gonna kill yourself with that," I said.

"Speaking of which, Claudia Garibay slipped into a coma last night. Where was Roland Delgado?"

"In the hospital. We need to talk to the guys on that list, Moon."

"We?"

"That's right."

The detective sliced a corner off his Spam, soaked it in runny egg yolk. "Not a good idea," he said. "We may need them as witnesses later. I don't want them interacting with you."

"So, what? I stand down?"

"Yeah. I'll call you afterward. We'll go over their statements together when I'm done."

My silence made him look up from his plate. "You're not going to stand down are you?"

I smiled, though seeing him suck down his breakfast was making my stomach turn. I looked at him over the edge of my cup of steaming tea.

"Probably not," I said.

*　*　*

Roland Delgado's bed was empty when I arrived at the hospital. The remnants of his morning meal were still on the tray at the foot of his unmade bed. I stepped out to the nurse's station and caught the attention of the woman at the desk.

"Could you tell me where Roland Delgado is?"

She looked me over in a way that left me surprised when she actually answered. "He's been released."

"When?"

She glanced at her watch. "About an hour ago."

"A little early in the morning for that, isn't it?"

"We take care of our own, Mr. Travis," she said, the hint of a contemptuous smile touching the corners of her eyes.

*   *   *

Both cars were in the carport when I pulled into the Delgado's driveway.

The curtains over the front windows were closed, and a blind had been drawn down over the green bottle glass inset in the front door. As I reached for the doorbell, Susan Delgado's voice came at me from inside.

"Go away, Mr. Travis," she said. Her tone was case-hardened steel.

"They called and told you I was coming."

"Leave us alone."

I stepped behind a row of skeletal shrubs that poked up from the dry soil of the planter in front of the living room window. I shouted loud enough so that Roland would hear. "Roland, we need to talk. Now."

"I won't tell you again," his mother shouted back. The shell of her composure was beginning to crack. "Get away from my house."

"Your school locker is empty. So is Ashley's. What did you take, Roland?"

"Don't make me call my lawyer," she threatened. "I'll sue you for harassment."

I moved back to the landing and spoke through the door. "Ashley Logan is dead, Mrs. Delgado. Her system was full of Schedule One hallucinogens, the same kind that Kalani Pawai was selling. I'd ask him about it, but somebody shot him. Roland needs to come clean on what he knows."

She was silent for several long moments. Her tone was an icy whisper when she finally spoke.

"Don't you dare ever threaten my son again," she said. "Now you have five seconds to get off my doorstep."

*   *   *

I HAD nearly reached the top of the hill, where the access road to the Delgado's house met the main highway, when my cell phone rang. Caller ID told me it was Moon, so I pulled onto the dirt shoulder, a shady area between the kiawe trees where spring water seeped out of the rocks and dampened the asphalt.

Moon and two uniforms had served the warrants for Kalani Pawai and Claudia 'Honey Girl' Garibay's lockers. The uniforms had logged the contents while Moon interviewed Pawai's three pals.

"They all tell the same story," he said.

"And?"

"The kid wasn't all bad. Played uke and sang in a local band, danced at the Luau on Thursday and Sunday nights."

"And deals hallucinogenics when he's not being Mr. Hawaii?"

"These guys say that's a new thing. Claim they didn't know he did anything but smoke a little 'lolo from time to time."

"Uh huh."

"I don't know, Big City, I kind of believe them. They said he started acting strange at some party a couple weekends ago."

An outsized stake bed truck heaped with macadamia nut husks passed the intersection in front of me, trailed by a half dozen slow-moving cars. A *haole* man in a straw planter's hat was last in line, pounding the wheel of a rental convertible.

"Something happen?" I asked.

"Not real clear, just said he'd been hinky since then."

"Hinky?"

"Yeah. My word."

"Tell me about the party."

"We got a map and an address off a flyer we found in Garibay's locker. It's down in Ocean View."

"They confirm it's the same one we're talking about?"

"Yeah."

"I'll go check it out. I'm halfway there already."

*   *   *

Ocean View was originally designed as a master-planned resort community a good hour and a half south of Kona. It occupied a wide swath of rough lava and scrub brush that ran from the coastline all the way up to the foot of the volcano. It didn't bear much resemblance to the sales brochures featuring calm blue lagoons and coconut palms that had been foisted off on buyers all over the Midwest. The original developer was nowhere to be found.

On the plus side, there was plenty of room between the homes that had ultimately sprung up out of that rough-hewn rock, and it was a favorite of artists, free spirits, and bohemians of every stripe. It took me over an hour to get there and another to find the place I was looking for.

I pulled onto a long gravel driveway whose address had been spray-painted on the rusted shell of an abandoned VW bus. In the distance, I saw the house, a rambling, one-story structure built of wood that was so blasted by wind and rain and rot that it looked as if it would be soft to the touch. It was tucked into a nook formed by a natural outcropping of stone and surrounded by an overgrowth of lehua and dry weeds.

The sky overhead was a cloudless blue so deep that it could have been water, but the near-constant wind had stripped the withered trees and shrubbery nearly bare. I could see how this could work as an illicit party spot; not a soul nearby to complain of loud music or parking problems. A haze of red dust kicked up off my shoes as I jumped down from the Jeep and made my way up the rutted footpath to the door.

Around the side, an old truck was propped up on concrete blocks, looking out across a broad, empty expanse of tamped-down soil. Piles of discarded rubbish were caught in the odd patches of weeds that sprung up amid the criss-cross of footprints etched in the dirt.

I pounded on the door with the ball of my fist until I heard the sound of someone moving around inside.

"Fuck off, I'm sleeping."

I didn't say a word, just kept hammering until the door swung open on a rail-thin, redheaded man I made for a twenty-something junkie as soon as the daylight landed on his face.

He was shirtless and pale. A lank tuft of hair sprouted at the center of his narrow chest like a bad patch of grass. The jeans he wore were unbuttoned and hung so low around his hips that his pubes were clearly visible as he stood there scratching his greasy scalp. His lean face was deeply scored by the pattern of cheap upholstery, the hair on one side matted as though he'd been sleeping for days.

"You own this place?" I asked.

"I rent it. Who the hell—"

I stepped past him as he stood in the open doorway. I never offered to introduce myself or shake his hand. His eyes didn't register the insult. They didn't register much of anything at all.

"What's your name?"

"Brian Susman."

"I want to know about a party down here a couple Fridays ago, Brian."

The air inside was stale with cigarettes and beer and the thick, drowsy smell of dope smoke. The nauseating odor of dried sweat and body fluids hung so heavily in the room I could almost see it in the diffused half-light that crept in behind the drawn curtains.

"I don't know what you're talking about," he said. When he barked his dry laugh, I saw the dull glint of a steel-ball stud through his tongue.

"Which part has you confused? I'll go over it again real slow."

"You walk into my house and treat me like an asshole?"

Susman was nothing more than a gas-huffing yard punk, his arms and chest smeared with a red rash that had scabbed over in places where he had scratched too hard.

"How many times you been down?" I asked.

His face twitched like it had been touched by electrical wire. "You're a pig?"

"You mean a police officer, Brian? Unfortunately for you, no. I'm a P.I. We don't have near as many rules as cops do."

"Get out of here."

"See? There's one of them. I'm already in. And I'm not leaving until I get what I want."

"I'll file a complaint."

"Use my phone," I smiled. "Of course, I'll have until the cops get all the way down here to bust your probation. You think I'd find anything interesting around here in that kind of time?"

His eyes shifted inward on a thought I don't think I could even guess at.

"What do you do for a living?"

"I'm a deejay."

"And you spin the music for these raves you put on?"

"They're not raves."

"Call 'em the Running of the fucking Bulls if you want. You deal a little on the side, Brian? You and Kalani Pawai?"

I knew I'd hit a nerve when I saw those dead eyes jangle inside the sockets.

"It was Kalani's party, man. Like a big blowout before school started up again. I just let him use my place."

"You were here."

"So were about two hundred other people."

I slid Roland Delgado's picture from my pocket. "This guy?"

He looked at it for less than a second. "I don't know. I don't think so."

"Honey Girl Garibay? Or a girl they call Sweet?"

"That skank? Yeah, she was here. They both were."

The stench in the room was beginning to make me gag. "How about this girl?" I showed him a picture of Ashley Logan.

His eyes narrowed once, then voided themselves of expression. I shoved the photo in front of his face again. "Was this girl here?"

He nodded. "She was a mess, man."

"More. Now."

Susman scratched at his arms, his breathing suddenly coming hard and fast. "Pawai was working her hard. He was spiking her drinks."

"You knew this? You saw it?"

"Not 'til after."

"After what?"

"After they was done with her, man. Jesus."

I felt another hot jolt rush through my veins.

"Who's 'they'?"

"I don't know. Pawai and a couple guys. They took turns on her in the back room."

"But not you," I hissed. He was closer to death than he'd been in his life, and he didn't even know it.

"No! It's like you said, I was spinning tunes."

Heat rose on my neck like red flames, and my vision spun down to a point. I turned to leave before I did something that would cost me more than he was worth, but he grabbed hold of my forearm. I felt his nails dig into my skin.

"We're square now, right?" he said. "I told you what you wanted."

I shook his hand off me. "You facilitated the gang-rape of a teenage girl. You couldn't see the near side of 'square' with a fucking telescope."

-34-

M y hands were still shaking as I turned south on the highway, directly into the afternoon sun.

I checked my phone every minute or so for a clear signal, the harsh black landscape and windblown trees nothing but a blur in my peripheral vision. I had driven nearly thirty miles before I could get a call through to Edita.

"I need an address for one of Honey Girl's friends. Crescenciano Perreira. They call her 'Sweet.'"

"Uncle Mike? I can barely hear you."

"Edita, I need an address!" I was hollering over the wind in the unprotected cab of the Jeep. "You've got a school directory, right?"

Her hesitation was so long, I thought I'd lost the connection. "I think I know where Dad keeps it. Yeah, here it is. Hold on."

Long seconds ticked by. "What's the last name you said?"

"Perreira," I said, and spelled it.

"What's going on? You don't sound too good."

"I'm fine," I said. "But I need that address."

She read it to me. "I think it's down off Alii—"

"I know the street, Edita." Sweet lived in the same neighborhood as Kalani Pawai.

*   *   *

The surf pounded the shoreline, rolled a mist of white water on an offshore wind, and filled the air with the smell of the sea and moss-covered rocks. A small group of teenage kids crossed the street in front of the Royal Poinciana Market to watch the surfers on the outer break. As I drove slowly past, I thought I saw Sweet sitting on the rocks with some friends sharing a forty-ounce Steinlager in a paper bag, so I pulled up another hundred yards and parked in a hash-marked no parking zone along Alii Drive.

The verdant smell of pakalolo floated on the same current that carried their voices, laughter, and the muffled hum of conversation. Somewhere not far away, two of their classmates were dead and awaiting burial, another lay in a coma on a hospital bed.

Sweet saw me from her perch on the rock. She said something I couldn't quite make out to a rangy, lank-haired *haole* boy who handed her the cigarette that had been pressed between his lips. The group drifted apart as she climbed down and started toward me.

She was small and slender, and carried herself with a round-shouldered slouch. There was something furtive behind her dark glasses. She took deep drags off the cigarette she protected from the wind with a practiced cup of her hand as she shambled barefooted through the sand.

"I remember you," she said. "From the hospital."

"What happened at the party down in Ocean View?"

She looked away, her expression blank and unreadable. "What party?"

"I talked to Brian Susman. He told me you were there."

Sweet kept her eyes on the surfers, but the muscles on her neck went taught. "He's fucked up."

I didn't disagree. "Kalani and Ashley are dead, Sweet. Honey Girl is in a coma. You don't want to get in the way of that."

She brought her cupped fist to her lips and pulled deeply at the cigarette hidden inside. She took the smoke deep in her lungs, exhaled slowly into the wind.

"This is rape and murder we're talking about," I said. "And you're one answer away from obstruction. You hearing me?"

When she finally spoke, she still had her back to me.

I came around in front of her, moving squarely into her field of vision.

"Say it again, Sweet. I didn't hear you."

Her mouth was set in a petulant sneer. "I said, 'it was just a goof.'"

"The party?"

"No," she said, waving my question away like a bad smell. "Afterward."

"I don't follow."

"I thought you said you knew what happened." Her tone suggested that I'd tricked her somehow. "She was so naïve."

"Honey Girl?"

"God, no," she spat. "Ashley."

As though she had lost the ability to remain standing, Sweet folded into the warm sand. She shook her head as she wrapped her arms around the legs she tucked in beneath her. I sat down beside her and watched a longboarder carve out a nice long left, then kick out where the white water met the inner reef.

"Ashley Logan," I said.

"Yeah. She came to me and Honey Girl a few days after the party. She wanted to know about pregnancy tests."

"Why you two?"

She answered me with a long look, slow burn.

"What about the tests?" I asked.

"She wanted to know how they worked, how soon you could tell. You know… after."

"So you helped her?"

"It was Honey Girl's idea."

I waited for more as I watched the surfer paddle back out through the white water, but nothing came. "You're going to have to use more words, here, Sweet. I'm not following you."

She hugged her legs in tight to her chest and heaved a sigh.

"Honey Girl told Ashley that we'd get her a test kit. You know, so Ashley wouldn't have to buy it herself. She was afraid of her mom finding out. Anyway, we met Ashley at my house after school. Honey Girl told her to pee on the stick and just bring it out—that she'd tell Ashley what it said. Ashley was really upset."

"And you told her she was pregnant."

Sweet took a last long drag on the cigarette and buried it in the sand beside her feet. "It was just a goof," she said again over a blanket of smoke. "Anybody would have known she wasn't knocked up."

"But you told her she was."

Sweet nodded, the afternoon light landing hard on the acne scars that colored her cheeks.

"Ashley knew it wouldn't be Roland's baby, didn't she?"

"She knew it couldn't be Roland's," Sweet said, a thin strand of disgust in her voice. "Them two was as cherry as you can get."

She stood and walked away from me, back to the friends who had regrouped at the rock. I watched as she took the paper bag from an outstretched hand and tipped the bottle to her lips.

I took one last look at the incoming set, and started back for the Jeep.

"How much trouble am I in?" she called after me, her voice barely audible over the rumble of the waves.

I didn't answer, didn't even turn around.

I had no way of knowing that Honey Girl Garibay's heart gave out in her hospital bed at the same moment I left Sweet standing in the sand, the green neck of the Steinlager poking out from the top of the paper bag she clutched so tightly in her hand.

*   *   *

I punched Moon's phone number as I pulled out onto the road. Five rings later, I was switched over to a voice message system.

"Moon, it's Travis. It's about four o'clock, and I'm heading to Roland Delgado's. Call me. It's important." I tossed the phone on the passenger seat, then thought better of it, and left a 9-1-1 on his pager, too.

I called the hospital next. When the operator came on, I asked for Susan Delgado.

"I'm sorry, Ms. Delgado is off today." I recognized the voice of the nurse from Pediatrics who'd brushed me off before. "You can leave a message, or try back tomorrow."

"Tell her Mike Travis is going to talk with her son. She might want to be there. I know how you like to take care of your own."

*   *   *

Both cars were in the lot again, but when I felt the hood of Mrs. Delgado's car, it was cold. Maybe the hospital hadn't been lying.

The shades weren't drawn across the windows, so I looked through the distorted glass for motion inside as I pressed the doorbell and hammered the door. "Roland! It's Mike Travis. Open up."

There was no sound.

"We need to talk, Roland," I said, pressing the doorbell again. "I know what happened at the party. I know about Ashley Logan."

I thought I heard some kind of movement and the desperate tones of a hushed conversation. I leaned on the bell this time.

A warped shadow passed in front of the door, and in the background, I could hear Susan Delgado's anxious voice. "Don't you dare open that door," she said. "Roland, I mean it, don't—"

I pushed my way past him as soon as he twisted the knob and found myself standing in a cramped and untidy living room. Roland shut the door and regarded me wordlessly.

"Talk to me, Roland," I said. "No more bullshit."

The bruises around his eyes had faded to sickly green, and the mark that encircled his neck was now nothing more than a bad rash. He pursed his lips and looked at the floor. "She wasn't supposed to be there alone—"

"Don't you say a word to that man!" Her shout came from a room down the hall. "Not one word!"

His face was bland and expressionless. His eyes shone with the glassy-wet look of painkillers as he moved from the foyer and into the room. "I was supposed to—"

Susan Delgado came out of nowhere, a quick burst of motion from the end of the darkened hall. My hand went instinctively to the Beretta.

I slipped it free of its holster as she stepped into the diffuse light, a matte-black hunting rifle pressed firmly against her shoulder.

But she hadn't counted on Roland's slow reactions, and it left him standing squarely between the barrels of our guns.

"Put it down, Ms. Delgado," I said.

Half of her face was obscured by the scope affixed to the rifle, but her uncombed hair framed her head like a tangled mane and imbued her with the look of a lunatic.

"Get that gun out of my son's face!"

I held the Beretta in a two-handed stance, and spoke to her evenly. "You know I can't do that."

Even with her cheek pressed against the black stock, I could see her eyes were illuminated with feral madness.

"Step to one side, Roland," she said. "I've got a clean shot."

"Mom—" His voice was plaintive, childlike.

"It's over, Susan," I said. "You've done what you set out to. You've protected your son."

Roland made a move to turn, and I saw the whiteness on her knuckles, the pressure against the Remington's trigger.

"Don't look at me!" Her voice was hysterical.

"Mom—"

The room bristled with the brittle energy of a standoff, with Roland as an unintended hostage, though for Susan Delgado or me, I didn't know. I kept my Beretta trained on her forehead, saw the rifle barrel begin to waver as the sound of her short, quick breaths and the sour smell of fear filled the musty air.

"You don't want to hurt anybody," I said. "And neither do I. Just put it down, Susan, and I'll do the same."

She shook her head slightly, kept that mean black rifle leveled at my chest. "I'm not afraid, Mr. Travis. I'm already a killer. Those kids nearly cost my son his soul."

"Ms. Delgado—"

"Don't speak to me! You brought this into my house!"

The tension in the room squeezed time to a pinpoint, every fiber of my body and brain focused tightly in the heavy silence.

Then all hell broke loose when my cell phone rang.

Roland startled badly at the sound, and I saw his mother's eyes lock down. Whether she mistook his sudden movement for mine, I'll never know. But a fraction of a second later she squeezed off a shot that creased Roland's shoulder, passed through muscle and tissue, and sprayed his blood across the side of my face.

Susan Delgado flinched as her eyes cut away for the fraction of a second that it took to throw myself at Roland's midsection. He went down like a feed sack, his head bouncing hard off the floor as his mother fired a second shot that passed so close to my head that I felt the funnel of hot wind cross the back of my neck. I wanted to shout something, but there was no time as I saw her swing the barrel around on me again.

I two-tapped the nine-mil, saw my first shot go wide and gouge a nasty hole in the living room wall. The next one took her high in the chest and spun her around sideways. As she went down, a sympathetic squeeze on the Remington's trigger sent a third magnum round through the ceiling, as a perfect blossom of blood spread across her blouse.

My phone was still ringing as I rolled onto my side and planted a hand in Roland's back, pressing him to the floor. The dark patch on the collar of his shirt was spreading fast. "Stay on the fucking deck. Don't move."

I kicked the rifle away from his mother's hand and watched it clatter onto the hard linoleum of the kitchen. I kept my pistol trained on Susan Delgado's stunned and twitching face as I reached for the phone with my free hand.

"Get down here code three with an ambulance," I said. I knew it was Moon. "We got two people down."

She blinked as she stared up from the floor, the first gout of arterial blood beginning to bubble at the corner of her mouth. I knelt down and turned her head to one side to keep her from drowning, even as she was trying to speak.

*   *   *

She was gone long before Moon got there, the blue light bouncing hard off the walls of the house. Roland sat on the floor, his back braced against the wall, nearly catatonic as we watched the EMTs go through the motions on his mother.

But it was Susan Delgado I still heard in my head. I had barely been able to make out the words as I felt her slip away, but she had repeated them again and again.

-35-

I knew it would be a couple days before all the disparate pieces of the story could be worked together into any sort of report that Moon could file, and probably much longer than that to make any real sense of it.

I've never been a believer in coincidence, but I have an entirely different conviction with respect to the notions of karma, or fate, or the power of events once set in motion.

It had been an innocent plan: that Ashley Logan would sneak out of her house and meet up with Roland Delgado at a party that was meant to celebrate the last days of summer. But the first thread came loose when Roland's mother came home early from the night shift, stranding Roland at home with no way to reach Ashley, to tell her the whole thing was off. It was as simple and innocent as that, but the events that unfolded from that single detail set up a chain reaction that began with gang-rape and ended in suicide and murder.

On the day she died, Ashley Logan made one last stop before she stepped into the sea and swam straight for the horizon. She dropped a letter in a postbox, addressed to Roland, and told him everything. Her words were imbued with shame and humiliation, but absolved Roland of any blame he might be inclined to take upon himself; it was her parents she knew she couldn't face. As far as I was concerned, Ashley Logan was killed by her own mother and father, and the unforgiving field of vision that defined their lives.

Around ten o'clock, I stepped outside with Moon. There was a brush-fire burning on the slope of Hualalai that cast an unnatural orange light in the night sky and filled the air with the smell of wood smoke. He leaned against the substation's rough concrete wall and shook a cigarette from the pack he kept in his shirt pocket.

"You don't have to stick around," he said. "I can call you tomorrow if I need you."

I shook my head. "I'd rather get it over with."

Moon dragged deeply on his cigarette and squinted his eyes. I turned my face to the burning sky and watched the play of light against the clouds.

"It's the mother," he said finally, plucking a loose bit of tobacco from his tongue. "I just don't get her."

"Which one?"

"Roland's."

"Mama Lion," I said. "She found the letter Ashley had sent to her son. He tried to kill himself the day he got it in the mail."

Susan Delgado never got to write her son a letter, or even share with him her last thoughts on Earth. But I had heard them clearly enough. The words she repeated softly as she died. *Mortal sin.*

I want to believe he understood the passionate purity of her motives, if not the malevolence of her actions. Two young people were dead as a direct result of her intervention, yet I couldn't look at the tragedy without seeing a tiny ring of light around its edges. Sometimes you had to move across the line in order to right the scales. I would never condone Susan Delgado's actions, but I could certainly understand them.

"Roland's mom was a devout Catholic," I said. "The way she saw it, Kalani Pawai and Honey Girl were responsible for Roland's attempted suicide. If her son had succeeded, he would have forever forfeited his soul. Since he didn't, Roland might've even ended up killing Pawai himself."

"You think she took them off the board for the church?"

"No, not for the church. To avenge her son's commission of one mortal sin and prevent him from committing another."

Moon crushed the butt under the heel of his boot. He regarded the glowing sky for a long moment before he spoke again. "You've never struck me as a church-going man," he said.

"Every Sunday," I said. The wail of sirens floated out in the distance, in the direction of the fire. "Until my mother died."

A long silence hung between us, each lost in our own thoughts. I saw Moon reach for another cigarette, then think better of it. He heaved a sigh and buried his hands in his pockets. He fixed his eyes on the asphalt between his feet.

"Did you see all the guns we found in the house?"

I nodded. "The ex-husband was some kind of hunter, I guess. It's how they met."

"Who?"

"Roland's parents."

"He tell you all this?"

"We had to pass a little time while we were waiting for you and the ambulance. I needed to keep him awake. He was loaded on painkillers and God-knows what all."

Moon shook his head, cocked one foot against the wall.

"What a clusterfuck," I said, feeling another heavy wave of fatigue come over me. "I've had it up to here with families, I swear to God."

"It's not always so bad."

"I just don't see it." Maybe it was the fear of some rogue gene in the bloodline. Or maybe it was simply the stains on my own conscience.

Marcus Aurelius said that the sins committed out of desire were worse than those committed out of anger. The angry man turns his back on reason out of a passionate kind of pain, an inner convulsion. But the man motivated by desire, one who is mastered by pleasure, is somehow more self-indulgent, less manly in his sins. It is he who deserves the harsher rebuke.

Or maybe there's no damned difference at all.

*   *   *

It was midnight by the time I got back to the *Kehau*.

Miles was standing on the afterdeck as I eased back the throttles on the skiff, waiting for me to toss him my bowline. He was showered and dressed in another one of the shirts I had bought him, and he smelled of aftershave and soap. Through the open hatchway, I could see the glow from the TV in the salon down below.

"I thought you'd be asleep," I said.

"I waited up."

I was struck by the realization that I hadn't made arrangements to get him from the pier to the boat that afternoon, and I felt vaguely guilty.

"How'd you get out here?"

"Got a lift from the parasail guys," he said, waving it away. "Listen, I need to talk to you."

"Sounds serious," I said. "I'm going to grab a beer. Want one?"

He shook his head, then glanced out the window, unsure of how to begin. "I'm flying back home this Saturday," he said finally.

I popped the cap off my Asahi, took a pull from the neck, and wiped my lips with the back of my hand. I was surprised by my own mixed emotions.

"I thought your school starts Monday. Aren't you cutting it a little close?"

"I told Edita I'd go with her to Ashley's funeral." There was a directness in his expression, and openness that hadn't been there before.

I took a long look at him, saw the changes that only two weeks in the islands had made. I reached out a hand, and when he took it, his grasp was firm and strong.

"I'm gonna miss you, Milo," I said.

The corners of his mouth turned up in a smile, a hint of amusement lighting his eyes. "You called me Milo."

"You said that's what you like to be called."

He glanced away. "Not so much, anymore."

"You grew up on me, bud," I said.

When he looked back, it was with an expression that said he didn't know what to make of what I had just told him.

*   *   *

An hour later, I was standing on the bow, alone, listening to what, for me, were the sounds of home. The rhythmic slap of water against the hull mingled with the strain on the ropes in the rigging, the snap of the American flag and pennant at the masthead. I gripped the chrome railing, slick with moisture and salt, and leaned into the wind that tossed my hair and pulled at the loose collar of my shirt. The moon was only a dim crescent rising over the shoulder of the volcano behind me, the sea a glistening black mirror that stretched all the way to where it met the sky along the far horizon.

I fixed my eyes on the stars and gave voice to the thought that had been occupying my mind all night. *"Pomaika'i a pau ole, Ashley,"* I said softly, and turned to go to bed.

-36-

1982. Los Angeles. Early Summer.

Reggie Carter lights a cigarette from the smoldering butt of the one he just finished. He cracks his window a little further, and the smoke trails out on the wind.

"Bother you?" he asks me.

"No," I say. It wouldn't matter if it did. I'm a rookie, and he's my training partner.

He's about to say something when we get the call. I take up the mic and respond as I have been taught. Reggie flips on the emergency lights and pulls a U-turn back to Figueroa, moving code-three to the USC campus.

Campus Security is already on the scene when we arrive, but there's no sign of the ambulance I expect. I'm up the stairs before my partner, taking them two at a time. The apartment door is wide open, and onlookers line the railing, trying to steal a glance. Inside, on the floor, lies a Caucasian male, early-twenties, long black hair matted against a red, sweating face. He's hyperventilating, nearly convulsing. I hear Reggie hollering into his shoulder-mic, calling again for EMS. I peel back the kid's eyelids and see that his pupils are dilated so wide there's nearly no iris. Another kid, his roommate most likely, is standing silent in the middle of the room. He's wrapped himself in his own arms, shivering.

"What the fuck happened? What's he on?"

The roommate looks at me dumbly.

"What did he take, goddammit?" I yell at him, but I can't get through. His eyes are glassy, mouth opening and closing like a dying fish.

EMS arrives, pushes through the growing crowd along the stairwell, elbows me out of the way.

* * *

The night is hot, the window of my apartment thrown open to catch what little breeze comes up off the beach below. The tide is rumbling against the wide, white swath of Zuma beach like distant thunder behind the music I've got playing on the stereo.

I've been drinking since I returned home from typing up the reports that followed our OD call-out. It had taken the remainder of our shift. I stand at the balcony rail, look out across the Pacific and barely make out the dim lights of Avalon across the channel. I upend the bottle of beer in my hand. As I walk back inside for another, it hits my brain like a hammer blow.

I pick up the phone and dial.

"You killed her, you sonofabitch," I say. There is a throbbing, red ache behind my eyes.

"Mike?"

"It was Belladonna. Nightshade. You fucking killed her, Valden. You killed Stacy Thorne."

He calls me back two hours later. He is almost as drunk as me.

"It wasn't supposed to happen that way," he says.

"Fuck you."

There is a wet, mewling sound coming over the line. I am about to hang up when he speaks again. "It was just supposed to make her miscarry. Mike, I swear to you."

I listened to my brother cry.
I never wanted to hear it again.

-37-

Three days later, ballistics confirmed that the bullets that killed Kalani Pawai and Honey Girl Garibay had come from Susan Delgado's rifle, a Remington Model 7 AWR chambered for a 7mm magnum round. The report came out the same day as Ashley Logan's funeral. I didn't attend.

Miles spent his last night in the islands at Tino's, in the shadow of the home in which his father and I had spent so many summers as kids. Unlike his father, though, I sensed the place had burned an impression on his character, and that he'd carry his days in the coffee fields, and his nights with Edita, with him for the rest of his life. It was impossible not to see myself in that.

I saw Miles off on a Saturday morning whose skies had been washed clean by the rain. I watched Edita kiss him gently and place a fragrant plumeria lei around his neck. She had picked the flowers and strung it herself. Edita and I waited outside of the screening area and watched him pass through Security. He turned and gave us one final wave, a hollow feeling in my gut as I watched him dissolve into the crowd.

A few days later, I woke at dawn as has always been my habit, still alone aboard the *Kehau*, and watched the sun spill warm yellow light across the ripple of gray clouds that shrouded the coastline. I walked barefoot and shirtless to the bow and sat cross-legged on the deck still damp with evening mist. Kona was just coming awake to a new flock of tourists eating room-service breakfasts on ocean-front lanais, or hoisting ice coolers over the stern rails of the sportfishing fleet. That night they might take their seats at long tables, fill their glasses with Mai Tais and their plates from the luau buffet, having no idea whatsoever that there were four fewer sets of footprints on these shores. But I would. Every time I heard those beating drums.

The girl they called "Sweet" got probation in exchange for the names of the two boys who, along with Kalani Pawai, had so viciously violated Ashley Logan. Once their trial is over, I will make it my business to be sure word gets out on the yard. Known sex offenders don't do well in prison.

Cady's mother, Sheila, moved Cady to an all-girl boarding school at the far end of the island. Edita told me she's allowed home once a month. The day I heard that, I came across a book of names and their origins. As I leafed through the pages, I stumbled across the name "Sheila." Its root is Gaelic: its meaning is blind. I thought that nothing could have been more fitting.

They never made an arrest in the bombing of Rosalie's car, which left me with some serious doubts about Arndt Ogden Krupp and Detective Scott Riley. It was ruled an act of vandalism, which was pure bullshit, but she and Dave ended up getting about three grand out of their insurance company— just enough to replace the shattered windows in their house and go out to dinner afterward. Rosie didn't mind, but I did. She figures she'll be in the center of one firestorm or another for the rest of her life. It's the way she seems to like it.

Roland Delgado dropped out of school, got rid of his truck, and left instructions with a local realtor to sell his mother's house the minute it clears probate. He was last seen at the Kona airport. Nobody knows where he went, but I like to believe that he took whatever college funds his mother had saved up and bought himself a ticket to a new life, and that somewhere along the way, he will finally forgive himself.

*   *   *

Lani finally met me for lunch at an open-air seafood restaurant at the southern edge of the bay. It had been more than two weeks since we'd really done any talking.

The water was clear and sparkling with light, the silhouettes of fish and sea turtles visible inside the clean line of swells that rolled toward the shore and broke into fine white cascades of spray and foam.

We took a table in the shade of an umbrella adorned with the Polynesian-girl logo of Hinano beer. Lani slid the sandals from her feet and ran her toes through the warm sand. Her long hair was pulled back in a ponytail, revealing the smooth skin of her neck.

"Your eyebrow is almost healed," she said.

I touched it involuntarily. "I think it's going to leave a scar."

A small smile touched her lips, but it was shot through with melancholy. Her manner was soft, solicitous to a point approaching pity. I hadn't seen her since the demonstration march at the gates of Ogden Krupp's development, and the sense of something coming to an end came back to me in full. I was struck by the things I don't think I had ever told her, that she had taught me a new meaning of time, and of gentler things. Like the lingering heat from the sun on my skin, or a lazy Sunday spent in bed together. I wondered what I was to her now, what it was she might have drawn from me.

Two young women pushing strollers took the table next to ours and I brushed my gaze across the tiny faces laced safely inside. After our waitress took our orders I fixed my attention on Lani.

"It's time to talk, Mike," she said but her eyes slipped away from me. I watched as she stared out across the water.

I ran my hand down the length of her arm, bringing her back from the silence that had overtaken her.

"I had this whole speech I was going to give you," she said finally.

I looked around the place again, at the tables decorated with colorful cocktails in tall, shapely glasses, and I felt out of place in my own town, unwashed and callous and numb.

Our iced teas arrived and I stirred mine aimlessly, then touched the rim to Lani's.

"I want to hear it, Lani," I said, which wasn't exactly the truth.

She seemed to steel herself for something, her eyes reaching inside mine as she spoke. "I'm going to have a baby, Mike. I'm pregnant."

My gaze slid from her face and rested on the children at the table beside us again. I felt something catch inside me. Maybe it was the innocence I found so difficult to absorb, like I was unworthy and somehow undeserving. It wasn't so much their helplessness that troubled me. It was the promise, the stainlessness I saw there. Maybe they were still too close to eternity, still somehow in possession of a piece of it.

"You've known for a while, haven't you?" I said.

She nodded. "I didn't know how to tell you. All I've ever heard from you is how much you dislike children."

"Yeah, well," I said, my eyes following a lone frigate bird floating on the wind. "You've been away for a couple weeks, Lani. You missed the part where I grew up."

The smell of salt air and the sound of the waves filled my senses, and I felt disengaged from the earth in a moment of singular clarity. I stood and crossed over to her, knelt in the sand beside her.

"I love you," I whispered, and placed my hand on the warm, smooth curve of her belly.

"This is what you want?" Her voice was so low it was nearly carried off in the breeze.

I kissed her gently, the taste of the tropics on her lips. "I love you both."

"Please don't say it unless you mean it, Mike," she said. "Unless you mean forever."

Her eyes shone wetly and I felt as though I could see inside her.

"Lani," I said, brushing soft kisses across the smooth planes of her face. "You're the only thing I know about forever."

Epilogue

The late-October lull had settled over town, the shops and restaurants nearly deserted in the weeks leading up to the holidays when it would all start over again. The days were short, and the nights came early, and when the wind was still, the air grew heavy with the smell of roasting coffee drifting down off the mountain.

I had spent most of the evening with Lani as she worked her shift at Lola's, so it was late by the time I pushed through the batwing doors at Snyder's. The place was almost deserted, the jukebox sitting silent in favor of the local FM station. Radical Rod was playing something sweet and slow by Karla Bonoff.

Snyder plucked an Asahi from the cooler as I took my seat at the rail. He brought it over with a tall glass of ice.

"You see the front page?" he asked as he tossed the daily paper across the bar at me. It was a photo of a D-9 earthmover, fire-blackened and smoldering in an un-graded section of Arndt Ogden Krupp's golf estates project. "Article says somebody destroyed all four of those tractors they had working out there. Says it's gonna delay the project by at least three months, cost the developer a ton of money."

"Hmm," I said, and handed the paper back to Snyder.

He eyeballed me for a couple seconds longer than necessary. "You don't seem surprised."

I shrugged. "Karma is a powerful force."

"Karma," he parroted, the creases of a smile showing in the corners of his eyes.

"Damn right."

"A powerful force," he nodded.

"A force to be reckoned with," I said, and lifted the Asahi to my lips.

*   *   *

We talked for another half hour, Snyder and I, but when last call came, another beer just didn't hold any appeal. An aimless kind of restlessness tugged me back out into the quiet night.

I walked slowly beneath heavy branches of banyan and the thick ropes of vine that hung from its limbs, past flickering pools of light spilled across warm pavement, through the smoke that trailed from the tips of torch fires.

From time to time, I caught my own reflection in the darkened windows of the shops, diaphanous and hollow, disappearing as I moved on, as if I had never been there at all. A friend of mine says that life will come and get you if you try to stand still, and I know it to be true. The future and the past spend eternity in collision, and we spend the whole of our lives in the center of it.

I climbed up on the seawall and took a seat among the rocks and let the silence of the night overtake me.

I gazed across the throat of the inlet and watched the boats pull at their mooring ropes. I watched the waves along the strand and the endless cycle of the tide. I watched the running lights of night fishermen along the horizon, and the slow course of satellites as they traced their way across the sky like falling stars.

A stir in the breeze carried the sound of a distant aircraft to my ears, pulled me back from the edge of nothing.

I lifted my head at some movement caught in the corner of my vision, a momentary flicker among the dark silhouettes of riffling ficus and coconut palms. A lone set of headlights wound slowly along the empty road.

They left their echo in my tired eyes when I finally turned and headed home.

Acknowledgments

Mahalo nui to all the members of the Hawaii County Police Department and the Hawaii County District Attorney's office, especially Capt. Dale Fergerstrom (ret.), Officer Stan Haanio, and Cynthia Tai—you bring honor and dignity to your amazingly difficult jobs.

To Christina, for being the best wife and partner any man could ever hope for. To Martha Weir for the world-class video. You're a pleasure to work with. And to David Merker, Don Merker, and Patrick Partridge who have been there from the very beginning.

A special mahalo to Roger McGee and his lovely wife Adele for the generous donation they made to Pua Plantasia and KOC in return for having your name used as a character in this novel. I hope you enjoy your fictional alter-ego, and continue your good work for such worthy causes. A debt of gratitude is owed to Don Winslow, Randy Wayne White, T. Jefferson Parker, Nichelle Tramble and Gary Phillips—spectacularly talented authors all—for your kokua, support and encouragement.

To Noland and Diane Palacol of Quinn's (a.k.a. Snyder's) for all the hospitality and aloha; and to Daniel Russell, Jon Griesser, Joe Danko, Jonathan Hood, Bridget Andrew, Ellie Harvey and Anna Caudell just for being so damned cool. And a heartfelt mahalo to Barry Martin for giving me some very good advice a long while ago.

Finally, and most importantly, there's this: in the early chapters of this book, Mike Travis makes a statement that he never saw the upside of having children. Those are his sentiments, not mine. He's wrong. It's all upside. I have been blessed with three children of whom I could not be more proud, and whose love and enthusiasm has been the keystone of my adult life. A very special and grateful thank you goes to Allegra, Raider and Britton with all my love. *Aloha pau ole.*